Everyday Lies

Editing, Design, typesetting and publishing by UK Book Publishing
www.ukbookpublishing.com
ISBN: 978-1-914195-57-0

Cath Cole had a working-class childhood in Bolton. She trained as a nurse and health visitor and subsequently as a further education lecturer and nurse tutor. She enjoyed a successful career in further education, which culminated in her becoming the principal of a further education college. After working with college staff to rescue a college judged to be failing, she was awarded the OBE.

The impact of State Registered Nurse training has underpinned her professional success. She was awarded a Master of Arts (Creative Writing) from Edge Hill University in 2013. Her first novel *Home from Home* was published in 2015 and has reached #1 in the Amazon Medical Fiction charts in the UK and Australia.

Cath travels Covid-19 permitting, reads and spends time with family and friends. She is married and has a son and three grandchildren.

Also by Cath Cole
Home from Home

Everyday Lies

Cath Cole

"In certain trying circumstances, urgent circumstances,
desperate circumstances, profanity furnishes a relief
denied even to prayer."

Mark Twain

For Dave
(1955-2015)

Elaine

Wants her nice mam back. The mam who stroked her hair and kissed her cheek and laughed at the things she said. She doesn't want the bad mam who shouts at her when she hasn't even been naughty. She doesn't like being on her own with her mam. She wants to be with her daddy or her grandma and grandad. She wants to be able to play with Weary Willie and Tired Tim.

Arthur

Wants to live the dream he created during the war when he was on the run in the mountains of Yugoslavia. To be with Sheila his wife, and Elaine their daughter, and one, or perhaps two more kiddies. He wants a clean and tidy home and good food. He wants the Sheila he married: sparkling, vivacious, interested in him and his books. He wants to give something back; to make escaping from the war with his life meaningful and worthwhile.

Sheila

Wants to be the person she was before her dreams were crushed. She would have liked to have gone to the grammar school, but her dad wouldn't let her. She wanted to be a nurse, but her mam said no. So Sheila secretly signed on for the Land Army. She wanted to stay in Cornwall, but her mam got ill, and she had to come home to look after her. She wants to be a good wife and mother, to love and be loved, but…

This is their story.

Chapter 1

ELAINE'S BEST day is Tuesday. She isn't very sure when Tuesday is, but it is one of the days she doesn't feel sad. The sad days make a shuffly sound and mean she won't be going to her grandma and grandad's house. She can remember the order of the days of the week when she says them with her daddy: Monday, Tuesday, Thursday, Friday, Wednesday, Sunday, Saturday. Elaine's mam and daddy shout at each other on the shuffly-sounding days. Elaine hides under her bed with her Isle of Man Teddy.

Elaine wants her nice mam back. Her friend Christine has a nice mam who Elaine calls Aunty Vera. A nice mam would take her to Simmonds' shop and look at the penny tray with her and tell her stories from the olden days.

Elaine's mam is like a wicked witch who shouts at her and pulls scary faces even when Elaine is trying her very hardest to be good and quiet like Isle of Man Teddy. Elaine likes her daddy. He gives her piggyback rides and calls her his precious girl. He takes her to the library and reads to her.

Elaine's other friends – Weary Willie and Tired Tim – live under the weeds in her grandad's garden and work under the stalls on Farnworth market. She would like to see them but her grandad has told her 'they're mischievous little buggers who keep themselves to themselves.' Elaine's tummy feels fuzzy and her heart makes a funny bump when Christine says they aren't real people.

Late one Saturday afternoon Elaine and her grandad caught the bus to Farnworth market. When they arrived, they scrambled about to look underneath the empty stalls for Weary Willie and Tired Tim, but all Elaine found was mouldy old cabbage leaves. Grandad had seen the 'little buggers' but they shot off, skipping and hopping on their short legs before Elaine had a chance to see them.

*

Sheila groaned. Her back ached from the effort of lugging a pile of hearth rugs from one side of the furnishing department to the other. The deputy manager had insisted that she shift the stack of Axminster closer to the front door. He'd issued his orders, 'roll them up and carry them, don't drag them,' and disappeared, leaving her to the sweaty, back-breaking job. Muttering under her breath at his stupidity she braced herself and bent to roll another rug. *He's having a go, misery guts, acting big because Mr G's gone to a meeting.*

She hoisted a rug across her arms then balanced her weight before trudging toward the front door. She concentrated; it would be easy to miss her step and fall when she couldn't see where she was going with her chin resting on the rug. She focused on the rain lashing against the windows as she made slow, determined steps to the growing pile by the door. The rain ran in torrents like loopy lace curtains on the large windows. *And look at the soddin' weather, I'll get drenched going home.* The windows rattled as the wind and rain battered against them. With a sudden swoosh the front door sprung open, swung wildly and then slammed shut for a second before ricocheting open to swing to and fro.

'Sheila, the door. Get the door,' Mr Gorton spluttered as he hurtled downstairs. At the bend in the stairs that divided the upper and lower floors of the furnishing department, he stumbled, missed his grab at the banister rail and rolled down the short lower flight of stairs. In her haste to get to him, Sheila dropped the rug she was carrying, stumbled over it and was propelled to his side at the foot of the stairs.

'Are you alright, Mr G?' Sheila prodded the short, rotund figure lying at her side. 'Mr G?'

'A bit winded,' he said, rolling over and patting the floor around him. 'My glasses, can you see my glasses, love?'

Sheila glanced round and saw the glasses above her on the stairs. On her hands and knees crawling to fetch them, she glanced up to see the deputy manager at the top of the stairs – smirking. *Supercilious bugger.*

'Get up, Mrs Brooks and get back to work. I'll help Mr Gorton to the staff room to repair his appearance.'

'I'll get back to work when I've seen to Mr G, dusted him down and made sure he's alright. And you can bugger off.'

'Sheila!' said Mr Gorton.

'Mr G,' Sheila plonked herself on the bottom step next

to her boss, 'I'm sick and fed up of him ordering me about, giving me stupid jobs that don't need doing.'

'Mr Gorton,' the deputy manager puffed up his chest as he towered over the pair sitting on the stairs, 'I insist you reprimand her at once.'

As Sheila stared up at the deputy manager her heart thudded, her vision glazed momentarily, and she was surprised to hear herself growl.

'I'm worn out, jiggered, fed up to the back teeth,' she took a shuddering breath, 'and couldn't give a damn about you.' She flicked her hand in dismissal toward the deputy, 'or being reprimanded or anything else for that matter.' She wrapped her arms around her legs and with her head resting on her knees, she sobbed.

'Sheila, come on love, calm yourself.' Mr Gorton gave a tentative tap-tap on Sheila's arm. 'What if a customer comes in?' His voice dropped. 'Come on, that's a good girl, I expect we could both do with a cup of tea and a breather. Let's go to the canteen.'

'And who will be here to assist customers?' said the deputy.

'You, my dear man. It's what you're paid for.' Mr Gorton eased himself into a standing position and touched Sheila's bent head. 'And while we're away you can move those rugs back where they came from.'

*

As Mr Gorton led the way upstairs Sheila turned and looked down to see the deputy manager watching their progress. Her heart was heavy; she was bone weary, her arms and back ached. She met his stare and stuck her tongue out. *You daft ha'p'orth, he'll get his own back sooner or later.*

With the fuss of ordering the tea and finding a seat sorted, Sheila and Mr Gorton faced each other across the table. Sheila concentrated on the ingredients listed on the HP sauce bottle. Mr Gorton shuffled in his seat. He coughed then stirred his tea.

'Sheila, tell me to mind my own business,' he chewed his lips, 'but that outburst … well it isn't like you to get upset like that. We all know he gets above himself at times…'

When she raised her head to meet the faded, grey eyes of the man who had been more like a kindly uncle rather than a boss to her since she was fourteen, self-loathing, fear and shame washed over her. She turned her attention back to the sauce bottle.

'You've not been yourself for a while … months,' he said in a quiet voice.

'I'm tired, Mr G. So very tired. I can't sleep. I don't know what to do with myself half the time.' Sheila hesitated, concentrating on her hands as she wrung them. She paused her twisting and squeezing and glanced up. 'And now I've done something daft … something I shouldn't have done.' *Forgotten you're a married woman, you trollop.*

'Is it to do with work, with what happened earlier?'

'No, it's… Have you ever made a mess, Mr G? Buggered things up? Sorry, swearing and that.'

'Made a mess of things?' Mr Gorton looked somewhere in the distance. 'I'd like to meet the man who hasn't made a mess at one time or another.' He focused his gaze back onto Sheila. 'Is it something you feel you could talk about, love? This mess? I don't mind, or there's Vera.'

'Vera knows about it, and thinks I'm stupid for letting myself get involved…' She hesitated, hunched her shoulders and rubbed her forehead. 'I don't know what to do, Mr G. I can't sleep for going over and over everything looking for answers. Trying to find where it all went wrong.'

'Everything?'

'How we were, me and Arthur. We couldn't wait for the war to end so we could be together. I were that excited,' she shook her head, 'and frustrated and in a lather, waiting for him to be demobbed.'

'I remember. You couldn't talk about anything else.' Mr Gorton nodded.

Sheila raised her head, sighed and slumped against the back of her chair. 'I were that proud of him when he went up to London for his medal,' she dragged her hands down her face, 'and now I don't know who he is any more.'

'In what way do you not know…?'

Sheila gazed over Mr Gorton's shoulder, her eyes half closed. 'It was hard when we were first wed, living with my mam and dad all squashed up in that little house.' She reached out to pick up a teaspoon and push sugar round the sugar bowl. 'We got a council house and then they started,' she glanced at Mr Gorton, 'the bloody nightmares.'

'It wasn't his fault, love. The war…'

'I know that, Mr G, but they've changed everything. His screaming and shouting and thrashing about … he thinks he's being shot down, that he's going to burn to death. He's buggered all the time, and so am I. I can't think straight.'

'Sheila, love, what can I say? What can I do?'

'Nothing. They've stopped for now, but he's disappeared inside himself. He's only there for our Elaine. I can't get near him,' she gave a shuddering sigh, 'I feel lonely and shut out.'

She fiddled with the cruet set, changing the position of the salt and pepper in relation to the vinegar. 'I can hardly put one foot in front of the other, I'm that done in.' Sheila gulped. 'And now I've done this daft thing, but it makes me feel alive … not lonely.'

Mr Gorton reached out an arm toward Sheila then pulled it back and settled it on his lap.

'I'm stuck in this mess I've made,' Sheila's voice fell. 'I want to go to sleep and never wake up – ever.' *Well, other than Wednesday afternoons. I can't let him go.* She batted away the welling tears. *Don't kid yourself, you know the answer. Tell him it's over and done.*

'Sheila? You were miles away… I was saying don't say that. What would I do without you?' Mr Gorton shook his head so hard his jowls wobbled. 'Why don't you get home, get some rest?'

'No, please, Mr G. Don't make me go home. I'm better here. I can cope when I'm working. At home, I don't know what to do with myself.'

'Alright, but take it easy. Tidy up downstairs.' Mr Gorton stood to go. 'It's stopped raining. Take the rubbish out, a bit of fresh air will do you good. And Sheila, whatever you think you've done, surely Arthur and Elaine are more important? Remember love, war leaves scars that can't be seen. Believe me, I should know.'

'Thanks, Mr G.' *If only you knew, you wouldn't think so much of me. Tomorrow has to be the last time.*

*

As the train passed the cooling towers of the power station, the workers from the Chloride who lived in upper and lower Kearsley rose from their seats as one body and shuffled, in their usual sequence, toward the doors of the train. They trooped out of the station muttering goodbyes. The surging tree trunk of bodies fractured into branches and then into twigs that became individuals making their way up the garden paths of the villages and streets of the urban sprawl that was Kearsley.

Arthur strode out, parade ground perfect, his overcoat folded across his arm. As he rounded the corner near The Grapes he stretched his neck to look round the bloke striding out in front of him whose pace was more infantry than air force. He waved when he saw the two specks in the distance that were his daughter and mother-in-law. Once he reached Carter's shop the excited little body was released by her grandma and came barrelling toward him.

'Daddy, Daddy, give me a piggyback, p-l-e-a-se?'

'You are getting far too big for your old man to carry you on his shoulders.' Arthur bent down so that Elaine could scramble onto his back. She hooked her left leg over his left shoulder.

'Where's your other leg? Here it comes. Hold on tight to my head.' Clutching his arms around Elaine's legs, Arthur walked the final hundred yards with his shoulders hunched and his overcoat threatening to slip to the floor.

Settled at the table Arthur rubbed his hands in anticipation of the potato pie and poverty pickles his mother-in-law was dishing up, while Elaine attempted to wedge herself on the corner of his chair.

'Let your daddy have his tea in peace. Why don't you come with me to fill the coal scuttle?'

'She's alright, Mrs C. I don't see much of her, let her stay.'

'Suit yourself, love. That card's for you.' Mrs Crompton nodded to the envelope propped against the vase on the sideboard. 'Happy Birthday for tomorrow.'

'Thanks a lot, Mrs C. I don't suppose anybody else will have bothered.'

'Do daddies have birthdays?' The incredulity on his daughter's face made Arthur smile.

'Every year believe it or not, precious girl.'

Elaine shook her head in disbelief and turned to scrutinise his face. 'How old are you?'

'Thirty-one,' Arthur sighed.

'Don't be sad, Daddy.'

'What makes you think I'm sad?'

'The corners of your eyes; they're flat instead of crinkly.'

Arthur reached out and pulled his daughter onto his knee. He buried his head into her neck. 'How wise you are,' he mumbled against his daughter's hair.

'Can I play with Christine when we get home?' Elaine was wise enough to know when she was on to a good thing.

'For half an hour so long as you don't make a fuss when it's time to come home. You can play at Christine's until both fingers on the clock point to six. Your mam will be home from the Co-op by then.'

*

'Let's play schools. I'll be the teacher,' said Christine.

'Why can't I be the teacher for a change?' Without waiting for a reply Elaine plonked herself on the lumpy cushion that signified the pupil's chair. Christine bent down and, huffing and puffing, hauled a lurid yellow child's chair from under the kitchen table. She settled herself majestically and, brushing imaginary debris from her shorts, she looked down at Elaine.

'Because you're mousey and I'm a bossy little bugger.'

'Aw, that's swearin', you'll get your bum smacked,' said Elaine.

'Won't. Anyway, it's what my grandma says.'

'What does "mousey" mean?'

'Dunno.' Christine shrugged her shoulders.

Elaine watched Christine search through her toy box. There was an old baker's tray that Uncle Bert had brought home from his bakery for firewood, but Aunty Vera had said it was too good to burn. Elaine and Christine had helped rub down the sides of the tray to make it smooth and ready for painting. Aunty Vera had used a big piece of rough brown card she said was called sandpaper. She'd made Elaine and Christine special rubbing blocks from old matchboxes.

Elaine would have liked her mam to make her a toy box and paint a little chair for her, even if it was a funny colour. She would like dolls clothes and knitted cardigans and new frocks in material that matched her mam's frocks, but her mam was 'bloody useless with her hands.' Elaine knew this because that's what her mam said when Aunty Vera told her mam to 'get your soddin' finger out.'

Elaine sighed when she saw Christine lift *Well Done, Noddy* from the pile of books, wax crayons, dolls and teddies.

'I don't like *Noddy*. It's for babies and anyway, I've read 'em all.'

''Tis not. Anyway, BE QUIET Elaine Brooks or you'll be up here at the front and feeling the ruler on your hands. Now, come here and start on page one, and read every word.'

'Yes, Miss Webb.'

Elaine reached for the proffered book and settled down to start reading only to be interrupted by a loud shouty voice coming from upstairs. Uncle Bert had an afternoon sleep because he got up during the night to bake bread and cakes.

'Vera, where the bleedin' hell are my fags?'

'By the side of the bed where you left them, I expect.' Elaine heard Aunty Vera clomping upstairs. 'Bert, for the thousandth time, will you please not smoke in bed; you'll burn the soddin' place down.'

The two girls stopped playing. Elaine was scared; she had learned that raised voices and swearwords meant trouble. She glanced at Christine who was leaning with her head on one side and her tongue lolling out, listening.

'I hope you don't intend smoking in bed when we move.'

'When we flit from this godforsaken place I promise,

scout's honour that I will live like a gent, as befits folk who live in a betterclassofplace.

'What are they talking about?' Elaine whispered.

'Moving. We're moving.'

'What's moving?'

'Dunno.'

'I have to go home now,' Elaine looked at the clock. The big finger was nearly on four. 'I'll play with you tomorrow.'

Chapter 2

SHEILA CHECKED her face in the mirror of her powder compact. *Bloody hell, a love bite. How could I be so stupid? The last time. It must be the last time. Who's to know?*

'Come on, luv, stop admiring yerself in that mirror and give us a kiss before I take you back.'

'You've had more than a kiss, Fred Baker. Get this car moving. I'm going to be late picking Elaine up as it is. I hate Wednesday teatimes.'

'Just one.' Fred reached out his left arm and pulled Sheila toward him. She felt his right hand working its way up her legs under her skirt. His fingers crept over her suspenders and into her French knickers. For a second or two she rested back, the dark shadow of her self-loathing and hate dimmed by the promise of losing herself in the moment.

'No, Fred. There'll be all hell to pay if I have to fetch her from the classroom. You know what Miss Webb's like. The snotty bugger always had it in for us when we were at school. You'll have to wait until next Wednesday.' *No, not next Wednesday. Tell him now ... tell him you can't see him.*

Fred slowly drew his hands from between Sheila's legs. As he straightened up, he swirled the index finger on his right hand in front of Sheila's nose.

'Smell that pretty pussy, umm taste that pretty pussy,' he said, sticking his finger in his mouth and sucking provocatively.

'Stop buggering about and get going. You're going to have to run me over the bridge now and drop me at the bottom of Church Road.'

Sheila muttered under her breath as the car crossed the bridge over the Irwell. Anxious to be out of the car and at the school she fidgeted in her seat. When she saw a woman dragging one child by the hand and pushing another in a battered pram stop and gawp at the car, Sheila flicked her head sharply left to satisfy the sudden interest she'd developed in the effluent swirling down the river.

'Nosy cow, she's got an eyeful.'

'Ignore her, what's wrong with a man giving his old friend a lift home?'

'Because, Fred, she and every other person in these three villages knows we went out with each other from being at school.'

'We did that, right up until the war started and I joined up and you had your head turned by that stuck up lot. And look where that's got you.'

'Shurrup, Fred, it's too late now.' Sheila jerked at the handle of the car door and had it open before the car stopped. 'I'll see you tomorrow, when you deliver.' She leapt out of the car to scuttle up the incline of Church Road. Her head down, her elbows pumping and her bum swaying, she hurried past the large terraced houses that faced Holy Trinity Church and the gardens of the primary school. She was sweating cobs and out of breath when she reached the school gates. She took one look at Vera's face and knew she was in for it.

'Bloody hell, Sheila, you're playing with fire,' said Vera as Sheila rested her hand against the gate post. 'I saw him dropping you off.'

'Don't start. I'll only be a sec, hang on.'

'No, I won't. Walk home on your own. You're married, Sheila, for good or ill, and it's time you…What's up, Christine, love?'

'I want to wait for Elaine. Pleeease, Mam, let's wait,' Christine said, pulling at the skirt of her mother's coat. 'Look, Miss Webb's seen Aunty Sheila and let Elaine go, she's coming. Look she's nearly here, running up the path.'

'Where've you been, Mam?' Elaine mopped away tears and snot with her coat sleeve. 'Miss Webb wouldn't let me out until she could see you.' Elaine wrapped her arms around her mother's legs and rested her head on Sheila's creased skirt. 'Ew, you smell like stinky fish.'

'Is it any wonder?' Vera raised her eyebrows. 'They were supposed to be trying on their costumes for the May walks this aft but, well … come on girls, let's go and look at the penny tray in Simmonds' shop. You'd best get home, Sheila, and give your fish fillets a good wash down.'

*

Arthur glanced into the distance, down the road to his

in-law's house. There would be no little figure looking
for him today. Elaine would, no doubt, be peering out of
the front room window looking for him with one eye on
Children's Hour.

He was proud that they were one of the few families
in Hazel Avenue to have had a television set for the
Coronation. Although Sheila had been in her element,
lauding it over the neighbours who'd crowded in to peer
at the snowy pictures of Princess Elizabeth as she became
Queen, she had soon got fed up of the pomp and ceremony
and abandoned Arthur to the liturgy while she helped to
set up the street party. Arthur had been disappointed with
his wife. She had no idea of the significance of the solemn
occasion, the dawn of a new Elizabethan era with optimism
and hope for a better future.

She was more interested in the party and the singing and
dancing. Arthur hadn't seen her after he'd excused himself
from the festivities to put Elaine, who was dropping on
her feet, to bed. He read for a while and then had fallen
asleep on the couch. Sheila told him the following day that
she hadn't wanted to wake him, so she'd covered him with
a blanket and gone to bed. And now, the best part of a
year later, what had become of them? Not much hope for
a better future or for another kiddie the way things were.
What had happened to the vivacious girl he knew before
the war? Where had she gone?

Arthur looked and looked again. He couldn't believe his
eyes, but lo and behold, there Sheila was, standing on the
doorstep, smiling, with her arm around Elaine's shoulders.

'Hello, Arthur luv, we were just going to set off to meet

you. Weren't we, Elaine?'

Elaine glanced up at her mam, shook her head, opened her mouth to say something but abandoned speech when she saw her daddy bend his knees and open his arms to her. She hurtled to him to be lifted high and twirled around.

'Come on you two, at this rate it'll be breakfast time before we have our tea.'

Arthur looked around the front room. Surely he was seeing things; the room looked, well, clean and tidy. Sheila was no housewife. Arthur spent Saturday mornings while Sheila was working at the Co-op, dusting and Ewbanking.

'I thought it would be nice for us all to have our tea together for once.' Sheila handed Arthur the card she'd found pushed down the side of the settee, 'especially with it being your birthday.' Sheila busied herself turning on the gas under the chip pan. 'Egg and chips, something warm and home cooked. It'll be a bit tastier than tripe and a tomato. Elaine's had a sauce buttie to put her on, and look, Arthur; I found a bottle of beer in the pantry. ... Arthur, are you okay?'

'Fine, Sheila, I'm fine. Bloody marvellous in fact.' He bent to kiss his wife's cheek. 'You look lovely; I like that scarf round your neck, very jaunty.'

'Well it's nice to make an effort once in a while.' Sheila patted the knot in the scarf. 'Here, drink this while I fry the eggs. You never know, we might feel like an early night.' Sheila smiled up at Arthur.

Sitting at the table and tucking into his tea, Arthur looked from his wife to his daughter. This was what he'd dreamed of, this is what had kept him going on those dark days and nights on the run in Yugoslavia: the thought that he would make it home to be with Sheila and their children. He would like more kiddies, but none had come along after Elaine. He managed to keep his mouth shut as Sheila piled chips onto a slice of bread, folded it over and proceeded to dip the buttie into her egg yolk. He wanted a better life for his family and that meant mixing with better company who knew how to behave. *One thing at a time, old man*, he told himself.

'Daddy, what's Moving?' said Elaine.

'Don't speak with your mouth full, love,' said Arthur.

Elaine chewed, swallowed and gulped.

'Now, what did you ask?'

'What's Moving?'

'Moving?' Arthur shook his head. 'I don't understand, love.'

'Aunty Vera and Uncle Bert are Mo-v-ing,' Elaine twisted her mouth and hesitated, 'from,' she hesitated again and then in a rush said, 'from Godforsaken place to Betterclassofplace.'

'Have you heard anything about this, Sheila?' Arthur ruffled his daughter's hair. 'You are a funny little thing.'

'But Daddy, what's Moving?'

'Bert's got a bee in his bonnet about flitting out of the village,' said Sheila.

'I can't say as I blame him.'

'What's wrong with the village? It was good enough for us all when we were growing up, and you liked it well enough when you used to come down here before you signed up.'

'Yes, well I agree with Bert.' Arthur nodded his head. 'I

think we should start saving for our own house.'

'Why?' Sheila said. 'We're ordinary working folk and besides, it's where I belong.'

'But, Daddy, what's Moving?'

'Shut up about moving will you, Elaine?' Sheila said as she abandoned her chip butty and reached for her fags and matches. Elaine hung her head and closed her eyes.

'Come on, Elaine. Let's help your mam by clearing the table.'

'No … it's alright. I'm sorry. I didn't mean to snap. You put Elaine to bed, and I'll sort this lot out.'

Anxious to recapture the earlier mood, Arthur reached out for Sheila's hand. She made to snatch it away but to his surprise relented and returned his squeeze.

'I know,' he said, 'let's save up and go to Cornwall for our holidays. Another year or two in the village won't harm us.'

'Arthur, are you sure? That would be marvellous, something to really look forward to; just like old times. Go on miss, up the wooden hill.'

Elaine slid off her chair and took tight hold of her daddy's hand.

.

Chapter 3

'HOLD HANDS and smile you two, you're supposed to be enjoying yourselves. I bet Bo Peep and Red Riding Hood smiled all the time,' Vera said to Elaine and Christine, who were standing side by side squinting into the sun. 'Here, be careful Bert, you don't want marks on them new slacks.'

Bert made to jump up from his crouched position and toppled over. 'Oops, watch my bloody camera, cost a bob or two did that.' He looked up at the two little girls. 'See, you can smile when you want to. Here, give us a hand up,' Bert clutched his camera to his chest and held out his other arm to his wife, 'and, Sheila you could light us a fag while you're standing there like Piffy on a butty.'

'She's a miserable kid at the best of times,' Sheila mumbled around the fag she was concentrating on lighting and nodded toward her daughter who was busy swapping her basket of apples for Christine's fancy crook.

'Sheila! Honestly. You're in one of them moods again. I don't know what's got into you. How can you say nasty

stuff like that? You never used to,' Vera said as she turned
to look more closely at Sheila. 'Are you alright? You look a
bit peaky and, if you ask me, you are definitely out of sorts;
you've got a face like a slapped ar-… backside,' Vera said
with a quick glance toward the girls.

'I'm okay, must be something I ate. Let's get these two in
the procession and then we can have a bit of peace for an
hour or two.'

'I thought we were walking with them and then coming
back here for our tea?' said Vera.

'Meat paste butties? I feel bilious at the thought,' Sheila
belched. 'Trust Arthur to disappear. Where's your Bert got
to? He was here a minute ago.'

'Arthur's over yonder helping the Mothers' Union sort
out their float,' said Vera, 'and Bert's over there. Why on
earth is he taking photographs of that woman and little
girl? Who does he think he is, Cecil, bloody, Beaton? Do
you know them, Sheila, that woman and the little girl?'

'Betty Wilson. She lives in Little Lever, near the canal.
She used to come down here before the war. Do you not
remember her? She had that kiddie with a soldier who got
her up the duff and left her in the lurch. He didn't come
back – poor sod. She called in't Co-op the other day and
made a point of telling me that she's moving down here.
Her little girl'll be in the same class as Elaine and Christine.'

Vera called over her shoulder 'Come on, Bert, I'm going
with Sheila to put Christine and Elaine in the procession.'

'Coming. I'm coming, hold your horses.'

Sheila, interested in Bert's lingering to talk to Betty
Wilson, turned around. *That's cash he's pushing in her hand.*

I wonder what all that's about.

'Watch your step, Sheila, you clumsy bugger,' Vera said as Sheila stumbled over a hummock of grass.

*

'Come on, Christine, Elaine, there's two places over here, get sat down.' Vera guarded the places at the long trestle table as the girls wound their way between Humpty Dumpty, Jack Horner, Snow White, Peter Pan and other assorted pint-sized characters and their parents. The carnival tea was in the Sunday school, a large building with vaulted ceilings that magnified the piping voices of the children who were frazzled by the excitement of walking in a procession in the May sunshine. The frustrated calls of their half-pissed parents who had been making the most of the extended opening hours of the village pubs and clubs while their sons and daughters trooped around the villages in their fairy tale finery mingled and added to the din.

'Is it alright if our Marion sits here?'

Vera smiled and nodded at the woman she'd seen Bert talking to.

'It would be nice if she could; she's going to be in the same class as your Christine and her friend,' the woman said.

'Help yourself. Shove up, luv,' Vera nudged a small boy dressed as Noddy. 'Stick her in here. Did Sheila say you're called Betty?'

'Yes, Betty Wilson. She's a one isn't she, that Sheila? Life and soul of the party; likes her fun, especially with the lads.'

'Shush won't you? That was before the war.' Vera nodded

pointedly at the man on the far side of the trestle table. He was intent on relieving Christine of her shepherdess crook and poke bonnet and Elaine of her red cape and straw basket. 'Arthur,' Vera raised her voice in an attempt to make herself heard, 'this is Betty. She's moving into Prestolee with her little girl. Betty, this is Arthur, Sheila's husband.' Vera said raising her eyes at Betty.

'Hello luv, pleased to meet you. You're not from round here are you?' said Betty.

'No, I used to come down to meet my friend Giles before the war. His dad was the manager at the Paper Mill.'

'That's how you met Sheila, isn't it, Arthur?' said Vera, her voice rising even further.

'Yes, and she introduced me to Vera and Bert, and Fred of course.' Arthur smiled at Vera. 'They're my friends now, and good friends at that. Isn't that right, Vera?'

'Yes, well yes ... me and Bert certainly,' Vera spluttered, 'Christine and Elaine are the best of pals. Just like me and Sheila were when we were growing up.' Vera contemplated the stranger. 'What's made you want to move to the village? Here luv, have a paste butty.' Vera moved the plate holding a collapsing mountain of soggy squares of white bread from the reach of Noddy's sticky fingers and pushed two onto the thick white plate in front of Betty's daughter. 'What's your name, luv?'

'Marion,' the little girl said around the mush in her mouth.

'Funny, that's what Bert liked when I was expecting, but I had my heart set on Christine.' Vera shrugged and smiled at Marion. 'What a pity you and Christine won't be able to play together.' She shifted Marion's plate and reached into the centre of the table to retrieve a lurid green jelly set in a glazed cardboard pot and plonk it in front of the little girl. 'Don't be shy, Marion. Dig in or these little terrors will eat the lot.'

'Why won't they be able to play together?' Betty barked across the table. 'I said why won't they be able to play together – my Marion and your Christine?'

'Sorry, I can't hear a bloody thing above this racket. Did you say why won't they be able to play together?' Vera looked askance at Betty. 'Are you alright, luv?'

'It's on then – the move?' Arthur cocked his head at Vera. 'I was saying to Sheila, I can't say I blame you – making a better life, buying your own house. Where is Sheila by the way?'

'She was feeling bilious earlier on. She's probably in the lavvy,' said Vera.

Chapter 4

SHEILA TURNED on the telly before staggering toward the settee. Settling back, she closed her eyes. *Perhaps I had too many brandy and lemonades when we finished up at the Working Men's. Drinking in an afternoon has never suited me. It was all my mam's fault saying they'd cure my bilious attack.* Sheila belched. *Still, it hasn't been a bad day; at least the rain held off. It would have been awful trailing around in drizzle, and feeling bilious got me out of helping with the teas. It's getting awkward with Arthur and Fred. Thank God Arthur had his head in a book most of the time. Fred's being a bloody nuisance though.*

I regret the day I ever took up with him again. I couldn't resist with being tired and feeling lonely. Like Vera said, I'm married for good or ill and Arthur sees him as a friend. It's a wonder my mam's not noticed when we're all together at the Working Men's. Him trying it on and me pushing him away. The guilt's driving me barmy. I should never have let him go all the way. Messing about is wrong, I know, but going all the way is ... sinful.

Arthur? Well he is my husband when all's said and done and let's face it, I've made it up to him, letting him hoist my nightie up whenever he feels like it. It's kept him satisfied and stopped the awful nagging voices in my head telling me I'm a good-for-nothing trollop.

'It'll be a while before she goes to sleep; they've had a marvellous day.' Arthur patted his wife's head as he squeezed through the space between the settee and the utility sideboard.

'Do you fancy a cuppa? You look done in.'

'Yes, that would be lovely, and a cup of liver salts.' Sheila belched, again. 'I must have eaten something, my belly's still upset.'

'I'll butter us a couple of cream crackers as well, then we can settle down to watch that new play – *Dixon of Dock Green.*'

*

The church bells clanged into Sheila's consciousness. Her head bumped and thumped, she felt like death warmed up. She threw back the covers and bolted toward the bathroom, just in time – she spewed and sweated with her head over the sink. When she finally lifted her head, the room swam. She needed a wee. *What did Arthur say he was going to do? Build a rock garden with Elaine. Who in Prestolee had a rock garden?* Sheila hitched up her nightie, perched herself on the side of the bath and relaxed as a stream of warm urine splashed against the porcelain. When she finished, she retrieved a pair of her old knickers that had metamorphosed into a mop cloth, and a bottle of bleach

from the airing cupboard and wiped around the bath.
Arthur had banned the jerry and insisted that they all use
the lavvy. He expected them to traipse downstairs through
the front room into the kitchen and out of the back door
to use it – even during the night. Why the council couldn't
have had the gorm to put lavvies in the bathroom, instead
of outside by the back door, God only knew. Still, she felt
better now and ready for a bit of toast. Replacing the bleach
and the mop cloth in the airing cupboard, she spied a box
of *Dr. White's. Hang on!* She staggered back until she hit the
side of the bath, her head spinning. *I can't be, can I? Bloody
hell – NO.* In a blind panic Sheila racked her brains. *When
was I last on?* She couldn't think straight. *Hellfire, not since
that Wednesday; weeks ago. Why now after all this time?*

The smell of toast began to make her mouth water. *I'm
hungry, really hungry. Is it any bloody wonder?* Standing in
front of the dressing table Sheila yanked her nightie over
her head. Peering into the mirror her blue veined breasts
told her what, deep down, she already knew.

'Sheila, what's keeping you?'

'I'm coming. Keep your hair on.'

Her bra was tight, even on the first hook. She checked
in the mirror as she pulled up her knickers. *Christ. I'm
showing. There's nothing for it I'm going to have to tell him
… and Fred. Dear God, I don't want another kiddie. Elaine'll
be turned seven. I can't stay at home. I need Vera and Mr G.
God forbid; how am I going to cope?*

'Sheila, what are you doing up there? You're not feeling
bilious again are you?'

'Stop mithering.' She dragged her nightie back on over

her underclothes. 'I'm coming down.'

Arthur turned around from the sink to find Sheila leaning on the frame of the middle door. 'You look ashen. You'd best go and see Dr Kelly tomorrow. Sit down and I'll make a fresh pot of tea.'

'Where's Elaine?'

'Playing in the garden… Sheila, I do wish you'd give her a bit more attention and care.'

'What does it matter? Pass us my fags.'

'She'll grow up thinking you're not bothered about her. She's a lovely child; surely you could make a bit more effort? After all, she's all we've got.'

Sheila drew on her cigarette; she held the smoke in her mouth and then, taking her time, blew it out. 'Not any longer she isn't. I'm three months gone…'

Arthur paused from spooning tea into the teapot.

'What did you say? He dropped the packet of tea onto the kitchen table and loose tea spilled across the oil cloth. 'I can't believe it… Sheila, love, that's the best news ever. When are you … when will it…?'

'I don't know for sure; I'll go and see Dr Kelly after work tomorrow.' Sheila traced her fingers through the spilt tea. *Arthur, please don't cry. I can't cope with you, with me, with any of this bloody mess.* 'I hope this doesn't put paid to us going to Cornwall?'

'Cornwall … there are more important things to think about now.' Arthur took Sheila by the shoulders and guided her toward the settee. 'Come on, sit down, I'll bank the fire up then you can have a bath.'

Sheila pulled the neck of her nightie toward her nose. 'I

do pong a bit.'

Arthur wrinkled his nose. 'It doesn't matter. Nothing matters except you and the baby and our Elaine,' he lowered his voice, 'my family.'

'I could murder a cup of tea,' Sheila said as she flicked through the pages of *Woman's Own,* 'and will you fetch me my fags and matches?' she called from her reclined position on the couch.

'Let me finish banking the fire then I'll get the brisket in the oven and make a pot of tea.'

*

Elaine smiled because her daddy was smiling. It was Sunday, an S-sounding day and her daddy's eyes were crinkly – he was smiling. Her mam looked pretty; she'd rolled her hair and painted her nails. She wasn't smiling, but she wasn't cussing either or saying she felt Billy Us. Elaine wasn't sure what her mam meant when she kept saying she was feeling rotten, feeling Billy Us. There was a boy called Billy Greasley in Miss Webb's class, who sat behind Elaine and Christine, but she couldn't see how Billy Greasley fitted in with the naughty boy who made her mam feel poorly. Her mam and daddy didn't like her to play with naughty boys and girls.

'Mam, where is Billy Us?'

'What? Bilious? It's gone. Gone for good, I hope.'

'Was he a naughty boy?'

'Elaine, what are you going on about? Here, Arthur,' Sheila twisted her head and shoulders to shout toward the middle door, 'Elaine thinks the baby's going to be a boy.'

Arthur appeared in the doorway with a knife in one hand and a potato in the other. 'You haven't said anything to her, have you? I don't think we should tell her yet. Six months is a long time for her to wait.'

'Course I haven't. I'm not bloody stupid.'

Elaine glanced from her mam to her daddy and decided the best place to be was under her bed with Isle of Man Teddy.

201 Hazel Avenue
Prestolee
Radcliffe

Dear Mam and Dad,

I hope you're both well. We're all very well and have wonderful news that I know you will be pleased to hear. Sheila is expecting again. We had given up hope that we might have another child after more than six years. You had better get the knitting needles out, Mam. We are not altogether sure when the baby is due. Sheila has only told me the news this morning, she will ask off work early to the doctor's on her way home tomorrow.

Do you think you will be coming to visit, Mam? It seems a good while since I last saw you and Elaine and Sheila will be glad to see you.

It would be good to see more of you and Dad. Elaine is growing up fast. She's as bright as a button – always on the go, asking questions and that. Her teacher Miss Webb says she is one of the cleverest in the class. I have high hopes that when the time comes she will pass the exam for the grammar school, but that's a long time off.

I hope things are going well on the camp. Have you got more buyers for the chalets now that everything is settling down and people have more money?

We have booked to go to Cornwall for the summer Wakes Weeks or we would come and see you. I am hoping that Sheila will see sense and change her mind about us going to Cornwall, but I doubt it somehow. It's funny she says she doesn't want to move out of this village, but she'll traipse all that way to see her friends.

Our friends Vera and Bert are moving. Bert's bakery business is doing well and he can afford a deposit on his own house. He's even talking about sending Christine to a posh school. We will all miss them when they leave the village, but we'll still have our other friend Fred nearby so it won't be too bad.

Anyway, that's all for now,

Your loving son,

Arthur

P.S. I have enclosed a photograph of Elaine with Christine. They had a lovely day at the May walks dressed up as Red Riding Hood and Bo Peep.

*

Sheila peered at the envelope on the sideboard. *He's written to his mam and dad to tell them. Not that they'll be much use stuck in Singleton in that dump of a field. How his dad thought he'd turn that into a chalet campsite for the gentry of Bolton, God only knew. The Brooks family have some strange ideas; moving house, fancy manners and chucking that rich uncle's money away on a field next to a muddy riverbank and hoping to make a fortune. Some hope. Still, one or two stuck up types have signed up and for some reason I can't fathom leave their posh houses on a Friday to go and spend two days skittering about on brown mud on that miserable riverbank before wandering back to their little white prefabs with, of all things, outside privies. Why posh folk would leave their swanky houses with an inside lavvy and all mod cons to live in a cardboard box and go outside in the wind and rain to do you know what in a big bucket with no flush and which, into the bargain, pongs to high heaven, beats me. His mam and dad will be neither use nor ornament minding two littl'uns. Still, thank heaven I can always rely on my mam and dad, especially my mam to help out, because come hell or high water I am going back to work, no matter what Arthur says. Fred! I'll have to tell him tomorrow. If he hears he'll be round.'*

'Sheila, love,' Sheila stiffened as Arthur hugged her from behind, 'you were miles away, staring out of the window. What were you thinking about?'

'Nothing, just…,' Sheila forced herself to relax and sag back against Arthur.

'I know, you're imagining our new family, aren't you?'

'I am that.' Sheila turned and nodded toward the letter. 'You've told them then?'

'I have, love. I couldn't wait. They'll be over the moon. I expect my mam'll be here before you can say Jack Robinson.'

'Mmm.' *Bloody hellfire, just what I need.* 'Where's our Elaine got to?'

Chapter 5

SHEILA RANG the cash for a vase into the till. 'I hope your aunty likes it,' she said as she pushed redundant pages of the *Bolton Evening News* into the body of the vase. 'If you've any more shopping you can call back for it. You don't want it broken, do you?'

While the woman hummed and hawed about lugging the parcelled vase around the market, Sheila kept half an eye on the door to the back shop.

'Here, take it with you then.' Sheila shoved the package across the counter toward the surprised customer. 'There's somebody I have to see,' and leaving the woman to her shopping, Sheila tottered through the length of the furniture showroom to the door with the legend **Staff Only**.

'Fred, hello,' Sheila shuffled her feet, 'have you … do you?'

'What's up, love?' Fred perched himself on a bedding box. 'You look as though you've got ants in your pants. Come here,' he patted the space next to him, 'and let me cheer you up like I used to, while there's nobody about.' He fluttered his eyelashes, grinned and held out a hand.

'I can't, I have to keep my eye on the shop.' Sheila stood on tiptoe to peer through the square window set in the door.

'A minute or two won't do any harm, come here.'

'Fred, will you shut up and listen?' Sheila turned to face Fred as he moved toward her. 'I don't know how to tell you but…'

'What is it, love? What's up?' Fred nodded toward the door and Sheila's backward glance caught the deputy manager advancing through the shop.

'I'd best go. Meet me in the boiler house at twelve o'clock.'

In the hope of encouraging the hands of the clock to whizz to her dinner break Sheila set about dusting the sideboards, dressing tables, bedding boxes and wardrobes. *Fred, you know you've always been special to me. No, that won't do. Fred, you know the day we … that I let you… Well, Fred, I'm going to the doctor's tonight…*

'Sheila?'

'Vera, I didn't see you there.'

'I know. You were gone with the jolly robins muttering away to yourself. Sheila, I've been trying to catch you.' Vera chanced a furtive glance around the deserted showroom.

'Something's up with you, you're not yourself. You haven't been for weeks … months. Come on, what is it?'

'Bloody hell, Vera. What do you think it is?' Sheila sagged against the sideboard she'd shone to perfection. 'I'm bloody well expecting – again.'

'Again!' Vera cocked her head. 'After all this time? So, you're not bilious then?'

'If only, Vera, if bloody only.'

'G-i-r-ls, leave the gossip until we close for dinner and, for that matter, what are you doing downstairs, Vera?' Mr Gorton said from halfway up the staircase.

'Come and get me at dinner.' said Vera heading for the stairs, Mr Gorton's shaking head and barely concealed smile, the towels and bed linen.

'I can't, I need to see Fred.'

'Fred?' Vera paused in her journey and made a slow turn. 'What's he got to do… oh bloody hell, Sheila!'

'Girls! How many more times? Strange as it may seem, you are paid to work not fraternise. The divvy doesn't grow on trees you know.'

*

Sheila looked left and right as she stepped gingerly over the cobbles. The Co-op yard was notorious for being treacherous underfoot. The square formed by the rear of the tall buildings kept the sun and warmth at bay on the balmiest of days. The flotsam and jetsam from the separate Co-op departments managed to seep from the designated dump to help the unwary skid on offal, mouldy veg and the droppings of the cats and dogs that foraged in the refuse. With a furtive look around Sheila unlatched the door to the boiler house and stepped inside.

'Ow!' She yelled as two hands came from behind her to grasp her breasts. 'Gerroff, that hurts.' She twisted out of Fred's grasp and stumbled backwards onto a pile of coke.

'Now look what you've done,' said Fred laughing. 'Give us your hand, you silly bugger, and anyway, what's up with you? You didn't used to mind a bit of fun.'

'No, well, that was before… I'm not usually three months gone, am I?'

'What?'

'You heard, Fred. I need a fag, let's get out of here.'

'No. Sheila,' Fred rubbed his forehead, 'are you saying what I … is it mine? Is that what you're telling me?'

'I don't know, and what's more I don't bloody well care. I'm going to the doctor's tonight. I have to go now, I need a wee.'

'Sheila, talk to me. Sheila!'

'Leave it, Fred. I've enough on my plate, what with Arthur and Elaine and one thing and another. His know-it-all mother will be round to stick her nose in before you can say boo to a bloody goose.'

'Let me hold you.' Fred held his arms out.

'Just leave it, Fred. Leave it.' Sheila unlatched the door and, glancing down, noticed that her nylons were laddered. *Shine on; what next?*

Chapter 6

SHEILA HESITATED in the corridor outside the door to the doctor's surgery. No matter how many times she went to the doctor's, she never knew whether to walk straight in or knock. She chanced a knock and sidled around the door in answer to the 'come in'.

'Sheila, I haven't seen you in a while. How's that husband of yours, and young Elaine? I saw your mother last week – she called in and left us one of her coconut cakes.' Dr Kelly nodded to the chair next to his desk. 'Come on, sit down girl and tell me what I can do for you.' He paused to answer a brisk knock on the door. 'Come in. It'll be herself bringing me a cuppa,' he said as his wife sidestepped into the room and set a mismatched cup and saucer precariously on a pile of papers sitting in the middle of his cluttered desk.

Sheila creased her lips in preparation to smile at Mrs Kelly. *She looks as though she's sucked a bag of lemons. He deserves better than her, miserable cow.*

'Thank you, dear. How many more are waiting out there?' Dr Kelly asked.

'Eleven … maybe twelve.'

'What time is it now?' he said, scrutinising the watch nestled on his paunch. 'Half seven, should be in for my supper by ten.'

Mrs Kelly gave Sheila a wan smile and melted back through the door.

'She'd rather be back on the wards bossing the nurses, than a doctor's wife with five kids, but we make our beds.' He shrugged his shoulders. Dr Kelly was popular; his patients knew that if required he could, and would, walk through fire for them. His time was their time when they visited his surgery. Sheila had arrived at the surgery at twenty past five, it was now half past seven and she was tired, hungry and close to tears.

'Well now, let's see, when was your last period?'

'How do you know?'

'It's my Irish magic. Now, my dear, jump on the bed and I'll have a look at you.' Dr Kelly confirmed Sheila's pregnancy, gave her a letter to send to the hospital, reminded her that she would need to take a sample of urine to her appointments and suggested she had a bottle of Guinness each night because she looked a touch peaky. Sheila lurched out of the surgery toward the front door of the Edwardian terraced house. The bright evening sunshine dazzled her.

'Sheila, where have you been?'

Sheila squinted toward the voice.

'Fred? What the blazes are you doing here?'

'Waiting for you. I missed you at the Co-op; I've been here since quarter to six.'

'Why?'

'Why! You could be having my kid and you need to ask me why?'

'Fred, I can't. I don't know if it's yours or Arthur's and, to be honest, at this minute I don't care either way.'

'Come on get in, I'll run you home.'

'You must be off your rocker; leave me, I'll get the bus.'

'No, you can say I was driving past, whatever. You'll think of something, you have before.'

'Yes, well that was before,' Sheila settled herself in the passenger seat. 'Now is bleeding well after, whichever way you look at it.'

'Leave Arthur and come and live with my mam and me.' Fred blurted. 'Elaine can come as well.'

'How can I? Elaine and him ... well, she's his salvation. I can't leave him, and like as not it's his anyway. Drop me here. I'll walk the rest of the way.' She launched herself onto the pavement, made to slam the passenger door, then hesitated and bent down to peer back into the car. 'Fred, try and look pleased when Arthur tells you. There's no way I can leave him. My mam and dad, they'd kill me.'

With one thing and another I'm asleep on my feet. Thank God, it's half-day closing tomorrow, I could sleep for England.

Chapter 7

ELAINE REACHED up to unhook her coat. The little lamb on the picture above her peg looked sad today. Elaine looked at the lamb and knew how it felt. It was one of the days her legs didn't want to run and skip, and her head was all buzzy. It wasn't an S day, or her daddy would be at home all day and he was never at home on school days, he would be at work making batteries. Saturday and Sunday were the names of the S's days. Today was the day her mam would be at the school gate … on her own. Aunty Vera and Christine had gone. They'd moved to betterclassofplace. Elaine sat next to Cynthia now. Cynthia sniffed a lot and had green teeth. With a sigh at the thought of the penny tray at Simmonds' Elaine shoved her arms down her coat sleeves and followed the other boys and girls to the top of the steps that led to the playground. She hopped down the first two steps and then remembered it was a sad day.

One, two and a jump and there she was on the edge of the playground. She dragged her legs around the corner of the building and up the long path to the gate. Her hair ribbon was undone; she'd cop it. Christine would have reminded her and helped her tie it back into a bow. It was too late now. Elaine dared to lift her head. All of a sudden, her legs started to skip and her head forgot to buzz.

'Grandma Brooks!' she ran toward the plump, smiling lady who was holding her arms open wide. Elaine's coat flew open behind her as she ran into the safe squashy haven to be enveloped, warm and safe. 'Grandma Brooks, it's you. You're my fairy grandma.'

'What a welcome.' The lady with the grey plait looped over the crown of her head stooped down to look into Elaine's eyes. 'Let me look at you, my big girl. My, you've grown. Oops, Elaine, you'll have to help your old grandma back up.'

Hand in hand, Elaine and Grandma Brooks set off up the road.

'Your mam said you'd be pleased to see me. I got a bit lost and went in the wrong door but the headmaster told me where to go and said he'd make sure your teacher knew that I was waiting for you. Your mam's having a bit of a rest. You don't mind me picking you up, do you?'

'Can we skip, Grandma?'

'You can, love; I'll follow on behind.'

'Are you staying forever, Grandma?'

'No, love, only until after tea and then I'll have to go back to your grandad.'

'Can I come with you to see Grandad?'

'No, my love, you have to stay with your mam and daddy and go to school tomorrow.'

'I don't want to…' Elaine felt her tummy dip and her eyes

go prickly. 'I don't like my mam any more; she's wicked. Like a bad witch.' Elaine threw her arms around her grandma's legs so that the two stumbled. Grandma Brooks leant against a garden wall. 'Please, let me go home with you.'

'Elaine, love, what on earth's the matter? I've never seen you like this before. Come on, dry your eyes and let's go and look in the toffee shop.'

*

As he rounded the corner into the keyhole Arthur nodded to a neighbour contemplating his immaculate garden. No one knew why the local council had taken it on itself to build a group of houses in Hazel Avenue in such a peculiar formation as opposed to the straight roads that ran through the rest of Prestolee. Living in one of the two keyhole formations was seen as something special. Arthur craned his neck on the lookout for Elaine. The late afternoon sun was in his eyes. He looked and looked again.

There she was in the front garden, her little body bobbing up and down intent on something or other and she looked to be nattering to someone. *Surely Sheila isn't on her hands and knees in the garden?* He quickened his step.

'Mam, oh Mam, I can't believe it. What are you doing here?'

'Hello son, I got your letter and before I had a chance to write back your dad said he was going into Preston and could drop me at the station, so, as you can see, I'm here.'

'Can you stop for tonight?'

'No, love, your dad's meeting me off the eight o'clock train in Preston. I'll have to go to catch the bus back to Bolton soon.'

'Surely you'll have your tea with us?'

'We've eaten, love. Well, Elaine and I have. Sheila said she wasn't hungry. I brought a rabbit pie and I told her it was good meat. Your dad shot the rabbit himself. We've left yours in between two plates for later.'

Chapter 8

EXCEPT FOR the red double-decker buses that trundled through the village every twenty minutes Market Street was quiet, even with all the local children on school holidays. The times of the buses – five past, twenty-five past and quarter to the hour – and Fletcher's Paper Mill whistle set the rhythms of the three villages of Ringley, Stoneclough and Prestolee. The twelve o'clock whistle at Fletcher's Paper Mill brought a whirl of activity. Workers bustled home to the terraced mill cottages that lined the busy road through Stoneclough.

Shop workers flicked their signs to closed and pulled down their blinds. During the school holidays, as well as regulating the workers, the piercing whistle called children in from the fields, canal and riverbanks, playground swings and the backyards of their friends to head back home for their dinners. For an hour, a hush blanketed the three villages.

'Please may I leave the table, Grandma?' Elaine clattered her knife and fork onto her plate.

'Wait till your grandad's finished and then you can take all the plates into the kitchen for me.'

With a deep sigh, Elaine slumped against the back of the upright chair.

'Let her go, Maisie, she's eaten up and she'll do nowt but turn them big brown eyes on every mouthful I lift to me mouth.' He turned to Elaine. 'Settle yourself on the settee, love. Take your shoes off and let your dinner go down.'

Elaine slid off her chair, hauled herself up onto the prickly settee and arranged a cushion for her head. 'Can I have your coat over me, Grandma?' She snuggled down in anticipation of the heavy weight of her grandma's everyday coat being tucked in around her shoulders. The familiar smell of the coat, her thumb in her mouth and a full tummy was lulling Elaine to sleep when banging on the front door jerked her awake.

'Who the bloody hell's that at dinner time?' Grandad swayed back to crane his neck and peer out of the window. 'It's Vera and Bert's kiddie. I thowt they'd flitted,' he said as Grandma went to answer the door.

'Can your Elaine come out and play?'

At the sound of Christine's voice Elaine threw back the coat and scrambled off the settee, her tiredness forgotten. She edged around her grandma in the poky vestibule.

'My grandma says we can play on her front so long as we don't get up to any bother.'

'It's dinner time, love. Are you sure your grandma says you can play out?'

'Yes, she's standing at the front, she watched me down the road.'

'Aw go on, let me, Grandma. I want to play with Christine while she's at her grandma's. Please.'

'Alright, but don't go away, and don't talk to anybody you don't know.'

'Who the bloody hell will they not know, Maisie? Thee's lived down 'ere for nigh on 35 years and thee's still not gor it in thi y'ed as folks knows every bugger down 'ere and every bugger's business for that matter,' Grandad said as he rootled in his pocket. 'Here's some coppers, you can buy yourself some toffees when Simmonds' opens.'

'Mr Crompton?' said Christine with her head on one side, one eye half shut and a hand on her hip. 'Do Weary Willie and Tired Tim really live in your weedy garden?'

'Christine, luv, as anybody ever told thi that thees spittin' image of thi dad, in more ways than one – cocky little bugger that he is?'

'Tell her, Grandad. Tell her,' Elaine's brow furrowed as she threw her arms in the air. 'She doesn't believe me.' Elaine turned her head, blinking rapidly. Christine would call her a softy baby if she saw wet eyes.

'Where else would they live? It's taken me years to get them weeds to grow as high as that. But it's for me to know and you to guess when they decide to come down from Farnworth market to have a holiday in my special garden. Now bugger off the two of you so as I can have my afternoon's sleep in peace.'

'Let's look if Weary Willie and Tired Tim are here,' Christine edged along the narrow path that skirted under the front window of the house. 'Come on slow coach, help me look.'

Christine looked back over her shoulder at Elaine who hovered at the edge of the garden. The girls glanced up at the rat-a-tat on the bedroom window.

'My grandad wants us to shift, we'd best go and play at your grandma's like she said we could.'

The two girls skipped up the road, stopping to jump over cracks in the pavement and walking three steps forward two steps back to keep the bogey man away, until they reached Christine's grandma's house. The terraced house sat in a prime location on the corner of Market Street and Bridge Street. Christine unlatched the door and yelled up the dark hall.

'Elaine's here. We're sitting on the front. Can we have a jam butty?'

'No, you've only just finished your dinner,' a bad-tempered voice from the depths of the house shouted, 'sit on the front and play and let folk have a rest, will you?'

'Let's have a concert. You sit on the wall and watch, and I'll be the turn and sing.'

'Why?' said Elaine as she hitched herself onto the low wall.

'Because a Y is not a Z, and anyway, I go to singing lessons now.'

Elaine wriggled further onto the wall and stuck her thumb in her mouth while Christine turned to position herself on the kerbstones that had metamorphosed into a stage.

'Elaine Brooks, stop wriggling and take your thumb out of your mouth.'

'Yes, Miss Webb,' Elaine parroted, adjusting her position

on the rough bricks.

Christine counted herself in: 'One, two, three, *onbarefootdays*,' she warbled, '*whenwewerejust*,' deep breath, '*acoupleofkids-oh*,'deep breath, '*onbarefootdays, O boy, the*' deep breath, '*thingswedid*,' deep breath. '*We'dgodowntotheshadybrook. Withabentpin...*'

At the sound of a car slowing down behind her Christine turned, wobbled and managed to right herself with a foot in the road. Elaine leapt off the wall, scratching the top of her legs on the rough bricks.

'Watch what you're doing, little girl. You were nearly a goner then,' said the man, looking at them through the open window of his car. He bent sideways to open the door nearest the pavement. 'Would you and your little friend like to come for a ride in my car? I've got some toffees here ... look.' He held out a white bag.

'What sort are they?' Christine leant into the car.

'Pear drops. Do you like pear drops?'

'I do. She doesn't,' Christine nodded toward Elaine who hovered behind her, 'they make the top of her mouth sore.'

'Christine,' Elaine yanked at the back of Christine's cardigan, 'come on, we'll...' As she glanced up and down the quiet, deserted street Elaine felt sick rise in her throat. She gulped and swallowed. Her heart beat fast. She rubbed the top of her legs to quiet the sharp prickle of the scratches. 'We'll be in bother...'

'I've got dolly mixtures as well. Climb in, next to me; come on, both of you. Get in. We'll go for... what the hell's that?' Fletcher's whistle pierced the stilled villages. 'Come on, quick. Climb inside.' The man reached for Christine's arm.

'Gerroff.' She pulled away as front doors opened, and mill workers popped out of their doors like figures out of cuckoo clocks.

'Ouch,' Christine shouted as the door grazed against her shoulder on its way to being pulled shut. She tumbled over onto Elaine who fell backwards onto the pavement. The shiny black car drifted down the street. Two women marching arm in arm as they rounded the corner onto Market Street all but fell onto Elaine and Christine, who were sprawled in the middle of the pavement feeling dazed and confused.

'What the blazes are you two playing there for, you daft little buggers?' one woman said.

'Sooner they're all back at school the better,' said the other.

'Talk about teacher's rest, mother's pest. You can't get a minute to yerself one way or the other.' Without a backward glance the women stepped around the two girls and scurried on their way.

'My shoulder hurts.' Christine struggled out of her cardigan. 'Look there's a big scratch on my arm where that door banged into me. I'm going to tell my grandma.'

'Don't. We'll get into bother,' said Elaine, thinking about the shouting at she'd get if her mam found out she and Christine had been talking to the strange man. 'Put your cardigan back on, we'll go and play round the back. Look at my socks; they're mucky where you stood on me.'

''S'not my fault – you should have moved out of the way,' Christine scrutinised Elaine's socks. 'Come on, take 'em off and we'll give 'em a rinse through in the outside lavvy.'

*

Elaine closed her library book and slid off her daddy's knee as the familiar music that signalled the end of *The Archers* and the start of bedtime came out of the radio.

'Come on, precious girl, it's time you went up the wooden hill.' Elaine slid off the settee and made toward the middle door through to the kitchen and outside to the lavvy for a wee.

'Elaine, don't forget to give your mam a goodnight kiss on your way back,' her daddy said, nodding toward the settee where her mam was flicking over the pages of a magazine.

'I'm not sure I want a kiss from a very bad little girl who tells lies and flushes her socks down the lavvy.'

'I didn't flush…' Elaine clamped her mouth shut. With her head bent she glanced upward. From under her eyelashes she took in her mam's snarly face with its pursed lips and narrowed eyes. Why didn't a good fairy come and whisk her mam away to never-never land or perhaps a wicked witch could boil her in a cauldron?

'See, she's telling more lies. Come on then, tell us, how the hell did your socks get from your feet into the lavvy then?'

Under her still-lowered eyes Elaine watched her mam's lips press together and her shoulder wobble from side to side as she reached out for her fags and matches, 'Money doesn't grow on trees, you know. There'll be no more penny tray at Simmonds' for you, my lady, until you're back at school.'

As she watched the familiar wagging finger Elaine felt her daddy grip her shoulders and turn her towards the door that led to the stairs, bed, Isle of Man Teddy and safety.

'Go on up, love,' he gave Elaine a little shove, 'and start getting yourself undressed.'

'Sheila, she's six years old.' Elaine dawdled on the stairs to listen. 'Couldn't you try and be a bit gentler with her?'

'Bugger off, Arthur. It's well past her bedtime.'

Elaine scurried upstairs. She dragged her hand across her wet face. Weary with the shouting and telling off, she wriggled out of her clothes making a pile of her shorts, blouse, vest and knickers. She knew her daddy was cross because he was making a lot of noise banging things round in the bathroom. Washed down and with her nightie on, Elaine was ready to climb into bed when her daddy knelt down in front of her.

'Sit on the end of the bed, love. I want to talk to you.'

Elaine squirmed backwards onto the low bed.

'Look at me, Elaine. I want you to tell me again what happened when you were playing with Christine.'

Elaine tried hard not to cry. She'd told Christine they'd cop it; talking to the man and then trying to rinse the muck off her socks by pulling the lavvy chain.

'It was Christine – she talked to the man, not me – and I wanted my socks to be clean so that I wouldn't get in bother.'

'Tell me about the man again.'

'I'm tired, Daddy. I want to go to sleep with Isle of Man Teddy.'

'Climb in then. You do know that you must never talk to strange men, don't you?'

'Yes, Daddy.' Elaine rolled over. She was the most fed up she'd ever been. Fed up of trying hard to be a good girl and her mam telling her she was a bad girl. She heard herself sobbing. The sound seemed far away. She buried her head in the soggy pillow. She was fed up of crying, fed up of being quiet, fed up of the stiff, tight feeling in her head when her mam shouted. Perhaps the man in the car was a wizard who'd really come to take her to never-never land to be with Peter Pan and Wendy. She liked dolly mixtures. She reached out for Isle of Man Teddy. He never shouted or bossed her about. He was there when she needed him. Elaine kissed his snot and tear-stained face and closed her eyes.

*

In the bathroom, Arthur fished the soggy block of soap out of the washbasin and rinsed out the face cloth. Passing Elaine's bedroom, he glanced in. She was fast asleep. With a heavy tread and a heavier heart, he made his way downstairs. He was going to have it out with Sheila. There was something in Elaine's story about the man in the shiny black car that she couldn't have made up. If it hadn't been for the mess with the socks, like as not she wouldn't have said anything.

'I'll put the kettle on,' said Arthur to Sheila, 'then I want to talk to you about the man in the car.'

'Please yourself, but it's a pack of lies. They've made it up. Christine's always been an old busybody. It's all your fault – well, you and my dad.'

'What have me and your dad got to do with anything?'

'Weary Willie and bloody Tired Tim that's what. Taking her to Farnworth market at teatime on Saturdays to crawl about under stalls. And then you and your fancy books; taking her to the library at her age. What's wrong with *Noddy*? It's no wonder her head's full of all sorts of old tripe, like telling your mam I'm wicked. I ask you, what was all that about? Let the blasted thing alone, Arthur. I'm sick and tired of hearing about it.'

'Please yourself, Sheila. You usually do these days.' Arthur checked himself. His neck prickled and sweat coated his top lip, sure signs that danger threatened if he didn't back off. 'I'll make the tea and then I'm going to the phone booth to telephone Bert and Vera. Where did you put that telephone number Vera gave you?'

'I've told you till I'm sick of telling you, you're making something out of nothing. Leave it and I'll talk to Vera at work tomorrow. It's her last day. Bert says she's to stay at home from now on. Why she kowtows to him, I don't know.' She knitted her arms and snarled, baring her teeth. 'He's stuck to his word; I'll give him that. Now he's made a bob or two he thinks he's better than the rest of us with his telephone and bathroom suite. He'll soon want nowt to do with the likes of us.' Sheila paused to draw breath. 'Are we having that cup of tea, or what?' Sheila closed her eyes and steadied her breathing. *I'm sick and tired of being like this. I'm trying to change. I avoid seeing Fred. I hate myself, who I am … bad-tempered and peevish. I need to be different. I want to be different, but how?*

Chapter 9

SHEILA EDGED her way between the boxes in the back shop of the furnishing department. She held one hand over her abdomen to protect it from the sharp edges of the piles of furniture waiting to be released from their brown paper shrouds. She sidestepped around the obstacles, determined to get to Mr Gorton before Vera arrived at work. *He's bound to see the sense of persuading Vera to stop on until I've had this baby; then she can leave to do nothing but twiddle her thumbs, and then Bob's your uncle, I can have my job back.* Sheila was chuffed with her idea and was sure Vera would jump at the chance to have an excuse to carry on working. She was bound to agree, especially if Mr G laid it on a bit. *He could tell Vera what crackin' girls we are, how he'd be lost, how the place wouldn't be the same. He could tell her he couldn't afford to lose one of us never mind the two of us what with the amount of work we do.*

'Mr Gorton.' Sheila scuttled across the shop, bending to fasten up the buttons that were beginning to strain the fabric of her turquoise overall. 'Can I have a quiet word?'

'It'll have to be quick, Sheila. I've a lot to see to, with that delivery to be unpacked.'

'It's about Vera.'

'Vera? She finishes today,' he harrumphed, 'and here she is, on the last minute as usual.' Mr Gorton pursed his lips and stood arms akimbo as Vera stumbled down the shop mopping her eyes. 'Whatever's the matter, Vera?'

'Mr Gorton, I…,' Vera collapsed onto a two-seater moquette settee.

The manager stepped forward, his hand flapping. 'Vera, you know very well we do not allow staff to sit on the furniture.'

'What's up, Vera?' said Sheila, dropping down beside her friend.

'Girls, girls, the furniture!'

'Mr Gorton, I've come in, but I don't think I can work today, not after last night.'

'Why, what's happened? It's not to do with our Elaine's socks, is it?' Sheila glanced up at her boss and sideways at her friend. 'I'm sick to death of hearing about the blessed things.'

'Socks! Is all this hoo-ha for a pair of socks?' said Mr Gorton, peering over his specs.

'Socks? What are you on about, Sheila? It's Marion, that little girl who was in the May walks with Christine and Elaine. She's gone missing.'

'Missing? What's that to do with our Elaine's socks?' said Sheila.

'Sheila, belt up about socks. It's nothing to do with bloody socks.' Vera rooted in her coat pocket and extricated a soggy hanky. 'It's that woman, Betty Wilson.'

'Betty Wilson?' *Bloody hell, it's true and Vera's found out. That little girl is Bert's kid after all. I knew it.*

'It was just after the war, Vera. Lots of stuff happened,' Sheila shook her head and reached out to pat Vera's arm, 'that shouldn't have happened.' *Believe me, I know about things that should never have happened.*

'Sheila!' Vera leaned back against the moquette and closed her eyes for a second or two. 'Belt up will you, my head's banging like mad.'

'Will one of you girls please tell me, in words of one syllable, what is going on? It is ten minutes past opening time and the front doors remain closed.'

'That little girl, Marion, I keep trying to tell you. She's gone missing.'

'Missing, missing what does that mean? And what is it to do with you, Vera?' Mr Gorton said, looking anxiously at the front door.

'She's gone, disappeared. They can't find her. Her mam, you know Sheila, that Betty girl,' Vera nodded as she looked to Sheila for confirmation, 'well she's started to work for Bert and they came for him last night ... the police I mean. They thought a man should be with her. He's in a right state; you'd think the kiddie was his, the way he's going on.'

'I'd put money on it,' Sheila muttered.

'What did you say, Sheila? You aren't half in a funny mood going on about socks and chunnering under your breath.'

'Nothing, it's just that, well...' *The man in the car with the toffees.* Sheila's hand covered her mouth '…bloody hell I feel sick.' *Dear God. I wouldn't listen to Elaine.*

'Please, stand up, Sheila. Get off that furniture,' said Mr Gorton, whirling his arms as though he held sparklers on Bonfire Night, 'I don't want that settee stained.'

'Did your Christine, by any chance,' Sheila belched into her hand, 'say anything about a man in a shiny black car offering her and Elaine some toffees?'

'Girls, I really must protest.'

'Hold your horses, Mr G, this is serious.' Sheila took a deep breath. Her heart was hammering and she could see stars floating. 'There's more to this than meets the eye.'

'Sheila, are you sure you're fit to be here?' Vera squirmed to sit sideways on to her friend. 'I tell you I've been up all night because some kiddie we hardly know has gone missing and you go on about socks and men in shiny black cars.'

'It is somewhat tortuous,' said Mr Gorton as he disturbed a dining room display by swinging a dining chair around to face the moquette settee. 'Sheila, start at the beginning and let us try and make sense of all this. Socks and all.' He glanced around the department. 'Then we can all get back to work.'

'I can't, Mr G.' Sheila rubbed her forehead. 'I'm beside myself; my little girl, my child,' she stifled a sob, 'my Ellie. I wouldn't believe her.'

'Ellie! Whose Ellie?' said Vera. 'Mr Gorton, she's poorly. It's with expecting; some women go funny you know.'

'My little sweetheart. She was telling the truth. I'm a rotten mother, Vera. She was nearly taken. I didn't believe her. Bloody hell.'

'Sheila, Vera, please! I'm going to open the shop. What would happen if the Chairman should drive past I have no idea.' Mr Gorton jumped up his jowls quivering and turned toward the door, jangling his keys. 'And then may I suggest we get this thing straightened out.'

'Sheila, I still don't understand what you're on about,' said Vera.

'Understand? What's to understand? That man, him in the black car, the shiny black car, he offered my little Ellie and your Christine some toffees to get in his car. Fletcher's whistle went and he drove off. Somehow our Ellie's socks got dirty and they tried to wash them in your mam's outside lavvy.'

'You look as though you've seen a ghost, Sheila.' Mr Gorton resumed his position on the dining chair. 'Now, where are we?'

'Why are you calling her Ellie?' said Vera, looking perplexed.

'I don't know something's come over me. I feel dead queer, like something deep inside me has caved in. My legs are like jelly.' Sheila covered her face with her hands and rocked backwards and forwards, squealing.

'Girls, I'm going to have to insist…'

'You'd best call the bobbies, Mr Gorton,' said Sheila through her hands. 'It seems obvious to me, my little Ellie and Christine were nearly taken by that evil bugger.' She sat upright. 'It just goes to show what a waste of space I am.'

'Sheila, you know I will never agree with you about … what you think about yourself. However, I do think the police need to be involved, with whatever it is you–' Mr Gorton waved his hands as though offering a nonchalant benediction to the two women, 'and Vera and your daughters appear to be involved in. However, I suggest you remove yourselves from the showroom,' he pointed toward the back shop. 'When I have telephoned the police station I will call the drapery manageress to, well, to come and see to you. While you are waiting you might stir yourselves and give that moquette a brush down.'

Leaving the moquette to its own devices, Sheila and Vera linked arms and ambled into the back shop.

'Sheila, I still don't really understand what you are going on about,' said Vera.

'Pull up that commode.' Sheila cleared a bundle of towels from a nursing chair and sat down. 'Ellie and Christine…'

'Ellie?'

'I can't explain, Vera, it's just that … well anyway, they were at your mam's playing on the front when a car pulled up and that filthy bugger offered them some toffees, Fletcher's whistle blew, somehow or other my little Ellie's socks got dirty and Christine gave 'em a rinse in your mam's lavvy.'

'Christine never said anything last night; course I don't suppose she would with all that fuss and bother about little Marion, although…' Vera's hand flew to her mouth, her eyes widening, 'come to think of it she did have a bruise on her shoulder, but I didn't ask her about it. Oh God, Sheila, they could … I should…'

✳

'Bloody hell that was quick,' Sheila said as a policeman's face filled the window of the door connecting the front and back shops.

The two policemen took Sheila and Vera through their stories. They were particularly interested in why Vera hadn't challenged Christine about the bruise on her shoulder and why the two mothers thought Elaine and Christine hadn't said anything about the man in the black car.

'Well … I expect they thought, well…' Vera looked at Sheila and shrugged her shoulders. 'They probably thought they'd be in bother,' Vera said, holding out her hands as if to surrender them to be cuffed.

'Why would they think that?' the one with the sergeant's stripes asked.

'We tell them…' Sheila sucked her lips, 'that they mustn't talk to strange men, don't we, Vera?'

'Or the bogey man'll get them,' added Vera, with a nod to the two men as if to say put that in your pipe and smoke it.

'So are you saying Elaine…?'

'Ellie. She's Ellie now. What's up, Vera, what's with the look?'

'Ellie? You're like a cracked record, going on about Ellie.' Vera turned to the sergeant. 'I think she needs to see a doctor.' Vera nodded toward Sheila, 'I don't like the look of her.'

For the remainder of the interview the two men struggled to keep Sheila and Vera in line as they digressed up alleys and down ginnels with their answers.

'I think we can call it a day for now, but we will need to visit you at home. We need to see Elaine, sorry Ellie,' the sergeant anticipated Sheila's protest, 'and Christine sometime today, as well as your husbands. From what you've told me I'm supposing your daughters are with their grandmothers.'

'Yes, but Ellie and my mam won't be at home. They'll have gone to the Working Men's to clean and get things sorted for opening time.'

'Prestolee Working Men's? Hmm, is your dad Billy Crompton, the bookie's runner?'

'Yes, so what?'

'Nothing, I don't suppose it's anything to do with this, but let's just say we've had more than one occasion to speak to Mr Crompton.'

'Yes, badgering him more like for trying to make a bob or two.'

'Sheila, leave it,' said Vera. 'My husband Bert's been out all day, helping search for that little girl … Marion.'

'Yes, that's very public-spirited of him,' the sergeant cocked his head to one side and closed one eye. 'Tell me, why is he so interested? It's unusual, isn't it, for a busy man … owns that bakery in Gladstone Road doesn't he, to be able to take time off? Is there something we should know … how should I put it … about your husband's relationship with Mrs Wilson?'

'Relationship, what do you mean?' Vera sat up straight, her head wobbling and her shoulders twitching. 'She works for him, that's all. He's good to his staff.'

'Hmm, that's what I heard. Come on, lad, we'd best be going.' Without further word or explanation, the two men rose. The 'lad' stuffed his notebook into his top pocket and they exited the way they had come in.

'I don't know about you, Vera, but my head's mazy with all this, that kiddie missing, then Ellie and Christine, a man in a black car with toffees, and what's it got to do with my dad and God only knows what else?' *Less said about Bert and that Betty the better.*

'Here comes Mr G with Lady Syddall,' said Vera as the two managers' shadows darkened the external window of the back shop.

'Well, Sheila, Vera, this is a fine mess we're in,' said Miss Syddall through puckered lips.

'Sorry, Miss Syddall, we didn't know about our girls and all this business of the missing child.'

'I mean the mess of the staffing, not your home circumstances. Married women working leads to, well, it leads to staff shortages. Your going home for the day will mean,' Miss Syddall pushed back her shoulders and stood as tall as a five-foot woman could. Her cantilevered chest quivered, 'that Mr Gorton and I will have to tend to the needs of the customers ourselves. Let me tell you, ladies, the drapery department is my life and I resent abandoning it to cover for your absence in the furnishing department.'

'Miss Syddall, I think we need to remember a young child is missing and…'

'Mr Gorton, what has that child got to do with the inner workings of my department?'

'I'll tell you what it's got to do with you and your bloody department, Miss Syddall, you stuck up cow…'

'Sheila!'

'Mr G, you can belt up too. Even you are more interested

in the soddin' divvy and what the Chairman will say than in our innocent kiddies being taken by a bloody nutter.' Sheila paused. Her heart was hammering, and she had a blinding headache. 'So you can stuff your job. Come on, Vera.' Without a backward glance, Sheila marched toward the stairs, the staff room and joblessness.

'Sheila! Oh my God, Sheila? Hang on, wait for me,' Vera said as she stumbled along in Sheila's wake.

The staircase shifted and swayed as Sheila attempted to put one foot in turn on each step. She reached out for the solid support of the banister rail in her attempt to haul herself up the mountain. The sanctuary of the staffroom felt miles away. She belched. *I'm going to die.* She lost her footing and lurched against the rail. *Poor Ellie; no mam. She'll be better off on her own, with Arthur.* Vera was pulling at her arm and saying something. Sheila heaved, belched again and crumpled to the floor. *Where's Vera?* Hand over hand she pulled herself upright and, with her sights on the staffroom door, made a sudden and determined spurt. She pushed against the door. Vaguely aware that the door banged shut behind her, she lurched toward the sink. The ground came towards her. *I'm dying. I don't want to die.*

'Stay where you are, Sheila. The ambulance is on its way.' Mr Gorton, on his knees on the floor beside Sheila, patted her shoulder. 'You can go back to your blessed department, Miss Syddall. You've done enough damage and caused enough upset. I'll manage here, these are my girls. Vera, do something useful, there's a good girl, go down and turn the sign to Closed.'

'I really do insist that I take over...'

'Miss Syddall, please leave us. These girls are like daughters to me.'

'Mr G,' Sheila said attempting to sit up, 'where's Vera?'

'I'm here, Sheila,' Vera said as she joined Mr Gorton on the floor, 'I've turned the sign but the door's still unlocked. Lie down again, Sheila. Try and keep still.'

'Vera, I feel all wet between my legs.'

'Sheila, surely you've not lost control of yourself?' Miss Syddall said, wrinkling her nose while she glanced toward Sheila's crotch.

'Miss Syddall, will you please just go,' said Mr Gorton.

'Vera, my belly hurts. What's happening?'

'Don't cry,' said Vera, hastily brushing her own damp cheeks. 'The ambulance won't be long. Will it, Mr G?'

Chapter 10

ELAINE, ENCASED in one of her grandma's pinnies, was standing on an upturned beer crate at the sink in the bar of the working men's club. She had her hands in warm soap suds intent on the job of ladling and teeming water from one pint glass to another. She stretched high with one glass while she held the other steady under the water. She was vaguely aware that her tummy felt damp through the pinny and her layers of clothes, but it wouldn't matter. She was with her grandma who had set her up at the sink and left her to play while she cleaned the bowls room.

Elaine wasn't allowed in the bowls room. She was sad that she was no longer allowed to touch the shiny black bowls that sat in their special racks. It took her both hands to lift the heavy bowls. It had been hard work for Elaine and Christine to lift all the bowls off the shelves and sort them out. They had dropped one or two on the floor. The bowls had made a loud thudding sound and rolled under the shelves where they couldn't be reached. Elaine had never seen her grandad cross before. He had said a lot of very bad words and threatened to lock her and Christine in the coalhole until Christmas. Now only Grandad, Grandma and the men who came to the Working Men's to roll the bowls on the bumpy green could go in the bowls room.

She wished her grandma would hurry up so that they could have their squelchy salmon butties with a bag of crisps and a glass of lemonade. Elaine sighed with happiness. Her grandma never shouted or raised her voice, but she would sometimes look sad if Elaine did something bad, like twiddling the dials on the gramophone.

Elaine's thoughts wandered and her mouth watered at the thought of the tangy vinegary taste of the bright pink salmon. Her grandad always told her to 'go steady wi' yon vinegar,' when she helped Grandma make up their dinner. Grandad had his on his own when he'd finished his rounds to pick up his bets. Elaine knew the bits of paper he called 'bets' had something to do with horses, dogs and football coupons. Sometimes, when it was school holidays and Christine was at her other grandma's, Elaine went around Prestolee and Stoneclough with her grandad to see his special friends. Elaine was interested in the 'friends.' Grandad didn't play with them or say very much to them. He took a piece of paper and some money from his friends and then put whatever they'd given him in a special bag that he showed her, but she wasn't allowed to touch. The bag had a special clock sewn onto the cloth. Elaine was perplexed by the goings on of grown-ups. Deep in thought, she jumped when the door to the big room banged shut and two policemen appeared.

'What are you doing, little girl?' the fat policeman said,

leaning over the bar.

'Ladling and teeming.'

'Where's your grandad?'

'Calling on his friends.'

'I'll bet he is. Who's looking after you then?'

'My Grandma. She's in the bowls room. We're going to have our butties soon.'

'That's as may be. Why don't you dry your hands and go and tell your grandma she's got company.'

'I'll shout for her. I'm not allowed in the bowls room. GRANDMA, GRANDMA.' Elaine hopped off the crate, tripped over her pinny and tumbled.

'Don't just stand there, go and see to her, you daft lump,' said the fat policeman. Elaine stared, fascinated, as the thin policeman's face hovered over her. It was covered in spots; some of them had joined together and were oozing yellow stuff.

'You've got a spotty face,' she told him. 'Is it sore?' She reached up to touch it.

He backed away. 'Come on, Ellie, we need to get you dry.' He reached toward a pile of pot towels on top of a tower of crisp boxes.

'I'll dry myself,' Elaine ignored the proffered pot towel and rummaged in her grandma's shopping bag to extricate a clean roller towel intended for the **Ladies**. Dabbing herself dry Elaine heard her grandma's voice at the other side of the bar; she was talking to the fat policeman. They were talking about her.

'Her name's Elaine, not Ellie,' she heard her grandma say.

'Elaine? Ellie? What does it matter? We need to ask her

some questions.'

'What sort of questions?'

'Nothing for you to bother about, Maisie.'

'It's Mrs Crompton to you, sergeant, and I will bother if it's all the same to you. I said, what sort of questions?'

'A kiddie's gone missing and we think Ellie, sorry Elaine,' he raised his eyebrows, 'might be able to help us; and before you get on your high horse and say anything else, her mam knows about us talking to her. She told us where she'd be. Now, how about a cup of tea while we have a quiet word?'

'I'm staying with her. You can ask your questions and then I'll make you a cup of tea, or perhaps something a little bit stronger?' Grandma inclined her head and creased her lips. Elaine felt the air around her shift. She sighed. She'd never heard her grandma sound really cross before. Grandma didn't seem to like the fat policeman who looked like PC Plod.

'Take these policemen and show them our special table,' said Grandma. 'I'll bring you a glass of lemonade.'

The special table had a carving of a man called W. G. Grace in the ironwork. Grandad said it was worth a bob or two and he was taking it with him when he retired. He told her that one day it would be hers. Elaine didn't like the look of W. G. Grace and tried not to sit near him. Careful to avoid the gruesome face, Elaine hitched herself onto a chair and the two men settled themselves facing her. The spotty one reached into his top pocket and pulled out a notebook and pencil.

'Are you going to draw?' asked Elaine.

The fat one gave Grandma a funny look as she sat down

at the table and handed Elaine a glass of lemonade.

'Elaine, love, you need to listen to the sergeant's questions and tell him what you know. The constable is going to write down what you say.'

'Why?'

'Mais... Mrs Crompton, we haven't got all day.'

'Elaine, love, just answer the questions and then we can have our butties.'

PC Plod asked Elaine to tell him about playing with Christine the day before.

'She was singing in the concert; she always sings, or be's the teacher.'

Mr Plod looked tired and fed up, just like her mam did when Elaine tried to tell her something important.

'What happened when the car pulled up?'

Elaine was surprised that PC Plod knew about the car. She and Christine would be in very big bother now.

'Christine wobbled and nearly fell in the road.'

'I thought the man gave you some toffees.'

'He didn't. It's bad to take toffees from strange men, and anyway, I don't like pear drops – they make my mouth sore.'

'Did the man offer you some pear drops?' PC Plod looked very cross.

'Christine told him I didn't like them, so he said I could have dolly mixtures instead.'

'What happened next?'

Elaine closed her eyes and tried to see pictures in her head.

'I pulled at Christine's cardigan; she was being a bad girl talking to...' Elaine glanced at her grandma for confirmation.

'Mrs Crompton, please can you help?' the fat policeman said.

'Elaine, love, why don't you tell the sergeant how your socks got dirty?'

'Fletcher's whistle went. Then people started to go back to work. The man banged the door shut. We fell over each other, and my socks got mucky. We tried to wash them in the outside lavvy. Christine's grandma's got two lavvies, one inside and one outside. Christine pulled the chain, to give 'em a rinse, and they disappeared.' Elaine bent her head in shame. She didn't know that PC Plod came to see children who flushed their socks down the lavvy. Perhaps there was something in *Noddy* stories after all.

'Elaine, have you ever seen the man in the car before?' said Grandma.

Elaine lifted her head slightly. What had the man in the shiny black car to do with her socks? Her top lip trembled.

Chapter 11

ARTHUR STARED out of the window at the cooling towers of the power station. The rhythm of the train changed as the scene shifted and the sewage works slid into view.

'Kearsley next stop,' the guard announced, passing through the carriage on the way to his van at the rear of the train. The lone passenger at the station, Arthur looked around; he felt strange without the tide of other workers that usually carried him down the station steps and onto Station Road for the brisk march toward the centre of Stoneclough. His sense of being in another world increased as he made his way through the village and glanced up side streets and alleys. Women were busy pegging and unpegging washing on lines strung from one side of 'the backings' to another.

Children darted in and out of flapping shirts, sheets and tablecloths. He didn't know this scene that belonged to the world of women and happy-go-lucky schoolchildren who were free from the constraints of school for five weeks.

Arthur glanced from left to right, hesitated, and then swept his eyes over the scene again. His shoulders tensed, he was on high alert. What would come at him next on this bizarre day? His manager had taken him to one side and told him that Sheila had collapsed at work and an ambulance had been called. He'd been allowed to use the telephone to call the hospital, but he was still none the wiser having been told that Sheila was waiting to be seen by a doctor and he should bring her night things at the evening visiting time. He attempted to ask for more details but was politely bidden goodbye and the phone went dead. He was frustrated in his effort to ring the Co-op from the phone box outside the railway station. He'd been about to press button A, but then saw the train coming and made a run for it. Now here he was, adrift, feeling out of time and place, wandering through a village life he didn't recognise, perplexed about Sheila and trying to make sense of Elaine's mixed up story. Why had Sheila collapsed? What did collapsed mean? What about the baby? What was that strange story Elaine had told about her socks and a man in a car. Had she imagined it, like Sheila said? His thoughts bumped and crashed into each other.

'Mrs C, Elaine,' Arthur shouted when he saw two familiar figures turning the corner from Bridge Street onto Market Street, 'wait for me!'

'Daddy.' Elaine ran toward him, her arms spread wide. 'Two policemen have been to see me about my socks. I told 'em I didn't be a bad girl.'

'Elaine love, what are you on about?' Arthur gave his mother-in-law a quizzical glance.

'Never mind your socks, love. Arthur, what are you doing here in the middle of the day? What is it?' Mrs Crompton seized Arthur's arm. 'Sheila! Dear God, has something happened to our Sheila?'

Arthur glanced around the street. 'Come on, Mrs C. Let's get you home.' He reached to put his arm around the little woman's shoulders.

'Tell me now, Arthur. Please.'

Elaine looked from one to the other of the grown-ups. Something bad was happening. The two best people in the whole wide world were very sad. Her nose prickled, she sniffed, a big juicy tear escaped and rolled down her cheek. Her daddy bent down and rubbed her cheek with his hanky.

'She collapsed in the furnishing and they've taken her to Townley's Hospital.' He crouched down. 'Climb aboard, little one, let's get you to 125.'

As they toiled down the road and into the house Arthur took his mother-in-law through the events of his morning, ending with the need to collect Sheila's night things for a stay in hospital. As Arthur knew she would, Mrs Crompton suggested that Elaine could move into 125 for however long it took for events to get back to normal.

'Do you think she might have lost the baby?' Mrs Crompton asked as she came out of the kitchen of 125 with two cups of tea.

Elaine pricked up her ears. She was sitting on her daddy's knee turning the pages of her library books. Lost? A baby? She didn't know her mam had found a baby. Out of the corner of her eye she saw her daddy flick a glance at her and then shake his head at Grandma.

'Little ears,' he said. 'What's all this about two policemen?'

'PC Plod is very cross about my socks?' Elaine hung her head. 'I telled him I was…'

'Told him. It's told, not telled,' said Arthur. 'Why are you talking like a baby?'

'Elaine love, shush, it's nowt to do with your blasted socks,' said Grandma. 'Don't cry, love, I'm not vexed at you. It's them bobbies, Arthur, poking round making snide comments about a man as is trying to make an honest, well … almost honest living.'

At Arthur's frown and puzzled shake of the head Mrs Crompton took a deep breath, sighed, and set about recounting the morning's events.

'… So it seems that our Elaine and Christine might not have been romancing about the man in the car after all. According to that sergeant, a kiddie called Marion has been missing since yesterday teatime.'

Arthur pulled Elaine close into his chest. 'God forbid.'

'What's romancing?' said Elaine.

＊

'Will this do?' said Arthur, emerging from the cupboard under the stairs holding a tartan shopping bag.

'It will when I've given it a wash down with a damp cloth. Honestly, Arthur, I don't know how you put up with our Sheila's slapdash ways. This house is a bloody midden.'

'She works hard at the Co-op … long hours and that.'

'It's no excuse for living in a pigsty, and the way she turns Elaine out in a morning is nobody's business.'

'I try to help where I can.' Arthur held out his arms and

bowed his head.

'I'm not having a go at you, lad. It's a woman's place to see to the house and her child. She's not been brought up to live in a tip; I've always kept a good table and a clean house.'

'I know that, Mrs C, but … well let's get hers and Elaine's things together.' Arthur felt drained. He was worried about Sheila and sickened to hear about the lost little girl. He shuddered at the thought of Elaine talking to some sick bastard in a car. The last thing he needed was a reminder that he lived with a woman who had come to disappoint him as a housewife and mother.

'While Elaine's with you tomorrow I'll give the place a good going over,' said Arthur.

'You'll not do it on your own. I'll be here early on and we'll set to.'

Arthur slumped backwards onto a chair, put his head in his hands and sobbed.

'Come on, Arthur, love, you're upsetting Elaine. Take her on your knee and tell her you're going to be alright.'

Arthur looked up to see Elaine with her head buried in her grandma's side. His little girl was sobbing and shaking.

'Come on, love. Your old man forgot himself for a minute.' He lifted Elaine to him and cradled her in his arms. 'How about we call in at Simmonds' and look at the penny tray on our way back to Grandma's?'

*

'It's her dad's fault, you know. He ruined her because we knew we couldn't have any more children,' Mrs C announced as she and Arthur watched Elaine ponder the merits of a sherbet dip as opposed to blackjacks. 'She could have everything she wanted. Well, except for her uniform for the grammar school.'

Arthur glanced around the shop, unsure of himself. He wasn't used to hearing confidences from Mrs C. The shopkeeper was in the back shop answering the telephone.

'I knew Sheila passed for the grammar school but...'

'He's not a mean man, far from it, but he insisted that the uniform was a waste of money for a girl who would only get married and have children...'

'Thank God, Oh, thank God.' The shopkeeper stumbled into the shop. 'That child ... they've found her curled up in the yard at The Horseshoe.'

Chapter 12

ARTHUR FOLLOWED the passengers dismounting from the bus at the terminus and followed them as they trudged through the hospital gates. He was dog tired from dragging himself through the endless day as one blow after another had thudded into him.

He hadn't felt like this since he was on the run, with Tito, in the Yugoslav mountains. Then, his salvation had been thoughts of home, of his mother worrying about him, his younger brother and their dad all fighting the fight and Sheila, his bright shining star, working on the land in Cornwall. She was like no other girl he'd known, vivacious, devil may care, yet kind and a good listener. She liked him to talk to her about the books he'd read. He'd been desperate to survive to get home to her, to propose and perhaps enjoy more fully her curvy body. The imaginings of what might await him in those warm, wet, secret places had cocooned him in the biting cold of the mountains. When had the star become tarnished? Was he as dismal to Sheila as she was to him? Mrs C's anger and shame at her daughter's housekeeping and mothercraft had jolted him awake to the lies he'd been telling himself about Sheila. He'd deluded himself and, as he trundled with his head down, he realised that he was worn out with the constant state of watchfulness he needed to keep an uneasy peace.

Elaine, his little treasure and the light of his life, had nearly been taken by that bastard of a man. Thoughts of being a tail end Charlie and the bombs that he had helped to drop defending his country sneaked into his consciousness, dragging him back to the evil scenes of horror and destruction. He'd been forced to take part in killing people, some of them innocent women and children – something that had haunted his days and devoured him in nightmares. The feeling of being soiled and rancid crept upon him when he was quiet and still. Arthur felt the familiar filth claw at his skin when he thought of the man in the black car. He told himself that if he ever got hold of that tosser he would wring his neck, hang, draw and quarter him and throw him into the flames of hell without a second thought.

'Sorry, I was lost in thought,' Arthur said to the man he bumped into.

'My fault, I'm lost too. Do you know if this is the way to the gy… women's ward?' The perplexed-looking man stood in the middle of the long hospital corridor gazing up at the signs suspended from the ceiling.

'Looks like it,' said Arthur. '1A, that's where I'm going.'

Arthur glanced left and right as he made his way from the outer entrance of 1A and up the corridor, past a linen cupboard, a toilet, a side-ward and the Sister's office. He hesitated, debating with himself whether to report to the Sister. He hovered outside the office; the Sister was busy talking on the telephone.

'Can I help?' A voice from behind him said.

Arthur spun round. A nurse carrying a carafe of water had paused on her journey into the ward. 'Yes, thank you, nurse ... my wife. I'm here to see my wife, Sheila. Mrs Sheila Brooks.' Arthur gulped, aware he was rambling.

'She's on the right, second bed. She's come round from her operation but she's still a bit groggy.'

'Operation? Oh my God.' Arthur reached to the wall for support.

'I'm sorry, Mr Brooks. Didn't you know? You'd better see Sister.'

'Sister?' said the nurse, stepping around Arthur to stand at the door of the office. A plumpish woman dressed in dark blue turned from her desk to face the nurse and Arthur. 'This is Mr Brooks. He didn't know his wife had been to theatre.'

'Thank you, Nurse. Mr Brooks, why don't you take a seat?' The Sister waved her hand in the direction of a chair adjacent to the desk. 'What have you been told about your wife's condition?'

'Er, nothing really – she collapsed at work. She works in the furnishing department at Farnworth Co-op. When I rang to see how she was I was told to come at visiting time and bring her night things.'

'I expect you knew she was pregnant.'

'Yes, of course. Was?' Arthur shook his head. 'I don't understand.'

'Mrs Brooks suffered an incomplete abortion. She's been to theatre to have the remaining products of conception removed.'

'The baby,' Arthur gulped. His hand shook and he felt his eyes prickle. 'It's gone?'

'I'm afraid so, but she's relatively young, and fit enough. Let her have a couple of periods and then try again. Now, if that's all, I need to get on with my report.' The Sister shifted her positon to face her desk. Arthur got the message, he was dismissed.

At the foot of the bed Arthur paused. Sheila was asleep, her head propped up on pillows and lolling to one side. She was as pale as death, her dark hair straggled round her face and her mouth sagged open as she whistled a soft snore.

'Help yourself to a chair from the pile by the door,' the nurse he'd spoken to before said as she approached the bed. 'I'll try to rouse her for you.'

'No, leave her. Let her rest…'

'Arthur, is that you?' Sheila opened her eyes.

'Mrs Brooks, how do you feel? Are you in any pain?'

'I could murder a cig and a cup of tea.'

Arthur shuddered. 'Sheila,' he snapped, 'the nurse wants to know if you're in pain. For God's sake, will you answer her questions?'

'It's alright, Mr Brooks.' The nurse offered Arthur a weak smile. 'I expect we can take it that your wife isn't feeling any discomfort. You can have a cup of tea after visiting, Mrs Brooks. I'm afraid your cigarette will have to wait until you can get to the day room.'

'I'm sorry, nurse. I didn't mean to snap, it's just that I'm a bit overwrought. I didn't know,' said Arthur.

'Arthur, love, come here. Don't cry, Arthur. Arthur, please, I need to talk to you, to tell you… Arthur, pass us your hanky. It's all my fault…'

Sheila had heard Arthur talking to the nurse, but kept her eyes closed. *He's here. I'm going to have to tell him the truth about the baby, about Fred, about everything being taken away from me. It's my punishment, I deserve it. If he forgives me, I'll be good, as good as gold … forever. Even if it kills me.*

The nurse was asking Sheila something. Sheila licked her lips; her mouth was dry. *I could murder a cig. Did I say that or think it? Arthur looks bloody miserable, what's he going on about? Bloody hell he's crying. What's that nurse blathering about?'*

'Arthur, it's all my fault. I'm a mess.' Sheila looked around, her eyes wild, her voice ratcheting up. 'I don't know what's good for me. Our little baby, it's gone.' Sheila screwed up her nose and, sniffing loudly, whisked her open hand under her nose; she stared at the gunge in her palm. 'Ugh, pass us your hanky.' Sheila slapped her lips together. 'And my teeth. God, I must look a bloody sight.' She grimaced. 'Arthur, how could you let anybody see me without my teeth?'

'Mrs Brooks, please try and calm yourself. The termination of your pregnancy isn't anybody's fault. These things happen, sometimes for the best…'

'What do you mean? You don't think I'm fit to be a mother, do you?' Sheila threw back her head and caterwauled.

'Sheila, try and calm down, everybody on the ward … they're looking at you.'

'What the bloody hell do I care? I've lost my precious baby and our lovely little Ellie… she was … that's why this has happened … the shock. But as well as all that,' Sheila gulped for breath, 'Arthur, I need to tell you…'

'Mrs Brooks, you need to take a deep breath or you will hyperventilate and lose consciousness if you insist on carrying on like this,' said the nurse.

'Sheila, come on. I know it's not what we wanted, but like the nurse said, these terrible things happen.'

'Arthur, you are the kindest man alive. How can I have done this to you? To us?' Sheila hung her head.

'I'll go and talk to Sister about a sedative,' said the nurse.

'Sheila, try and calm yourself.' Arthur hitched the chair closer to the side of the bed and took Sheila's hands. 'Try and take a deep breath and tell me quietly what's upsetting you.'

Sheila breathed deeply. 'I feel a bit light-headed.'

'Look at me. Now steady your breathing … that's better. Now try and tell me, very slowly, what happened.'

How can I tell him about everything when he's so honest and true? No good in bed though; a twiddle of my tits and in it goes for a quick roust about, it splodges out and that's it. Still, I've had my fun and now look at me: an unfit mother with her kiddie nearly taken and her poor little baby all mangled up.

'Sheila, are you listening? Sheila?'

'I'm a bad girl, Arthur, a bad mother and a bad wife. I wasn't like this before the war and when we were first married. I was nice then. I was, wasn't I?'

'You were more, I don't know, better to be with, laughing

and asking questions, more interested in things. Sheila, what are you going on about the war for?' Arthur rubbed his eyes. 'You were different. The war and its aftermath, it changed us all.'

'It didn't change you. Well, not that much. You're a bit quieter than you used to be; inside yourself. It didn't change Bert – he still thinks he's God's gift.' Sheila paused. 'Bloody hell, that kiddie, Arthur, did they find that kiddie?'

'Yes, she's here in the hospital. They found her at the back of The Horseshoe, that's all I know. Shei…'

'She's Bert's kid; that little girl.'

'Sheila, what are you on about?'

'You wait and see. It'll all come out.'

'Sheila, you're getting excited again. Come on, calm down. Have a drink of water.'

The clanging of a handbell penetrated the ward. 'End of visiting, thank you,' the nurse announced to the ward.

*

The taste of beer and cigarettes mingled with the musky scent of fresh sweat and Fred's tongue wet and searching in her mouth made Sheila groan with pleasure. She wanted more, much more. She groaned and squirmed then bit hard into Fred's neck.

'Mam.' Sheila felt a tap on her shoulder. 'What are you and Uncle Fred doing?' Alarmed at the unexpected voice, Sheila turned to find Ellie and Christine hanging over the front seats of the car staring at her and Fred.

'What are you two doing here in the back of the car?' Sheila said.

'Will you do that to me, Uncle Fred, give me a cuddle and tickle up my legs?' Christine said before she clambered over the seat and threw herself onto Fred's knee. Sheila watched dumbfounded as he started necking with Christine.

'It's not fair; she always goes first. I don't like Christine any more. I'm going to get into a big black car and go with Marion and the naughty man.' Sheila watched, frozen to her seat, as a sleek black car pulled up alongside Fred's car, the passenger door opened and a packet of dolly mixtures spilled out. Sheila shouted, but the shout stayed deep inside her chest. She clawed at her door handle which had turned into a giant pear drop. Elaine blew Sheila a kiss before she darted out of Fred's car and skipped up the pebbled pathway of coloured toffees and into the waiting car. The car tooted and took off into the distance, but not before Sheila had seen Elaine wrap her hands round the neck of the driver who, Sheila was staggered to see, looked like Mr Gorton.

'Now look what you've done, Sheila, with your slap-happy ways and your philandering. You deserve everything you've got, lady. Let me tell you you're no daughter of mine and your dad's. Bugger off and never darken the door of 125 again.' Her mother's voice was coming from somewhere deep inside Sheila, accompanied by the sound of her dad weeping and honking into his hanky.

The sounds of the ward seeped into Sheila's consciousness. She was swaddled in the bed clothes drenched in sweat.

Chapter 13

SHEILA GAZED out of the day room window across the narrow rectangle of lawn to the ward that ran alongside 1A. She watched the Sister in blue talk to the Sister in maroon. *They must be changing shift. I'd probably have been a Sister by now.* She glanced at the clock. Two o'clock. *Arthur should be here any minute.* Sheila straightened her shoulders, pulled on her cardigan and, resting her handbag on the windowsill, checked for her fags and matches.

She glanced again at the ward opposite; the Sisters were laughing together. She shrugged and let out a phew of regret at the sight of their success in life. They were qualified and happy in their work. *I bet their mams and dads are proud of them, I would be. Perhaps our Ellie'll be a nurse. I know one thing, for sure, if she passes for the Grammar she's going. She can be whatever she wants to be...'*

'Sheila, are you alright? What's the matter?'

'Arthur, I didn't hear you come in. Lend us your hanky; we don't want to keep the taxi waiting.' Sheila grabbed her handbag.

'There's no rush, take your time. Fred brought me. He's waiting outside in his car. He wouldn't hear of me coming for you in a taxi.'

'Fred!'

'It's good of him. He said he had some time off owing. Even so, we'd best get a move on, we don't want to keep him waiting.'

'Arthur, wait a minute, I want to say… I need to say… I meant what I said the other night. I am going to be different. Proper, like I know you want me to be. Like I want to be.'

'You've had a nasty shock, love. Let's get you home,' Arthur said as he picked up the tartan bag and guided Sheila toward the day room door.

*

Arthur stared out of the car window. He was bewildered, his thoughts jumbled. The loss of the baby – no matter what the Sister said Arthur couldn't help but think of it as a baby – had disturbed Sheila. She was remorseful, pleading with him to forgive her, saying she would change her ways, be a better wife and mother. It was what he wanted, what he yearned for … yet there was something in it all that was amiss. Something he couldn't put his finger on. At least she'd stopped that nonsense of insisting that Bert was the father of that poor child that had gone missing – taken by that evil, sod of a man.

He jumped as he felt a tap on his shoulder.

'Arthur, Fred's asking how long you'll be off work,' Sheila said from the back seat.

'Sorry, Fred, I was miles away. They've let me have tomorrow off as well as this afternoon.'

'So, you'll be on your own from Thursday on then, Sheila? I'll call in and make sure you're alright when I deliver in the village,' Fred said, glancing through the rear-view mirror and catching Sheila's eye.

'No. Don't.' Sheila shook her head at the eyes staring at her. 'There's no need. I'll be fine.'

'Sheila?' said Arthur squirming around in the car seat to give her a scathing look.

'Arthur, I've told you things are different now. I've my home and my family to see to … I'll have jobs to do, the tea to get and … and … well, I'll be busy.'

'Thank you anyway, Fred,' said Arthur. 'I appreciate your concern. Why don't you call in and see us on your way back from the football on Saturday? I know Elaine will be glad to see her Uncle Fred.'

∗

Elaine tugged on her grandma's hand. Her tummy bumped and her head buzzed. Something was up.

'Grandma, you're going the wrong way.'

'I'm taking you home love, your mam's at home now. Your daddy fetched her from the hospital this afternoon.'

'Has she found the baby?'

Grandma stopped walking and looked down at Elaine. Elaine looked up. Grandma was sad, like the little sheep on shuffly days. 'The baby's gone, love.'

'Have they looked behind The Horseshoe? That's where Marion was.'

'I think we'd best ask your daddy to have a little word with you.'

∗

Elaine lay in bed listening to the sound of the man next door mowing his lawn. The brr, brr, clunk noise of the mower usually made her feel snuggly and dreamy, but tonight she had a lot to think about. She had thought she might be better under the bed with her thumb in her mouth cuddled up to Isle of Man Teddy but Teddy was comfy, asleep against her shoulder.

Elaine knew he didn't want to move. She thought about the story her daddy had told her: Christine mustn't know that babies didn't come from under cabbage leaves or she would have said something. Perhaps she did know but with living in betterclassofplace she hadn't been able to tell her the new story. Anyway, her daddy said they came from a seed that the daddy gave to the mam. Why did Grandma say babies came from under cabbage leaves?

Elaine chomped on her thumb. It was a very, very silly story. Did the mam have a plant pot in her tummy for the seed to grow in? Was there a plant pot in the manger when baby Jesus was born? Daddy said he'd tell her more when she was older. The bad man had taken Marion to Ringley Woods, she'd run off before he could… Elaine tried to remember the words she'd heard her mam and daddy use … intofirewithher thankgod. What was a thankgod? Why was Marion near a fire in Ringley Woods? Little girls shouldn't go near the fire. There was a lot to think about. She wished she was a Teddy from the Isle of Man. Elaine snuggled down. She smiled. She was going to see Grandma and Grandad Brooks in Singleton. Cornwall would have to wait for another year. The snuggly blanket of sleep crept up over Isle of Man Teddy and Elaine.

Ellie? Why did mam call her Ellie?

Chapter 14

URING THE next week Sheila was on the receiving
end of a good telling off or two from her mam,
despite her delicate condition. She was left in no
doubt that her housekeeping was 'a bloody disgrace' and
that 'a man who worked hard and produced a regular wage
should be able to rely on his wife to keep a good table.'

Sheila rued the day that her mother and Arthur had set
about bottoming the house while she was in hospital. Every
cupboard and drawer had been turned out. The windows
had been cleaned with vinegar, the smell of Mansion polish
tickled Sheila's nose and a residue of Vim still clung to the
underside of the washbasin and side of the bath. Sheila was
pleased to be reunited with the knickers she thought she'd
lost. Her mam had found them festering at the bottom of
the wardrobe. It had been worth the earwigging to see her
mam's face when she handed over the washed and ironed
French knickers. Her mam had now insisted that Sheila,
with Arthur's help, stick to a routine for housework.

'I've never expected your dad to lift a finger, and before

you say anything, lady, you're not the only one who's worked and kept house. I've always worked.' Her mother harrumphed, 'least said about you keeping house the better, our Sheila. But, from now on you'll do as I say, is that clear?'

'Yes, Mam,' said Sheila, who had resigned herself to the inevitability of a life of drudgery and misery. 'I'm sorry. I know… well … I've had my punishment.'

'Sheila, don't set off crying again. That Sister said you were overwrought and had to rest. Come on, I've had my say. I'll make us a cup of tea and then we'll make a list of jobs for you to do each day.'

Sheila groaned.

∗

Over the next week or so life settled down for Sheila, Arthur and Elaine. Elaine started back at school after the five-week holiday. She had moved up a class, and although she still missed Christine, her longing for her bossy friend began to fade when her new teacher, Mrs Marsh, sat a girl called Ann next to her and asked Elaine to look after her.

Ann had moved into the vicarage with her mam and daddy, who was the new vicar at Holy Trinity. A little voice inside Elaine told her to try hard to make friends with Ann. The whispering inside her head said her daddy would be pleased. Mixed up thoughts of her mam – the wicked witch mam and the new, different one – and what she might think made Elaine's head go buzzy so she switched them off by carefully keeping her eye on Ann. Elaine watched Ann take a neatly folded blue hanky from up her cardigan sleeve to dab at her nose.

At break Elaine hid in the lavvy when she'd had a wee and folded and refolded the rag her grandma had torn from one of her cosy old nighties. Whizzy thoughts that she couldn't quite catch hold of were trying to tell her something. Something to do with Ann being betterer than her but that she, Elaine, was betterer than Cynthia who had green teeth and left silver snot threads on her cardigan sleeves.

When Ann smiled Elaine saw that her teeth were a milky white colour. Elaine took to watching Ann out of the corner of her eye when Mrs Marsh called her up to the front to read. She watched and listened as Mrs Marsh smiled at Ann and put her arm around her shoulders.

'Your speech is a delight,' she heard Mrs Marsh tell Ann. 'Not like these little heathens.'

Elaine said the word 'heathen' in her head. She didn't know what it meant but she was sure it wasn't a good word. Ann said 'my mummy,' not 'mi mam,' lunch instead of dinner and lavatory instead of lavvy. Tucked up in bed Elaine told Isle of Man Teddy, 'My mummy says we can have sauce sandwiches for our tea tomorrow, but only after we've been to the lavatory.'

*

Sheila was irritated, surprised and touched when Mr Gorton appeared at the front door on a Wednesday afternoon, two weeks after she had been discharged from the hospital. She was in the kitchen crumbling lard into flour when she heard the front door knocker. *Don't tell me, it's Fred. Bloody hell, I've told him he's not welcome when*

I'm on my own and besides that, what the hell is he doing hammering on the front door?

Sheila reached for the tea towel spraying puffs of flour over the oil cloth on the kitchen table. The door knocker banged again.

'Hold your horses, Fred. I can't move any faster.' She scurried through the middle door pulling at the sticky gunge still clinging to her hands. Her heart thumped; her breath was shallow. 'I've told you, Fred … Mr G! I thought … never mind, come in.' Sheila stepped to one side to allow Mr Gorton into the hall. 'Go through into the…' Sheila nodded toward the front room door.

'I'm making pastry … well, trying to,' she said holding out her hands.

'I can see that,' said Mr Gorton, holding out a bunch of white chrysanthemums. 'How are you?' Casting his eyes around the room he settled on the top of the television as a resting place for his gift. 'My mother suggested chrysanthemums, she likes her flowers does my old ma.'

What the hell do I do now? Why's he come? What if Fred turns up? A lump of the sticky dough took flight as Sheila waved her hands around. Sheila and Mr Gorton watched its flight path toward the sideboard. 'I'll just go and get this off my hands.'

'By the looks of it you've put too much water in,' said Mr Gorton. 'I'm a dab hand at pastry – always have been. I've cool hands you see.'

Sheila sighed and her shoulders sagged. 'Well I'm bloody useless at it, like most things…'

'Less of that talk, my girl.'

Sheila watched amazed as Mr G shook off his jacket and proceeded to roll up his shirt sleeves. 'Stop gawping, Sheila or you and that mess will turn to papier mâché. Come on, show me where the flour and lard are, and I'll set to while you sort yourself out, make us a cup of tea and put your flowers in water.'

'But I don't understand…' *No, I'm bloody flabbergasted.*

'Too old to fight in the last unpleasantness but did my time in the catering corp first time round,' Mr G said as he crumbled a fresh lot of lard into flour. 'Did your mam not show you to use only the tips of your fingers and never let the flour touch the palms of your hands?'

'No,' Sheila shook her head, 'Ellie likes cooking with her, but I never got the chance. She was always busy boxing and coxing with my dad's shift down the pit and hers at the mill … my jobs were always the ironing, still is for that matter, and donkey stoning the steps.'

'My mam's a good plain cook but she leaves me the baking to do on a Sunday morning while she's at church. I make a lovely Russian sandwich cake. I'll fetch you one next time I come… Now who's this?' said Mr Gorton in answer to a sharp rap on the back door. 'Are you expecting company?'

'Yes, no…' Sheila groaned as Fred walked into the kitchen. *Well that's got that sorted; there'll be no mithering me to go and live with him and his mam while Mr G's here.* 'Fred! What a surprise.' Sheila lifted her eyebrows until her eyeballs ached.

'Mr Gorton, I didn't expect to see you here … baking.'

'No, well that wasn't the intention, but Sheila was in

a predicament and I'm drawn to a lady in distress.' Mr Gorton wiggled his shoulders and pouted. 'Particularly when it's one of my girls. Where's your rolling pin, Sheila?' Mr Gorton cast his eyes around the kitchen, his wrists held carefully over the mixing bowl.

'I didn't think about that. I haven't got one.'

'Don't look so glum and start that daft talk again,' he nodded toward the draining board 'pass us that milk bottle.'

'What daft talk?' said Fred.

'She's got some funny notion she's no good at owt, daft girl. Best sales assistant I've ever had. That's one of the reasons I'm here, to persuade her to come back to the furnishing department instead of hiding herself away here in the village grocery.'

'She's good at important stuff.' Behind Mr Gorton's back Fred blew Sheila a kiss. 'Aren't you, love? And for what it's worth, Mr G, I agree that she's better off with us at the centre of things, in Farnworth.'

Sheila's eyebrows lurched into orbit again as she mouthed 'bugger off' at Fred.

At long last the early afternoon of bouncing back and forth between Fred's thinly-veiled flirting and Mr Gorton's helpful tips and hints on pie preparation drew to a close.

'Bye, Mr G, tell your mam I'll call and see her when I'm next in Harper Green,' Sheila waved to the retreating car. 'Bye.' *God only knows I deserve a fag after that. I thought Fred would never take the hint to run Mr G home.* She caught sight of the clock on the mantelpiece. *Hell's bells, I'd best get a move on.*

Grabbing her fags and matches and shoving them in the

pocket of her mac Sheila set off for the school gate. *Sorry Arthur, but if you'd had the afternoon I had you'd be smoking in the street.*

*

Elaine missed the little lamb. Now that she was a big girl in Mrs Marsh's class she had her name over her peg. The little lamb was in the babies' cloakroom at the other side of the school.

'Elaine, come on, put a spurt on we need to go and talk to your mummy. My mummy said she'd look out for her at the gate,' said Ann.

'Comin'.'

'Coming, it's coming**ggg**. Remember what Mrs Marsh said about sounding your **gs**.'

Elaine rarely thought about Christine these days. There was no need. She'd found another knowledgeable friend who was more than willing to guide her through life's playtime. When thoughts of Christine skipped into her head, she thought of how she was glad to be rid of *Noddy* and to be with Alice and her looking glass. Elaine really liked Ann, her big house, her noisy twin brothers and her mummy and daddy. She understood that being Ann's special friend pleased Mrs Marsh and her mummy, remember not mam she told herself, and daddy, especially her daddy. Now her tummy was tumbling round and round because she was nice scared. Ann's mummy had two special things to ask her mummy. Elaine liked her new mam … mummy with the lost baby – most of the time.

✳

Bloody hell, here she comes; the new vicar's wife. Sheila straightened her shoulders, took a deep breath and tried to smile.

'Hello. How do you do, Mrs Brooks, or may I call you Sheila?' The woman holding her hand out was the image of Grace Kelly. She unnerved Sheila.

God almighty. Sheila gulped. *She's bloody gorgeous for a vicar's wife, and posh. What's our Ellie gone and done?* With a quick skim of her hand down the side of her mac Sheila proffered her hand.

'Elaine's told me so much about you, you poor thing. You have been in the wars. Have you time to come back to the vicarage for a cup of tea? I expect we will have so much to talk about. I was in the Land Army, as I'm led to believe you were. Please, do say you'll come back and have a chinwag with me. I know so few people in the village. Look, here are the girls now.'

Dizzy from the verbal assault Sheila shook her head, in an attempt to clear it, as Ellie and a tall girl the image of her mother ran toward them.

'Where are my scallywags?' said the vicar's wife, looking around. 'Here they are,' she announced as two boys swooped up to them with their arms spread wide. 'They're going through a RAF phase; so much noisier than being submariners I find.'

'Arthur my husband … was in the R Hay Heff.' Sheila nodded aimlessly while she tried to think of something, anything useful to say to the tornado of a woman.

'I'm Jocelyn by the way but please call me Lyn. Come on, you lot, let's get home for scones, fresh from the oven.'

The boys swooped round the two women and the girls and then dashed ahead. As Ann took her mother's hand, Elaine reached out and tucked her hand inside Sheila's. *Dear God Arthur, I only hope I can behave proper.*

'Ellie and Hi like a schown of a teatime. Don't we, luv?'

'Scon? Scone?' Elaine muttered.

On the short walk to the vicarage, Sheila, hand in hand with Elaine trooped behind Lyn and Ann. Sheila watched Lyn nod and smile to all and sundry and saying 'good afternoon,' when people caught her eye.

'Mummy, your hand's sweaty,' Elaine announced as they pulled up sharp so that Lyn could speak to old Mrs Wardle who was standing at her garden gate.

'Mrs Wardle, how are you? Well – I hope. See you on Sunday. Goodbye.'

Sheila turned her head to smile at the old lady as the entourage swept on up the vicarage path. She swallowed hard to stopper the bubble of a nervous giggle that was threatening to burst.

'Do you feel Billy Us, Mummy?

'No love, I'm marvelhuss,' Sheila patted her chest, 'just a little tickle in my throat, that's all.'

'Come on in, Sheila. Do sit down.' Lyn turned to inspect the possibilities for seating. 'Let's shift this pile of clothes.' She lifted the untidy pile from a battered easy chair and dumped them on a tower of magazines and newspapers that spilled from a settee that looked set for a bonfire.

'Excuse the squalor, but I do find there are more

important things in life than housekeeping. Don't you?'

'Yes, I do, I do.' *Bloody hell, I wish my mam could see this tip.*

'I tell you what, Sheila, it's bloody cold in here. We haven't lit the fire yet, come on into the kitchen. It's the only place in this mausoleum that has any warmth. I'm dreading winter, like as not we'll all be frozen to death in our beds unless my pa…but well come on.'

I wonder if she ever pauses for breath. Sheila heaved a sigh. *Well at least I won't keep putting my aitches where there aren't any if she natters all the time.*

∗

Arthur paused and listened. The back door was ajar. He heard laughter and tuneless singing.

'Onward Christian soldiers, marching as to war … la, la, la.'

'What comes next, Mummy?'

Mummy? Arthur cocked his head on one side.

'…marching as to war … la, la … With the cross of Je-e-sus going… Arthur, love… Is it that time already?'

'Daddy, look I'm busy,' the kitchen chair balanced at the side of the sink wobbled. 'Oops,' Elaine said as she shifted her weight to regain the chair's balance. 'I'm washing the potatoes for my mummy.'

'I can see that.' Arthur took in his daughter's smiling face and his wife's apron. He'd never seen Sheila wear an apron. Above all there was a smell of food, hot food. He looked toward the stove, amazed.

'Arthur, stop standing there like Piffy on a butty and go

and hang your coat up and sit down in the front until your tea's ready.'

'Daddy, we've had a beltin', I mean belting**gg** time. Haven't we, Mummy?'

'Arthur, shift yourself. I need to set the table.'

'Sheila, I don't understand.'

'Understand! What's to understand?' I grant you we're a bit late getting the tea on the table, but we've been to the vicarage for our tea. Well, not our cooked tea but a cup of tea and a scone.'

'Scon. They say scon at the vicarage, Mummy.'

Arthur drifted through the front room, hung his coat in the hall and made his way back through the kitchen to visit the lavvy. He felt dazed, like that day he'd come home early and wandered through the village. His wife was busy; focused, laughing and smiling while she did jobs with their child?

Having finished his regular evacuation, he reached toward the nail for a few squares of newspaper. The nail was empty. Tutting and opening his mouth to yell, Arthur noticed a roll of lavatory paper up on the windowsill. 'I feel like Alice in Wonderland,' Arthur muttered as he watched the toilet flush. 'If I'm not careful I'll disappear down the drain.'

The kitchen table rocked as Arthur squeezed into the tight space between the wall and the table.

'This table's too small now our Ellie's getting bigger. I'll speak to Mr G about us saving for a new one, once I'm back in the furnishing. Here, Arthur, steak and kidney pie,' Sheila turned from the draining board where she'd been coaxing food onto plates, 'sorry it's slopped a bit, but well … I'll get used to it … this cookin' lark, especially when I've started at the classes.'

'Cooki**ng**, Mummy.'

'Classes? You're starting work in the furnishing again? The vicarage? Lavvy paper?

'Lavatory, Daddy.'

Arthur shook his head in disbelief. 'Sheila, I feel as though I've stepped through the looking glass. What's happened?'

'You can use it for tracing paper as well,' Elaine said.

Arthur shook his head and smiled.

With the tea things washed and dried, *The Archers* listened to and Elaine in bed with Isle of Man Teddy, Arthur and Sheila settled themselves in the front room with a cup of tea.

'Now we're settled and on our own, with our Little Sir Echo in bed, tell me again everything that's happened today,' said Arthur.

*

Arthur tugged at the sheet and blankets. Sheila mumbled as the tension of the pull dragged against her body. Arthur rolled over and closed his eyes. It was no good; he was awake. Stretching his neck to get a view of the fireplace, the luminous fingers of the alarm clock told him it was seven minutes past two. He sat up and pummelled his pillows. It was bouncing down outside.

He thought about the coming weekend in Singleton and prayed for fine weather. The thought of Sheila – even the new Sheila – cooped up in the chalet with his Ma and Elaine and rain drumming and rattling the corrugated roof made him shudder. 'Don't think about it,' he told himself. What was he going to do about work? He wanted a change; more responsibility, something exciting, something more rewarding. But without qualifications, what could he hope to achieve? His warrant officer's status stood for nothing. Then there was Elaine's growing friendship with the vicar and his family, her speech, and new habits. She wanted proper hankies, for God's sake.

Sheila having tea at the vicarage? All that stuff about wanting to go to classes on Wednesday afternoon and changing her mind and going back to work in the furnishing, instead of working in the village Co-op, Mr Gorton teaching her to bake and Fred being promoted to manage the drivers and look after the Co-op yard. Bert and Vera, it would be good to see them. What had happened to that woman and her little girl? Perhaps if he got up for a wee and a drink of water? He'd get drenched going out to the lavvy. He could go in the bathroom sink. Sheila would never know. Count from a hundred backwards: 100, 99, 98 … Singleton. It would be good to spend time with his ma and dad, perhaps he'd bag a rabbit or two, imagine Sheila skinning and cleaning rabbits – never. Where was he? 95, 94…

Chapter 15

'POULTON-LE-FYLDE NEXT station,' the guard's voice rose and fell across the words. 'Poulton-le-Fylde your next station stop.'

'We're here. Mummy, Daddy, we're here.' Elaine ran to the carriage door. 'Look there's Grandad.' She waved to the figure she'd seen on the platform. 'The smoke's covered him up and the train's left him behind. Where is he?'

'Don't cry love, he's still there. Look, he's here now, coming out of the cloud of steam.'

Elaine sniffed and wiped her cardigan sleeve under her nose.

'What about that big girl's hanky you made such a fuss about?' Arthur said raising his eyebrows and giving Elaine a lopsided smile.

*

'You look like Princess Anne sitting in the front seat with Grandad.'

'She's only a little girl, I'm like Prince Charles. He's nearly as old as me.'

'It's my birthday next week, Grandad.'

'Will you be five then, princess?'

'Seven, Grandad,' Elaine looked askance at the big bald man driving the car. 'I'm a big girl now. I'll be seven.'

'Grandad's teasing you, love,' Arthur said, reaching over the front seat to pat his daughter's shoulder.

'I like Grandad's car. It's nice and soft and cosy.' She wriggled back into the battered leather of the front seat. 'Not like the bastard's car.'

'Elaine! What did you say?' Arthur said leaning forward again.

'The naughty car, I don't like it.'

'Arthur, leave it. She's only repeating what you've said. What we've all said,' Sheila said with shrug and a questioning glance at her husband.

'Is something up with the little'un? What's going on?'

Arthur caught his dad's eye in the rear-view mirror, shook his head and nodded toward Elaine.

'Any chance of bagging a few rabbits while we're here, Dad?'

'I think I'll come with you, it's a while since I held a gun. Then I'll get your mam to learn me about skinnin' and that,' said Sheila.

'Skinnin**gg**,' said Elaine.

Arthur nodded momentarily speechless. 'It's teach, love, not learn.'

＊

Sheila braced herself. She wanted to go, and the only place

to go was the earth closet. There was nothing for it; she took a deep breath and unlatched the door of the wooden hut. With her hand covering her nose and mouth, she contemplated the job of getting her knickers down. *Bloody hellfire. Four days of this. As God is my witness I will only wee in this, if it's the last thing I do.* Sheila looked around. *Where the bloody hell is the newspaper? Buck up, Sheila, lavatory paper as they say at the vicarage – get it right.*

'Sheila, what are you doing in there?'

'Hold your horses, Arthur.' *Bugger, it's that shiny stuff that's neither use nor ornament. I am going to try and be proper. It's time for me to be a good wife and mother I know that, but dear God don't let them ask me to empty the lavvies.* Sheila gagged as, from habit, she looked for the chain. She swallowed the bile that rose in her throat as she turned round hit by the pong and sight of the contents of the closet. *Hells bells, who does turds that size?*

'Come and sit down, Sheila. You must be ready for a cup of tea. I've made a malt loaf; it'll put us on till teatime.'

'Grandma says it keeps you regular. What's regular?' said Elaine.

'Let's not talk about things like going to the toilet at the table.' Grandma winked at Elaine.

'Number twos are "keeps you regular",' Elaine said, pleased with herself as the penny dropped.

'Ellie!' Sheila choked back her rising irritation. 'Let's talk about something else.'

'Cor! I'll tell you what, that closet smells ripe,' Arthur said settling himself at the table.

If anybody else mentions that soddin' lavvy so help me I

will…

'You look a bit peaky, love,' Mrs Brooks looked over her glasses at Sheila. 'Why don't you and Arthur go out after tea? Have a walk along the riverbank and call in at *The Shard Bridge*. I'll give Elaine a wash down and see her into bed.'

'And read me a story. Please, Grandma.'

*

Sheila and Arthur made their way down through the campsite to the riverbank. Arthur nodded and smiled at people they saw. It was the start of the Bolton September Wakes Week and the evening was suffused with a wistful, languid air. The part-time residents of the Wyre Estuary clung to the last vestiges of summer. Chalet owners nattered to each other as they tended the late blooms in their patches of garden or surveyed their prefabricated palaces.

'Brooky? Is that you?'

Sheila turned to see a woman waving to them from one of the larger chalets, set back from the rutted road.

'Who's that?' she said.

'Pamela, Pam Davis.' Arthur set off toward the woman his arms open wide. Sheila lolloped after him. The galoshes Mrs Brooks had insisted she wore over her shoes made her unsteady and clumsy. By the time she'd stumped across the grass Pamela and Arthur were wrapped around each other.

'Come and say hello to Pam,' said Arthur, holding out an arm to Sheila while managing to keep his other arm round Pamela's waist. 'You've met before, haven't you?' he said with a grin as he turned his head from one woman to the other.

Pamela leant forward to peer across Arthur's face at Sheila. Sheila cocked her head and snarled sweetly at the woman protected by her husband's arm still held tight around the stranger's waist.

'No, if you remember you deserted me, abandoned me for Sheila and the RAF.'

What the ... who the hell is she?

'Don't tease, Pammy. You were never interested.' Arthur let go of Pamela's waist and shifted his arm from Sheila's waist to her bottom. 'She was after a posh lad down the road. I was somebody to knock about with. Like you and Fred.'

Sheila coughed, *bloody hell I hope not,* and offered a rictus of a smile to the two old friends.

With arrangements made for Elaine and Judith, Pamela's daughter, to play together the following day, Sheila and Arthur set off for the riverbank.

'Where's her husband?' Sheila said when they were barely out of earshot.

Arthur glanced backward. 'I'm not entirely sure there was one, something about a weekend leave wedding and then ... well he's nowhere to be seen. In fact, as far as I know he's never been seen.'

Just like Betty Wilson, up the duff and left to fend for herself. 'Was she your girlfriend? Did you fancy her?'

'No, not really. Not my girlfriend I mean. We lived in the terraced houses that backed onto their big house... She was part of the Sailing Club crowd ... I didn't really fit in.'

'But did you fancy her?'

'I liked her well enough, but … well I met you.'

At the top of the steps leading down to the river Arthur stepped in front of Sheila and held out his hand. 'Take it slowly and watch your footing.'

Tangled tree roots and large logs precariously held together with compressed clay soil formed a series of uneven steps that led to the bank of the River Wyre.

'I feel like a bloody giant in seven-league boots.' Sheila took her eyes off her feet for a second. 'Oops, bugger.'

'I've got you…'

Sheila and Arthur staggered backwards, sliding toward a gate marked **Private.**

'Sheila, are you hurt?' Arthur eased Sheila away from him so that he could see her face. 'Sheila, look at me. You're crying. What's wrong?'

'Me. That's what's wrong.' Sheila leant against Arthur. 'I'm bloody useless. Useless at everything. I can't even manage a walk without…'

'Come on, love, let's go back home,' Arthur kissed the top of Sheila's head, 'to my mam and dad's, I mean.'

'No. I don't want your mam or that Pamela girl to see me like this. Your mam already thinks I'm gormless. I'll bet you wish you'd stuck it out with her … that Pam?'

'Don't be daft. Come on, there used to be an old bench down here, let's have a sit down while you try and gather yourself.'

I feel like death warmed up. I am so bloody tired I don't know what to do with myself. He fancies her no matter what he says. I'm not blind. He's not smiled at me like that for years. Dear God, I don't want him to leave me, our Ellie would be heartbroken.

'Arty, you won't leave me, will you?'

Arthur turned, flabbergasted. 'Sheila, did I hear you right? Did you just call me Arty?'

'Did I?'

'Yes, you bloody well did, for the first time in years. Come here.' Arthur bounced his backside on the rickety bench, 'come on and sit down, it doesn't feel too damp.'

Sheila looked down at Arthur. She was puzzled. 'What's up? You look pleased with yourself. I don't get it … but then I don't… Arthur, I'm … I don't know what I am … useless, a waste of time and space.' She turned and began to walk away.

Arthur leapt up, skidded on a slick of mud, tumbled and ended up with his backside in the sludge as his head ricocheted against the seat of the bench. In her attempt to hurry to him Sheila trod one galumphing galosh on the other. She hurtled forwards and fell on top of her husband. Arthur groaned as Sheila's body hit his. In a mild panic Sheila, anxious to tend to him, rolled sideward to end up sitting with her back against the bench, her carefully rolled hair straggled over her face. They turned to look at each other. Arthur chuckled, Sheila spluttered and their chokes suddenly burst into united raucous laughter. Sheila quietened first. Her head flopped forward as hot tears brimmed and slopped down her cheeks. Her shoulders shook as sobs enveloped her.

'Come here.' Arthur pulled Sheila toward him, whispering 'shush, shush,' to the top of her head.

Sheila lifted her blotchy, wet face to gaze mournfully at

Arthur. 'I … can't…'

'Shush.' Arthur kissed her forehead, then her eyes, her nose and her mouth. His tongue delved into her mouth, urgent, probing and sucking. Sheila returned his passion in equal measure. Shifting her position, Sheila hoisted herself to straddle Arthur. She felt his dick hard against her. Leaning her weight on one knee she dragged the skirt of her frock from under her legs.

'What the blazes…'

'Let's get it out.' Sheila leant back and pulled at Arthur's belt.

'Here! Suppose…'

Sheila leant forward and stoppered Arthur's mouth with hers while riding against his groin. He reached up and pulled at the buttons on the front of her dress. *Hell's bells, he has got it in him after all.* When she'd wriggled her arms free from her bodice, she reached behind to unhook her bra.

'We need to stop. Suppose…' Arthur's eyes were wide, fixated on Sheila's chest.

'Not yet, Arty.' She leaned forward. 'Suck me,' she whispered.

As Arthur's mouth pulled and sucked at her nipple Sheila shifted slightly so that she could reach down and backward to grope between her legs. Her breast slipped out of his mouth as she squeezed and massaged his dick. He groaned. She smiled. *Good on you, Arty … what's he going to think?*

'What the…?' A black and white sheepdog peered from under the bench.

'Jess, here Jess,' a voice called from beyond the site gate.

Sheila swung herself off Arthur who whipped off his sports coat and tossed it matador-like round Sheila's shoulders.

'Bugger off, dog.' Sheila batted her hands at the dog as she staggered to her feet. It poked its nose up her skirt, sniffing. 'Go on, get gone.' She kicked out at the dog as she fled the scene.

'Jess... Sorry, is she bothering you?'

'No, no she's no bother,' said Arthur from his perch on the bench. 'My wife's just admiring the ... wildflowers.' He turned his head slightly toward Sheila who was half hidden in the riverside bushes.

'Has he gone?' Sheila hissed.

'You can come out now.' Arthur held out his arms to his wife. 'Come here, that was ... bloody marvellous.'

'I, er ... read about it in a magazine. You know how to make your husband happy when you have your monthly...' *Keep your mouth shut, you fool.*

'Sheila,' Arthur held Sheila away from him at arm's length. 'Let's try and start again. ... Get to know one another, like we were before the nightmares came back. Don't get upset again, love. Come on, let's sit down, that Sister said you needed to keep calm.'

'I need to tell you something.' Sheila turned her head away from Arthur. She watched the sun sinking over the opposite riverbank; orange and pink light dappled the sky. She paused and shuddered. 'Light us a fag will you, please, there's something I want to say.'

'You'll catch your death, come on let's get back.' He reached for her hand and pulled her to her feet. 'We both need a good wash.'

'No, wait. I have to tell you…'

'Sheila, whatever's bothering you – going back to work, that child being taken, the baby – it doesn't matter. Come on, let's get back. I don't know how we're going to explain why we're covered in mud.'

'You won't leave me will you, Arty? However bad I've been you won't leave me? Will you?'

'I love you.' He took a grip of his wife's shoulders. 'I always have, and always will.' He gave her shoulders a gentle shake. 'I've been doing a lot of thinking lately. We need to talk. Things need to be different for me as well as you.'

'What? Why?'

'You didn't marry a bloke who's wrapped up in himself and tortured by his thoughts. I know I've disappeared inside myself. I need, no, want something else … but well, like I said, we need to talk.' He reached for Sheila's hand. 'Come on, love. It'll be dark soon.'

Having explained to his mam and dad that Sheila had tripped over in her galoshes and that he hadn't been looking where he was going and had fallen in a bundle on top of her, Arthur stretched and yawned and pleaded the need for an early night.

His mam's nobody's fool; she knows there's summat up.

＊

'I like the flickering of the calor lamp,' Sheila said, standing at the side of the bed and reaching under the pillow for her nightie. 'It reminds me of Cornwall, all cosy and warm.'

'Come to bed.' Arthur flicked his eyes over his wife's body.

'There's no need to put that on, is there?

Sheila gasped. Suddenly shy she slipped between the thick flannel sheets and wriggled down into the soft feather bed. Arthur rolled onto his side, his hand reaching for her breasts.

'Earlier on, it was special, very special.'

Sheila saw his face blur as he moved toward her. He nibbled her lips.

I'm dreaming; how does he know about all this sort of stuff?

Sinking, sinking, losing herself in the moment she gave herself to the thrill of Arthur's finger rubbing and sliding in the wet slick between her legs. Satiated, Sheila watched the dark hump of a shadow on the wall slow its rhythmic rise and fall. *This must be making love, and by God it's even better than that one time with Fred.*

Arthur flopped onto his back, his eyes closed. He breathed deeply. As he opened his eyes he turned to Sheila, a luminous smile lighting his face. 'I don't know about you, love, but that was absolutely bloody marvellous. The only thing I want now is a cigarette. I'll light up for both of us.'

Sheila rummaged on the bedside table. 'There's no ashtray.' She held one hand under the other to catch redundant ash.

'Here, flick it into my shoe,' said Arthur straightening himself from investigating the floor at his side of the bed. He dropped the shoe between them as he put his other arm around Sheila and pulled her towards him.

'What do we do with the dog end?'

'Give it here; I'll squeeze it dead,' Arthur said as he tossed the shoe onto the floor. 'I don't want you burning your fingers.'

'No, I don't want any blisters,' Sheila wriggled down the bed to walk her fingertips towards Arthur's groin, 'they might stop me doing this.' Circling her fingers in his pubic hair she moved to stroke him. As Sheila pumped away Arthur lay back, moaning to the syncopated rhythm of her arm movement.

Well this is a turn up for the book. Ugh, bloody hell Sheila, keep your mind on the job. She transferred the gung on her hand to the sheet. 'Arty! Burning, what's burning? That fag end.'

'There's no damage done,' said Arthur sitting down heavily on the edge of the bed after his attempt at firefighting. 'Why don't you straighten the covers and I'll go and make us a brew? Then when we're settled, I want to talk...' he rubbed his forehead, 'I need to try to explain why I've been selfish, caught up in myself.'

Settled down to sleep with her arms around Arthur's shoulders and her naked breasts pressed against his back, Sheila nuzzled her husband's neck.

'Before you say anything there's something I need to tell you. I've been a bad woman Arty, a very bad woman.'

Arthur shuffled around to face Sheila.

'No, Sheila, I won't have it. I'll not hear you say anything bad about yourself. Like I said it's been me that's not been there for you. Me that's been lost, even to myself. It's a good job you've had good friends like Vera and Bert, and Fred. He's a gentleman always on the lookout for you and Elaine.'

'Arty?'

'Come on, luv, put your nightie on or you'll catch your death.'

∗

Elaine wiggled her toes in her sandals, the fine grit of the sand scratched under the holes of the cut-out flower pattern. She looked across at her mummy sitting in one of Judith's mummy's deckchairs. Should she ask if she could take her shoes off or just do it?

Her mummy was smiling, her arm stretched out to stroke her daddy's hair. They kept giving each other funny looks. Elaine felt squirmy inside; nice and soft and squirmy, like a vanilla slice with all the custard squelching out.

She settled her bottom on the brick ridge that formed the edge of the sandpit and bent to fiddle with a buckle.

'What's up, Ellie?' said her daddy crawling across the grass toward her.

Elaine paused, Ellie! Her daddy had called her Ellie. 'The sand's got in my sandals.'

'Take 'em off and wiggle your toes in the sand, like Judith. Enjoy yourself, love,' said her mummy shading her eyes against the sun, 'there'll not be many more days left like this... Ooh, Arty.'

Elaine watched transfixed as her daddy bent to kiss her mummy before he settled back down on the rug at the side of her deckchair. Something was up. It felt as though Father Christmas might pop out from behind a bush. Was something going to happen? Had her daddy found a seed and planted it in her mummy in place of the baby that was lost? Elaine looked around; there wasn't a plant pot to be seen, just the plastic bucket for building sandcastles.

'Come on, I'm fed up of playing in this sandpit,' Judith said, stamping on the row of castles she'd made. 'Let's play schools. I'll be the teacher.'

Elaine sighed. 'We could take it in turns?' she chanced.

'You tell her, Elaine, or is it Ellie?' Judith's mammy said as she came out from the chalet with a tray. She looked at Elaine's mammy and daddy.

'Ellie,' her mammy and daddy said together.

'I love my daughter with all my heart, but I have to admit she is one hell of a bossy boots. She needs a feisty friend who'll stand up to her and tell her what's what. Lemonade everyone?'

Elaine slurped her lemonade. She peered into the glass. She could see lemon pips and little bits of lemon. Could lemon pips act like a seed and make her grow into a new person; an Ellie who was a feasty friend? What did feasty mean?

'Daddy, what's feasty?' Ellie said, gulping as she forced herself to swallow a pip.

'Sorry, Ellie, it's feisty not feasty and means small and lively. A person who knows their own mind,' Judith's mammy said, smiling, 'just like you.'

'There you are, Ellie, and all that from a woman with a degree in English.'

'You be the teacher first,' said Ellie, needing the reassurance of old habits in the face of the puzzles created by grown-ups.

*

Washed down and settled in the narrow bed in the tiny bedroom Ellie turned on her side to face Isle of Man Teddy. She stared into his beady eyes. What would it be like to be a teddy?

'I know you're not real, you've never been a seed,' she told him.

He stared back. She pressed her nose against his. The hard ridges in the brown wool of his nose waggled against the wobbly bit at the end of her nose.

'Who do you like best,' Ellie shifted her head, staring closely at Isle of Man Teddy was making her eyes blurry, 'Ann or Judith?'

Ann's house was very big. It had loads of dark, dusty nooks and crannies for hide and seek. Judith's chalet was little, like a giant doll's house with its kitchen with room for only one person and the tiny bedrooms with cheerful red check curtains. Ellie liked both houses.

She liked Ann and Judith's mummies who were more like Aunty Vera, cooking and making things, than her mam. They talked different, like Mrs Marsh, sounding their g's and saying funny words. Why did her mam … mummy, talk funny when she was with them? Her new mummy was gooderer than the old one. Why did her mummy and daddy call her Ellie and how big was the plant pot for the baby seed?

'Let's go to sleep,' she said to Isle of Man Teddy. 'I'm very tired.'

*

Sheila shivered as she made her way across the path from

the privy to the chalet. *It'll be bloody freezing here in a week or two.* She paused and tipped her head back to stare into the night sky. *Home tomorrow, to a new start. I can never tell him about ... I've got to see Fred.*

Who'd have thought he was scared of me thinking he was, what was his word? Depraved, that's it–depraved. Well I bloody well like depraved. While she towelled her hands dry at the kitchen sink, under the noise of the music on the radio, Sheila heard muted voices. Whatever they were talking about it sounded serious. She inched her way toward the living room door and hovered. *It's me they're on about.*

'... well she's different, that's all I can say. More like she was when you were first married, but quieter,' said Mrs Brooks.

'The war has a lot to answer for, Mum. Look at Dad. Who'd have thought he'd be happy emptying privies and mowing grass all day instead of being a foreman in a factory?'

'True enough, son. I want a bit of peace and quiet after all,' said Arthur's dad.

'It's time to leave the past behind us. It's a new world. A different world,' Mrs Brooks said.

'... and me. Look at me. A washed-out version of who I used to be. Sheila's had a raw deal with me as a husband; introspective, self-absorbed. Looking for something, but not knowing what. I've been a dead loss as a husband. It's a wonder she's not looked somewhere else ... anyway, being here has given us some sort of second chance.'

'How do you mean love, second chance?' Mrs Brooks

said.

'To get things right. To be a proper husband and wife.'

Oops, surely, he's not going to tell them about the riverbank.
'Should I put the kettle on?' Sheila said, bustling into the
front room.

'Sheila, love, I was just saying how much we've enjoyed
you being here,' Mrs Brooks said as she turned to smile at
Sheila.

*

As the train chugged out of Poulton station Ellie hoisted
her legs onto the long seat, stuck her thumb in her mouth,
curled up with Isle of Man Teddy hugged to her chest and
fell sound asleep.

'Happy as Larry,' said Arthur nodding at Ellie.

'She's had the time of her life, playing with Judith,' Sheila
said, smiling at Arthur as he took her hand in his.

'Sheila, we're happy. Aren't we? You know … together?'

'I, I… Oh Arty, I wish we could go on like this forever.'
Sheila dipped her head while she fumbled up her cardi
sleeve.

'Don't get upset, love. Here, take my hanky. Give your
nose a good blow and wipe your eyes.' Arthur sat up
straight, gulped and took a deep breath as his wife tidied
herself. 'Sheila, I want to take you for my wife,' he held out
his hands, 'to love and honour you forever and forever…'

Sheila shoved the soggy hanky up her sleeve and grasped
the outstretched hands. 'And I promise to love, honour and
obey you, Arty, from this day forward for better or worse…
You'd best have this hanky back.'

Ignoring his tears Arthur pulled Sheila toward him. Emerging from the extended clinch Sheila opened her eyes to meet the stare of the guard as he goggled thorough the corridor window, a mesmerised smirk on his face. As his gaze flicked to the position of her hand Sheila followed his eyes and hastily snatched her hand back from the swelling in Arthur's crotch.

'What's up?'

'That guard, he was… watching us.'

Ellie woke to the sound of her mummy and daddy laughing together and the sight of her daddy with his back to her doing something with his pants.

'Are we nearly there yet?'

'Look there's the town hall clock; we're coming into Chorley, then it's Bolton next stop and then the bus home,' said Arthur.

'Can we go and see Grandma and Grandad?'

'Tomorrow, love. Grandma's making you a birthday tea. We'll go and see her after Sunday school.' Sheila winked at Arthur.

'Why did you pull that funny face?' Ellie said.

'Because… because, well because a y is not a z,' said Sheila, leaning toward Arthur to kiss his cheek.

'Your mummy means she's happy, we're both happy, we're all happy,' said Arthur, throwing his arms wide so that Sheila had to duck her head.

'Isle of Man Teddy is sad. He wants to see Grandma and Grandad when we get home.'

'Well we can't have you and Isle of Man Teddy in a sulk, so once we've got home and unpacked we'll walk down to the Working Men's and you can have a bottle of pop and a packet of crisps and say hello to Grandma and Grandad. You might even see Uncle Fred.'

Dear God, I hope not. I need to see him on my own. 'It's time he found a lady friend, I'll tell you that for nothing,' said Sheila with feeling.

'You don't think he could be … you know … like Mr Gorton?'

'Fred? Definitely not, I'm sure of it.' *Careful Sheila, best keep quiet.*

'Can Uncle Fred come to my birthday party?'

'If it's alright with Grandma, I'm sure he can,' said Arthur.

I'll have to catch him tonight and tell him it can never happen again. I'm a different person now. Well, I want to be different, I will be different. Then there's my mam, I'm going to sort things out with her once and for all.

Chapter 16

ONDAY MORNING the start of a new life, a fresh start. Sheila had been relieved when her mam had been busy with a bowls tournament and Fred was nowhere to be seen on Saturday evening. Ellie had her pop and crisps. Arthur had a pint of black and tan and Sheila a port and lemon and then they'd headed for home.

Ellie's birthday tea provided by her mam had made Sheila more determined to sort herself out and learn to cook. Her mam's baking was famous in the village and the Working Men's; coconut tarts, Manchester tart, malt loaf and any sort of pie, sweet or savoury you name it, her mam produced them. Since rationing had ended she'd been in her element using sugar and butter as though it might up and disappear again. She made cakes for anybody and everybody at the drop of a hat. Dr Kelly had only to wave at her when he was on his rounds and she was up at the surgery with a cake.

From now on everything was going to be different. No more shenanigans with Fred, he had to be told today. The messing about should never have started, but it had, and she'd paid for it. How, when and where the telling would be Sheila hadn't figured out, but it had to be done, somehow. Her mam, well it would be difficult, but Sheila had decided that she had to apologise about showing herself up with her housekeeping and letting things slide. She was sure her mam knew that things hadn't been proper between her and Arthur. Well, everything was different now: they were a man and wife who were, Sheila blushed when she thought about it, in love with each other. To prove it Sheila winced as she walked. Between her legs throbbed like hell. They'd even done it this morning and she was on her monthly. She thought about that poor little baby. *It must have been Fred's. That's probably why I lost it, as a punishment. That and Ellie nearly being taken ... well I've learned my lesson. All these years with Arthur without expecting and then once with Fred and I was up the duff. Still, Ellie was certainly Arthur's, the spit of him and seven tomorrow. Do we really want another kiddie? If I catch tomorrow there'd be the best part of an eight-year gap?*

Sheila baulked at the thought of the rubber Dutch cap springing all over the bedroom. Vera used it and said it had a mind of its own. Just as she thought she had it under control and was ready to push it up it shot out of her hand and she ended up grovelling under the bed and once she even had to climb behind the dressing table. *Perhaps Arthur could use something. Like as not, there's no need. Nothing's happened, and like as not it's not going to.* Thoughts meandered in and around the maze in Sheila's head as she paused to rest from lugging the suitcase of dirty washing. She smiled when she saw the white froth of foam, the effluent from the local cotton mills, as it spumed and sprayed its way down the Irwell. Ellie had been fascinated when her grandad spun her one of his fairy tales about the suds being the leftovers from the gypsies further upstream in Farnworth doing their washing on the banks of the river.

Part of the new set-up was Sheila and her mam doing the washing together on a Monday now that Sheila wouldn't be working on that day. They were going to wash together and then each do their own ironing instead of Sheila setting about the ironing for both families on Monday and Tuesday nights after work.

'Mam. It's me, I'm here,' Sheila called as she unlatched the front door of 125. 'It's like a Turkish baths in here.'

'Shape yourself, and let's get all that washing in piles. You do know how to sort stuff; cleanest first working through t'muckiest.'

Sheila bit back a retort. 'Yes, Mam, I do.'

'Well, shape yourself. The sooner the first lot are outside the quicker they'll dry. Water's on and I've set up the dolly tub and mangle.'

The two women worked in tandem in the hot damp air of the kitchen. Pans of water were set to boil on the stove. Her mother set Sheila to work at the sink scrubbing collars and cuffs, knicker gussets and Ellie's white socks with a block of *Sunlight* soap. Mrs C poured boiling water into the tub and then pounded and agitated the clothes with the posser. Heaving the clothes from the hot water with long wooden tongs she paused. 'I'll tell you what, I'll push em through t'wringers and you turn yon handle.'

'I think I'd rather be working full time,' said Sheila.

'That's as maybe but I'll tell you this for nothing, lady, it's a bloody sight easier two of us doing this than me doing it on my own.'

'Mam, I want … need to say summat…'

'There's time for natterin' when we've got stuff on the line and another lot waiting to go out. Keep at it for a bit longer then I'll make us a brew and butter us a slice of fruit loaf.'

With the bedding blowing fit to take flight in the back yard and clothing draped on the airer hitched up toward the ceiling as well as festooned on the maiden in front of the fire, mother and daughter were ready for a breather.

'I don't know about you, Mam,' Sheila said taking a slurp of hot tea, 'but I'm powfagged.'

'This is how it is, running a home. You've been yezzy about jobs in your house for far too long.'

'I know, don't keep going on. Don't you think I've learned my lesson?'

'Waterworks don't wash with me, lady. Never have done, and never will…'

'Mam, please?' Sheila rootled in her apron pocket.

'There's some rag in that top drawer,' her mother waved her hand in the direction of the sideboard. 'Here, while I'm thinking about it, why does our Elaine keep going on about proper hankies?'

Sheila cleared her nose and dragged the rag under her eyes. *This is it.* 'Mam, there's summat I … well … Mam?'

'What is it, love? You're not, you know … again, so soon?' Mrs C nodded toward Sheila's abdomen.

'No, not that. It's just I need to say I'm sorry for being

bad, not right, you know about being married, being a wife, the house and all that business … I'm, I don't know…' Sheila dragged the rag out of her apron pocket and gave an almighty blow.

'What are you saying? Is everything alright between you and Arthur? You know me and your dad … well we like him, always have done, even though he's quiet and a bit on the posh side.'

'Everything's … it's fine, better than it's ever been. Mam, will you please listen for a minute?' Sheila took a deep breath and turned her gaze on the tall weeds wafting back and forth outside the cottage window. 'I'm sorry I've been a trollop.'

'Trollop!'

'Yes Mam, trollop.' *In more ways than one.* 'I've not been proper as a wife, I mean housewife. But I am going to mend my ways.' Sheila sighed. 'Come on, let's get on with that next pile, and Mam, I'm going to talk to Mr G about us buying a washing machine when I go into work on Wednesday morning.'

'A washing machine! You've lost your mind, lady.'

*

Mrs Marsh opened the register.

'Quiet please, children. Remember the holiday is over.' She peered over her glasses and swivelled her head so that every child felt as though they had been suitably threatened. 'You are back in school not playing out in the street like urchins.'

'What's urchins?' Ellie said to Ann.

Ann lowered her eyes as Mrs Marsh's head snapped up and she glared in their direction.

'Elaine Brooks, was that you talking?'

'Yes, Mrs Marsh, and my name's Ellie now.'

'Ellie! What on earth are you talking about child?'

'Ellie, my mam says…' Ellie gave a surreptitious glance at Ann, 'I mean, my mummy and daddy say my name's Ellie now.'

'There's no need to get upset, child, but I still want to know what you were whispering to Ann about.'

'Urchins? What's urchins?'

'Ann, I am sure you can explain to Elaine, sorry Ellie, what urchins are.' Mrs Marsh placed emphasis on the word urchins while looking pointedly at Ellie and shaking her head.

'Erm,' Ann cast her eyes around the room, 'I … don't really know.'

'Come now, I think you are being bashful. Didn't your father have a parish in the back streets of Salford before he came to Holy Trinity?'

Ellie looked at her friend and then at Mrs Marsh. *Why is Ann sad?*

'It means… ragged children,' Ann said in a barely audible voice.

Ragged? Ellie played with the new word. *Ragged, ragged, ragged*, she said to herself. *Something to do with rags? I'll ask Ann at milk time.*

*

Children clustered around the pile of milk crates outside

the back entrance of the school. Ellie braced herself for the claggy feel of the milk on her tongue. She hated the taste of the lukewarm drink. It reminded her of the taste of sick. She hung back while Mrs Taylor the teachers' help jabbed the foil caps with her scissors. David Turnham, who smelt of something really horrible and usually had one hand down the back of his trousers, was in charge of straws. His well-practised technique saw him grasp the box of straws to his chest with one hand and, after licking the thumb of the other hand, reach into the box to flick up a straw and pinch it between his thumb and first finger before dropping his catch into the jagged hole in each bottle top.

'Elaine Brooks...' Mrs Taylor said with one hand on her hip the other hand holding her scissors, dagger-like, poised over a silver bottle top.

'Ellie,' half a dozen piping voices corrected in unison.

'Ellie? What rubbish. Are you sure? I'll check that with your mam, young lady. We don't want none of them snob ways round here.' Mrs Taylor paused and a look of dark accusation flitted across her face as she looked from one child to another. 'Now, where was I? Elaine, that's what it says on the register and until I hear different that is how it stays. Come and get your milk, girl. You as well, Ann, and no more of your fancy talk.'

'I. I...' Ellie looked at Ann, who shrugged her shoulders and held out her hand for her milk.

'Come on, Ellie, let's drink our milk and then play hopscotch.'

The two girls perched on the low wall of the raised flower bed and sucked away until they heard air slurping up their straws.

'Do you like grown-ups?' Ellie watched Ann think what to say.

'I like some. I like my mummy and daddy and gramps and grandma. I like my tickly grandad as well,' Ann lowered her voice, 'but I'm scared of my granny. She makes my mummy cry. I thought I liked Mrs Marsh, but she was unkind this morning. She said rude things.'

'About rags, raggy… ragged children?' Ellie whispered.

'Yes, my daddy says it's rude to point out that people are poor and boo, boo, boorish. Yes, that's it – boorish. He says it's not their fault they don't know any better.'

'Boorish?'

'Rough and common,' Ann paused at the sound of the jangling of the school bell.

Ragged, rough and common? Ellie was perplexed. She longed for Isle of Man Teddy and the cosy space under her bed.

*

I've got carried away with myself. Why the hell didn't I stick with working in Stoneclough, in the grocery? What made me say I'd go back and work for Mr G? Come on, Sheila, show a bit of respect. As always he's been good to you, getting your job back, having a word at that cookery class and all that. I don't know, now that it's come to it I'd rather not go to that class, but I'll have to. I can't let Mr G down and besides it'll keep Fred away. I hope to God he doesn't take it into his head to come and pick me up. I must see him today – first thing if I can – and tell him once and for all it's done. Over with.

'Sheila, wait for me.'

Sheila turned to see Fred emerging from the dimness of the shadows thrown by the high walls of the back yard of the Co-op buildings.

'Fred!' *Bloody hell this is it.* 'You look different.'

Arms open wide Fred made to pull Sheila toward him. She froze.

'New job. The suit.' He brushed his lapels. 'I had it for my dad's funeral. Come on, let's have a minute in the boiler house.'

'No.' Sheila shrugged Fred's arm away from her hand. 'I need to talk to you, but not in there.'

'Well where then?' Fred's glance took in the desolate square of dark buildings, the windows like eyes watching the exchange.

'Here'll do. Fred, it's over between us. Forever.'

'Hang on a minute. Not like this, not here, not now it isn't. You were having my…'

'Keep your voice down, will you.' Sheila turned to flounce down the yard toward the boiler house. 'I've got five minutes before I need to get my overall on and what's more you can keep that bloody door open.'

Fred, sentry like, stood in the doorway of the boiler house. 'What's up with you, love? I've missed you. I've never stopped thinking about you and Elaine. I've had a word with my mam.'

'You've what?!' Aghast, Sheila shook her fists and stamped a foot, her mouth wide open and her eyes staring.

'Well, I've told her I've got a lady friend with a kiddie.'

'You'd no right. Like as not she'll guess and then it'll be

all over Ringley, then Stoneclough and Prestolee. Dear God, Fred, have you no common sense?'

'I've nothing to lose and everything to gain. Why wouldn't I want to tell my mam?'

'Fred, for once and for all will you get it into your thick skull: I'm Arthur's wife.' Sheila threw her arms wide. 'I … I love him, not that it's any of your soddin' business.'

'You've changed your tune. When did all this love,' Fred crossed his arms over his heart and looked upward in a parody of rapture, 'business come about?'

'Since all that mess with Ellie and that bastard in the car. What's it to you anyway?'

'What's it to me? Sheila, we've been together since we were twelve years old.'

'No, we haven't. I married Arthur, remember? After you went off in the army and I didn't hear a soddin' word from you for the best part of a year.' Sheila shuddered. 'Then when you came home on leave you thought you'd start where you left off.'

'I did send you word. I always asked my mam to pass on my best, and anyway you had your head turned by that Giles and his toffee-nosed mates. You thought Arthur was something different.' Fred threw up his hands, tapped his foot, inhaled deeply and shook his head at Sheila. 'He's nowt but a miserable bugger who's more interested in his books than you. You've said so yourself, a million times. Or had you forgotten?'

'Belt up, Fred. I've told you, it's over. We've had our fun and I'm the one who's paid for it.' Sheila stepped forward. 'Now sod off and leave me alone.'

'You were always one for a bit of fun, a bit of slap and tickle. I wonder what Arthur would say if he knew?'

'You wouldn't tell him, would you? Please, Fred, I beg of you, please don't. I'm trying hard, we both are. Please, leave us alone.'

'And what about me, Sheila? What am I supposed to do? Stand on one side while you play happy families?'

'No, Fred, go and find a lass as'll make you happy. Then we can be friends, but I beg of you, for our Ellie's sake if nobody else's.' Sheila glanced at her watch. 'I have to go.'

'Why this calling her Ellie all of a sudden?' said Fred.

Sheila pushed Fred in the chest with both her hands. The surprise of the attack forced him to step back. Taking her chance Sheila shoved past him and ran toward the back door of the furnishing as fast as the slippery cobbles would allow.

She peered through the window that led from the back shop to the showroom. Mr Gorton was intent on unlocking the front door. She hustled into her overall, spat on her hands as an aid to straightening her stockings, pinched her lips together and pushed through the door into the showroom.

'Morning, Mr Gorton.'

'Morning, Sheila.' He peered at her. 'You're looking a bit flummoxed.'

'No, I'm fine, really I am. First morning back and all that.'

'Well take your time and get settled back in by whipping round with a duster.' He shook his head and looked sorrowful. 'I'm really sorry but I've bad news about that class. It's full … they can't take you. I'm so sorry. I shouldn't have promised, not without checking first.'

'Never mind.' *Thank you, God.* 'I'm sure…'

'I can see you're disappointed. I knew you would be,' Mr Gorton took a deep breath. 'So I've had a thought. Why don't I come to your house of a Wednesday afternoon and teach you myself? We could have a bite of toast and a cup of tea then get going.'

'Ellie, I'll need to pick our Ellie up from school.'

'No bother, we'll have finished by then. I can walk you to the school and then get off for my bus. How does that sound to you?'

Fred! I'll not be on my own. He won't be able to come and pester me. I have to keep away from him. He looked a treat in that suit. Sheila! It's over. You've told him. Sheila took a deep breath and paused. 'Mr Gorton, if it's not too much trouble I would really like you to teach me to cook on a Wednesday afternoon. If you're sure, that is.' She felt her shoulders drop as she relaxed.

'What were you going to make for tonight's tea?'

'Egg and chips.'

'We can do better than that – cottage pie. I'll make you a shopping list and you can take a minute or two to nip to the butchers and grocer's after you've done your dusting.'

*

Arthur smiled at the man facing him in the railway carriage. The man looked startled.

'Marvellous evening, isn't it?' said Arthur.

'If you say so,' the man said with an uncertain glance at the leaden skies and mist hanging over the Irwell valley.

The other occupants of the carriage turned to observe the controversial weather then settled back into their habitual going home stupor.

Arthur checked his watch; on time, he'd be home by twenty-five past five on the dot. Sheila and Ellie would be waiting for him. Wait a minute, wasn't it today Sheila was going to that class? There'd be something tasty to look forward to, or perhaps not? She wasn't the cook her mam was but, God help her, she was trying.

'Here we go,' said a man from accounts, sticking to his usual script as the train chugged into the station.

'Bye. Good evening. Bye,' Arthur chirruped as his travelling companions left the main branch of the crowd and split off for their own streets and avenues. He was oblivious to their taciturn faces. Life was good, life was spiffing as the squadron leader would have said, life was…

'Arthur. Over here, Arthur.'

'Is he shouting for you, mate?' said a man bracing himself to overtake Arthur as they rounded the corner of the station steps.

'Fred!'

'Do you want a lift? I can drop you at home.'

Arthur eased himself into the seat of the Ford Pop. He sniffed; beer.

'Is everything okay, you look as though you've been in a bit of bother?'

'Fine. I'm fine. A bit of a set-to in The Clock Face, some jumped-up bugger trying to tell me how to do my new job. I threatened to give him what for and that two-faced landlord shoved me out t'vault and barred me. Sod him.'

'That's not like you, resorting to a fight.'

'Resorting to a fight, la bloody da, you're not in the poncey RAF now you know.'

'I'm sorry. Forget it.' Arthur heard Fred sniff and saw his coat sleeve slide across his face. Not wanting to antagonise him further Arthur chanced a surreptitious peek at Fred. 'I say old ma…' Arthur bit back the RAF lingo. 'What's up? It's not like you to get yourself in a state about a fall out in a pub.'

'That's the least of my worries. Truth is, the love of my life, the only woman…Well she's told me to piss off, to leave her alone.'

'I didn't know you were seeing someone.' Arthur was taken aback. 'Who is she? Do we know her?'

'Know her, course you bloody know her. She's yo… Why she's…' Fred paused and shook his head. 'What's the use; it'll only make matters worse. I'll drop you here, I'm going to nip in the off-licence; hair of the dog and all that.'

Fred swung himself out of the driver's seat and staggered off toward the off-licence without a backward glance at Arthur still sitting in the passenger seat. Leaving Fred to wallow in his misery, Arthur set off to walk the rest of the way home.

Surely Sheila would know if Fred was seeing somebody, Arthur thought as he trudged up Hazel Avenue. They're as close as brother and sister. Why hadn't she said something? Arthur paused in his musing. Course, she could have said something, but would he have remembered? He decided he'd probably forgotten or that Sheila herself had forgotten with the upset when she'd lost the baby. The ward sister had said it wasn't unusual for a woman to be forgetful and depressed after a miscarriage, and then they'd had all that to do with that bastard in the car. Was it any wonder Fred's love life had passed them by? Now we're wrapped up in each other, the three of us. Nobody else matters. There they are, my lovely girls. He waved to the two figures waiting at the open front door and quickened his step. Home at last. Arthur bent down to catch Ellie and twirl her round. He groaned.

'I won't be able to lift you much longer, little one. I don't think my back will stand it.'

'Daddy, Daddy, we's going out for our tea on Saturday and I'm going to be a Brownie and Mrs Marsh is a bad lady because she said we was urchins,' Elaine gabbled as her parents smiled at each other over her head.

'Hello, love. How was the class?' Arthur said, one arm linked with Sheila and the other resting on Ellie's head.

'Daddy, urchins is bad, very bad. Ann's mummy said Mrs Marsh should be ... rep, rep ... repripaired.' Ellie hung her head. 'We's not bad, we don't wear rags. You and me and mummy, we're not bad. Are we?'

Arthur balanced himself on the corner stone of the rock garden and pulled Ellie to him.

'Whatever it is, love, I'm sure there's no need to get upset.' He raised his eyebrows and looked over the child's head at Sheila.

'As far as Lyn and me can make out Mrs Marsh called the class a bunch of urchins and then made matters worse by asking Ann to tell the others what urchin meant. Ann's been crying her eyes out because Mrs Marsh made her say her friends wore rags and Ellie because … well, she's taken it to heart being told she's common and now Lyn's up in arms and wants to complain to the headmaster, the Council and every other bugger she can think of.'

'Come on, love, you know you don't wear rags.'

'I've got rags for hankies.' Ellie sniffled and fished up her sleeve.

'You've not. Look, you've got a big girl's hanky, come on blow your nose.'

'Bloody hell,' Sheila scurried toward the house, 'the carrots…'

*

Arthur settled his knife and fork together in the middle of his empty plate.

'Thank you, Sheila, that was tasty, very tasty. Ellie, put your knife and fork together.' Arthur nodded toward his plate. 'If we are going to do things properly, and not behave like urchins, let's start with our table manners.'

Sheila made a surreptitious move to alter the layout of her cutlery.

'…and remember what I've told you about holding your knife and fork like a pen. Tuck the handles inside your hands.'

Ellie picked her knife and fork up for a quick practice.

'I don't like it, it feels funny, and Mrs Taylor'll tell me off for having snot ways.'

'Snot ways?' Arthur said.

'Gladys Taylor, the know-it-all, told Ellie that she had sno**b** ways.'

'What? Has Prestolee School gone mad? How can we be common, dressed in rags and snobs on the same day? I think I agree with your friend Lyn, something needs to be said.'

'Well…' Sheila twisted her lips and gave Arthur a wry smile. 'It's as well we've been practising our table manners 'cause… because Arty, you'll never guess, we're off to the vicarage for our tea on Saturday.'

'The vicarage? Not your mam's? I thought Ellie meant your mam's when she said we were going out.' Arthur shook his head in bewilderment. 'And what's all this about the Brownies?'

Sheila and Ellie recounted their tale of yet another afternoon of tea and scones at the vicarage.

'So, let me get this straight. One,' Arthur held up the thumb on his left hand and tapped it with the forefinger on his right hand. 'You've said about the classes and Mr Gorton.'

'Who's Mr Gorton?' said Ellie looking from one parent to the other.

'Mummy's boss,' said Arthur.

'He's teaching me to cook.'

'Why?'

'Because it's one of the many things your mam's useless at,' said Sheila

'Sheila, don't. Your mam isn't useless at anything. How can you be useless at something you've never practised?'

'Are we practising to be snots?'

'Snobs, love, and no we're not. We don't need to … because we are decent people, kind people.'

'Russfians. Is we russ…'

'Ellie, love,' Arthur took a deep breath, 'we are ourselves, that's good enough.'

'We don't have green teeth though.'

'I give up.' Arthur shook his head and smiled at his wife and daughter.

'Never give up, try try and try again – that's what you tell me,' said Ellie, her forehead furrowed as she contemplated her father.'

'That's told you, Arty.'

'And, it's made you smile,' said Arthur. 'Now, two,' he said striking his finger against his opposite hand, 'the Brownies and then three, tea and scones at the vicarage today as well as going there on Saturday, four, the washing up and five, precious girl, it's bedtime.'

*

Arthur fiddled with the television aerial until the snowy picture gave way to a man elaborately dressed in white tie and tails. The man spoke in flowery language and waved his hands about to the delight of the audience then introduced a troupe of dancers who, he told his audience to whistling and applause, were direct from the Moulin Rouge in Paris. Arthur backed away from the television, his brow creased and his mouth twisted.

'Arty, is something up?' said Sheila.

'Up? No, why?'

'Every now and then … in between all … you know … our Ellie, and her snots and ragamuffins and Brownies, and God knows what else–' Sheila looked at her hands as she rubbed them against each other '–you get that lost look. Have I done something wrong?'

'No, Sheila, no. Come here,' Arthur perched on the arm of the settee, his arm round his wife's shoulders. 'I didn't know whether to say anything.' Arthur shifted his position and bent to kneel in front of his wife.

'About what?'

'Don't look so worried, love. I'm fine, you're fine and Ellie's fine – that's all that matters to me.'

'What then?'

'Fred…'

'Fred!'

'See I knew you'd get upset; you've gone as white as a sheet.'

'Wha… what's–'

'He picked me up at the bottom of the station steps. Funny really, I had the feeling he'd been waiting for me.'

'Why?' Sheila's hands covered her mouth.

'He, well he seemed to want to talk, man to man. Turns out some woman or other has chucked him.'

Sheila managed a strangled sound from the back of her throat.

'Yes, well that's what I thought. It's obviously a surprise to you as well.'

'Did he say anything else?'

'No, he pulled up at the off-licence, staggered inside and I walked it home from there.'

'But what did he want? Why was he staggering?'

'He was the worse for wear; he's been barred from The Clock Face for fighting.'

Sheila felt light-headed. A brief shake of her head produced a burst of stars in front of her eyes. She sagged against the back of the settee.

'Tell me what he said, Arty. Now, please, I need to know what he told you.'

'So, you do know, I should have known, you two have always been as thick as thieves.'

Arthur pushed himself up from the floor to settle next to Sheila, and took her hand.

Christ Almighty, what's going on? Arty doesn't seem bothered about anything. Breathe, Sheila, breathe.

'He's desolate. Says the love of his life has given him the elbow, told him to "piss off" he said. Poor man, no wonder he was half-cut.'

Words failed Sheila. She tried to speak, gulped and with a squeak said, 'Did he tell you who she is?'

'No, I thought you'd know.'

'Me? I've no idea.' Sheila sat upright, her heart thudding. 'Knowing Fred, it'll be a passing fancy, he's always imagining he's found the love of his life and then before you know where you are, he's forgotten all about her. I think I'll make us a pot of tea, and take two aspirins. I've got a banging headache.' *Thank you, Fred. God bless you and thank you.*

Chapter 17

SHEILA LOOKED left and right as she edged her way through handbags and lingerie. She glanced at a display of camiknickers and shuddered. *Give me a pair of French keks any day.* Miss Syddall was nowhere to be seen. *Where the devil is the old bag?* She made her way upstairs, glancing down into the ground floor. *There she is, the miserable old bugger, smarming at a woman contemplating boxes of hankies. One honk and snot'll soak right through that linen.* Sheila bounded up the remaining stairs and glanced around as she reached the top. *Ah good, Joyce'll get me sorted.*

'Sheila, you daft bugger. What are you doing creeping up on me like that?'

'You were miles away.'

'I'm sorry, love. How are you? It's good to see you back.' Joyce took a step back, cocked her head on one side and smiled. 'You look … different. I don't know … happy.'

'I am happy.' Sheila paused. 'I really am.' She laughed and threw her arms wide.

'Did you want something or are you on a wander round?'

'I want a new frock.'

'Dress please, Sheila. We sell dresses here you know,' Joyce said with a wink.

'La bloody da. Come on then, show us what you've got.'

'What's up? Are you and that posh lad of yours off out?'

'He's not posh, he's quiet.' Sheila smiled to herself. 'He wants the best for us. There's nothing wrong with that is there?'

Joyce led Sheila to a rack of dresses, looked Sheila up and down and reached into the rail. 'These are new in.' She held out a dress. 'Where did you say you were going?'

'Out for our tea … our supper. To the vicarage.'

'Bloody hell here comes Lady Syddall,' said Joyce, nodding toward the top of the stairs.

Miss Syddall bustled over, her corsets out of synchronisation with her body movements.

'It must be jelly 'cause jam don't wobble like that,' muttered Joyce.

Sheila bowed her head to hide her smirk.

'You might well look ashamed of yourself, Sheila. What are you doing out of your department before closing time?'

'Mr Gorton said…'

'Well he would, wouldn't he?'

'She's buying a dress for the vicarage; she's going for her tea, sorry supper,' said Joyce.

'The vicarage? You? At a vicarage?' Miss Syddall reached out to steady herself against the counter. 'For your … supper?'

*

Arthur and Ellie set about making the beds, washing the breakfast pots, emptying ashtrays and putting out the milk bottles. A scoot around with the Ewbank and they were ready for their Saturday morning trip to the library. Pushing the back-door key into his mac pocket Arthur looked skyward to contemplate the late September weather. There was a nip in the air, a slight breeze, a light wind and clear skies; ideal flying weather. Ellie followed his gaze.

'What are you looking at?'

'Nothing really. I was just looking at the sky.'

'There's nothing there, just blue. Daddy, why is the sky blue?'

Arthur took a deep breath as his brain chugged into action. 'Let's see,' he took a deep breath, 'it's to do with the way particles … bits in the air throw blue light from the sun. Tonight, if we look at the sky before it goes dark, we'll see it's red and orange because the blue light is having a rest.'

'Does the sun have arms?'

'No, you know the sun doesn't have arms.' Arthur shook his head. 'It's round like a balloon.'

'How can it throw then?'

'Come on, quick march or we'll miss the bus.'

Kearsley library, a single-storey prefabricated building, sat at the top of the steep rise of Stoneclough brow behind a big house that had once been the home of a long-dead mill owner and was now the local authority clinic. The library and clinic served the local population in the sprawling urban district of Kearsley. The squat, ungainly building was saved from being drab by the skills of the library assistant who lovingly tended the garden in her spare time.

The two small patches of manicured lawn on either side of the path provided a background to the profusion of colour from snapdragons, milkweed and Michaelmas daisies. Well, Arthur thought they were snapdragons, milkweed and Michaelmas daisies. The library assistant was his muse, guide and mentor on all things gardening. She had guided him through the ins and outs of the rock garden, which was now an admired feature of the keyhole in Hazel Avenue.

'Monica Dickens?' The librarian looked puzzled as she stamped the book. 'Not your usual choice, Mr Brooks.'

'It's for my wife; she likes me to choose books for her.'

'I don't think I know her?'

'Sheila, was Crompton, she works in the furnishing at the Co-op.'

'No,' the librarian hesitated, 'that doesn't help. Mother and I rarely shop in Farnworth. We much prefer Kendal Milne in Manchester.'

Annoyed with himself for feeling put down by a simple comment, Arthur snarled inwardly. Cussing to himself he gathered his books, peered over the lower shelving in the children's section and, with an inclination of his head, mouthed to Ellie 'time to go.' Hand in hand father and daughter walked down Station Road toward the station steps and home ready to meet Sheila who was taking a rare Saturday afternoon off work.

*

After dinner Ellie and Isle of Man Teddy were packed off to bed for a rest. Ellie accepted her fate. She wanted to stay up late – half past eight had been promised if she was a good girl.

Sheila finished her ciggy, stretched and yawned. 'Let's get these pots washed and dried,' she yawned again, 'and then I'll put my feet up as well. You could always come and wake me up?' She raised her eyebrows at Arthur.

Arthur laughed, 'Sheila Brooks, you are the light of my life. Get yourself upstairs and I'll see to these,' he pushed himself up and away from the kitchen table. 'Sheila,' he paused, 'how posh … cultured are the vicar and his wife?'

'Posh? They're not posh. Lyn talks proper but the vicar, I can't bring myself to call him Rob, he talks like us. He comes from the other side of Bolton. Didn't I tell you that?'

*

Arthur dragged on his cigarette as he gazed out of the front room window. He was conscious of Ellie opening and closing the lid on her music box. Her rest had lasted all of half an hour. The tinny sound of The Skater's Waltz was setting his nerves on edge.

'Is Ann your best friend these days, or Christine?' Arthur said without turning around. The lid of the music box slammed shut.

'Best friend? Um, Ann, since the socks, and the naughty man, and Christine moved … to that other place.' The tinny music tinkled the skater's presence and stopped again as the lid slapped down. 'Uncle Bert doesn't like us, neither does Uncle Fred. I miss Uncle Fred.'

'Here's Mummy,' said Arthur at the sound of footsteps on the stairs.

'Are we going now?' Ellie sighed as she pushed the music box aside and scrambled off the settee. She watched her daddy looking at her mummy. His eyes were crinkly, and he was smiling. Her mammy looked pretty, like a picture in her *Woman's Own*. She was smiling as well. They didn't shout at each other any more. Ellie wasn't sure if she wanted to be a grown-up. There were so many things she didn't understand like where was Uncle Fred and why did Aunty Vera not bring Christine to see her grandma any more? Ellie paused. She'd rather be a grown-up than a tiny doll turning round all day inside a box.

'Come on, Dolly Daydream, I thought you wanted to be on your way to see your friend Ann,' said Arthur.

'Daddy, who's your best friend?'

'Mummy, of course.'

Ellie looked sideways at her daddy. Whatever would he say next?

Chapter 18

A S SHE pulled her coat on over her new dress Sheila became conscious of the amount of fabric in the skirt. The material refused to be squashed under her old coat. She thought about Princess Margaret who always looked happy and confident in her smart clothes. "Circle skirts worn below the knee" were the new fashion, according to a caption under a picture of the Princess in the *Woman's Own*. *I expect she has more than one coat and a good few fur stoles: still it's good of Arty to treat me for my birthday. We've never really made a fuss about things like birthdays and anniversaries but … well things are different now; we think about each other, care about each other. Perhaps I could look at a new coat; this old thing looks even more ancient against the lovely bright colours of this frock. Arty likes the colours though and I got a good bit off with my staff discount and it'll make a good bit of divvy. Dear God, we're here. Let me not show myself up. Let Arty be proud of me. Let him see I've changed.*

'She's a good cook is Lyn,' said Sheila as they mounted

the steps leading to the imposing door of the vicarage. 'She likes all that foreign stuff.'

'What's foreign stuff?' said Ellie as the vicarage door opened. The question went unanswered. Ann reached out and pulled Ellie inside. As the two girls scampered upstairs followed by a mangy-looking dog Arthur spotted two boys peering over the bannister. Whoops and laughter were quickly followed by the slam of a door.

'Well that's the little ones sorted.' Lyn held out her hand. 'I'm Lyn and you must be Arthur.' She pumped Arthur's hand. 'Sheila's told me so much about you. Rob won't be a tick, he's on the telephone. Sheila, don't stand on ceremony. Chuck your coat over the bannister and come and have a sherry.'

Sheila was surprised when Lyn opened a door on the left of the hall.

'Come into the sitting room. I've lit a fire.'

'Oh!' said Sheila.

'This is the grown-ups' room, rarely used I might add.'

Lanhydrock, it looks like a worn-out version of Lanhydrock, where we went that Christmas in Cornwall when we couldn't get home on leave and Lady Robartes invited us all round. Bleedin' hell who is Lyn? All this stuff's come from some big house or other.

'Sheila, Arthur, please do sit down.' Lyn turned from the sideboard holding a decanter in one hand and a small cut-glass goblet, not much bigger than a large thimble, in the other. 'The sun is over the yard arm, isn't it?'

Sheila glanced around. She admired the line of creamy candles in tall glass candlesticks reflected in the enormous mirror suspended above the high fireplace. She looked and looked again. *Bloody hell that's a grand piano! Them photographs'll take some dusting.*

'Are you both warm enough? This room is like a mausoleum. Mummy insisted that we had this furniture. I hate that bloody piano; it reminds me too much of the creepy chap who gave me lessons. Still, it's a useful place to keep the photographs.'

Sheila smiled. *What would lardy arse Lady Syddall say if she could see me now? Knocking back sherry.* Sheila took a gulp and coughed.

'The furniture, it's…'

'Seen better days and if you look closely it's full of moth holes and woodworm. Dreadful stuff,' Lyn said screwing up her face.

'What's dreadful stuff?' a voice with a laugh in it said from behind Sheila. 'You must be Arthur.' The vicar lolloped around the end of the settee to face Sheila and Arthur with his hand extended. 'It's good to meet you at last. Sheila and Ellie have become the best of friends with my girls.'

Sheila watched Arthur's shoulders drop as he took a deep breath and returned the handshake of the lanky man with a head of grey curly hair bending toward him. *Daft bugger's nervous.*

'I'm Rob, by the way.'

*

The table was set in the kitchen. Rob had objected to eating in the dining room because of the miserable outlook; the trees outside the window blocked out the light, it smelled of damp and the room needed decorating. He detested the Victorian furniture dumped on them by his mother-in-law maintaining it was fit for a museum, or preferably a bonfire, Lyn explained as she directed the four children to one end of the table, and the adults to the other end.

'Rob, pour the wine while I drain the pasta, will you?'

Arthur caught Sheila's eye. He'd been anticipating a plate meat pie, and brown bread and butter. *Wine*? *Pasta*? He twisted his lips ever so slightly and quickly looked away.

'Where's my knife?' Ellie piped up from the end of the table.

'We don't need knives for pasta,' Ann said to her friend.

'What's pasta?'

The table was deadly quiet and Arthur saw Sheila's cheeks flush. *We're out of our depth.*

'Oh dear, how crass am I? I'm so sorry, Sheila, Arthur, I didn't think.' Lyn looked mortified. 'It's just … oh I'm useless.'

'No… please, we enjoy new experiences.' Arthur ran his tongue round his dry mouth as the danger of attack subsided. 'Don't we, Sheila? Ellie?' Arthur nodded vigorously to his wife and daughter. 'So much so that Sheila is having cookery lessons.'

'… and Arty gets me books from the library, and Ellie is looking forward to starting Brownies, aren't you, love?' Sheila said.

'And I'm looking for … something … anything … a new challenge.' The words tumbled out of Arthur's mouth, as relief replaced the panic that had threatened to engulf him.

'So, Lyn, my love, like I told you, a bowl of pasta is not

going to defeat these gradely folks. And anyway, it's my fault. It's my favourite. I requested it, so let's stop talking and start twirling. Ellie, watch Ann and the boys – they'll show you how the Italians do it.'

'Not that the rest of us have been to Italy, we've just taken Rob's word for it,' Lyn said recovering her equilibrium as she plonked a large bowl of spaghetti and then a large bowl of what looked, to Arthur, like the bottom of a cottage pie in the middle of the table.

Arthur sniffed. 'Garlic,' he said quietly, 'I remember that smell.'

Ann helped Ellie tie her table napkin around her neck then demonstrated how to twirl her fork against her spoon and suck the spaghetti into her mouth.

'Arthur, I can't thank you enough for letting us borrow Ellie and Sheila. You must be very proud of them both,' said Rob between slurps of red wine.

'Yes, I am, but I don't understand what you're saying.'

'Let's just say they are the most unpretentious, charming, unassuming people I've met for a long time.'

Arthur shook his head. 'I still don't understand.' His brow furrowed.

'In my job, people want to know you for who you are, or who they perceive you are, and once they know who Lyn's dad is, they're even worse. For us to be with folk who are well, just like us, you know, ordinary. Well, it's bloody marvellous.'

'Language, Pops,' the boys shouted in unison.

'What are you up to, Rob?' Lyn turned from her conversation with Sheila.

'I'm telling Arthur how much we appreciate Ellie and Sheila.'

'Have another drink, darling. The first glass always makes him maudlin, and pass the carafe across here,' said Lyn.

The wine eased the grown-ups into relaxation as they tucked into their meal.

'Where do you buy that?' Sheila nodded to the empty spaghetti bowl in the middle of the table.

'I used to go into Manchester when we lived in Salford, but according to Rob there's a delicatessen in Bolton, on Chorley Old Road.'

'Lyn, honestly you're in Prestolee now. What in hell's name, whoops sorry vic… Rob, is a delica… whatever it is?' said Sheila.

'See that's what I mean, Arthur, no pretention, no guile, just honesty.' Rob opened his arms his palms upwards. 'It's a shop selling continental food, Sheila, and the only reason I know what it is is that I was brought up on Church Road in Bolton and passed the only one in the town, which by the way sells the best food ever, on my way to school,' said Rob.

'You went to Bolton School then?' said Arthur, his temple beginning to throb.

'Yes, more through good luck than anything, but it was thanks to the school that I got into Cambridge where I met Lyn's brother and then Lyn of course. What about you?'

'I went to Oxford Grove.' Arthur shook his head. 'I had to leave at fourteen, my mam and dad needed me to work.'

'As was the case with so many. My cousins were both brighter than me but ended up down the pit. Bugger…' Rob looked at his sons. 'Boys, why don't you play upstairs…?

And sorry, Arthur, I didn't mean to be patronising.'

'Don't apologise, it's as you said. It's what happened, happens, even now,' said Arthur.

'It's wrong, very wrong how some get the chance and others don't,' said Rob.

'Rob darling, not politics at the table,' said Lyn standing to clear the table.

'I'm interested, really I am,' said Arthur.

'You should hear him when Daddy's here.'

'Well, I can't resist baiting the old bear. High court judge or not.'

Arthur spluttered. 'Sorry … it's just that well…' He glanced at Rob and gave a nervous laugh. 'Sheila's dad's an illegal bookies runner.'

'Priceless, bloody priceless.' Rob spluttered as a deep laugh came up from his boots. 'The reason my parents,' he held his breath to control himself, 'could afford Bolton School is my dad's a bookie.'

'What's up with them two?' Sheila turned from the draining board.

'Something to do with Rob's dad and daddy. Come on let's join them, this lot can soak till morning.'

Rob eased the cork from another bottle of wine and poured.

*

Arthur was ferreting through the top drawer of the sideboard when Sheila dragged herself downstairs and into the front room.

'First thing I need is two aspirins,' she said reaching for

her handbag. 'My head's splitting.'

'Here they are.'

Sheila stuck her little finger in the neck of the bottle and drew out a plug of cotton wool. 'How much did we drink?' Sheila groaned. 'I'llniptothelavvyandmakeusabrew,' she muttered as she groped her way toward the kitchen. 'I feel sick.'

A pot of tea, a cigarette and a slice of toast later Sheila felt the sick feeling slipping away. She belched. 'That was the best night out I've had for a long time.'

'Me too,' Arthur said, glancing at his watch. 'Ellie as well, by the look of the time. I'll go and wake her.'

'No need, here she comes.'

'I need to go, I need to go.' Ellie barrelled through the front room toward the back door.

Over another pot of tea, and with Ellie furnished with a slice of toast, Sheila and Arthur were sufficiently recovered to set about examining their evening at the vicarage. They agreed that it was hilarious that Rob's dad was a bookie albeit a legitimate one with a successful business. Sheila wasn't sure what a high court judge was other than he sat in a court and passed out prison sentences. She was intrigued to know if he wore a black hanky on his head and condemned people to death.

'My mam's always saying my dad should have been a Philadelphia lawyer, with all his sayings. Do you think Rob's right, Arty, about them as has chances and them as doesn't? That it's money that matters?' Sheila watched Arthur as he pondered.

'Well, yes and no. It didn't help Lyn, did it? Her mam,

sorry mummy and daddy had the same attitude as yours. Except that her mam's reason for not letting her go into nursing was more snobby than your ma's.'

'Fancy and she really wanted to be a doctor. You won't be like that with our Ellie, will you?' Sheila said.

'Never in a million years, she can be and do whatever she wants. Although I'd like her to go to the grammar school.'

'I don't blame my mam and dad for denying me the grammar school and nursing. I never have, although I was disappointed. I sulked for weeks about the nursing, but they did what they thought was right for me.' Sheila paused to run her tongue around her mouth. 'Although I've never been sure about having all my teeth out for my twenty-first.'

'Grandad always knows what's best. I know because it was him that told me about Weary Willie and Tired Tim.' Ellie gave her parents an emphatic nod to reassure them of her faith in her grandad.

'He does that, love. Come on it's time you were dressed,' said Arthur.

'Arty, hang on though, what did you think of him? Rob.'

'I like him, not your usual sort of vicar. I liked what he believes in. I've got my doubts about Jesus and God ... the war and that, but he's certainly made me think ... about all sorts; friendships, serving the community, family, politics...'

'Let's have another cuppa.'

'Alright, but Sheila, I am proud of you. I want to make you proud of me.'

'Get away with you, I'm nothing, a nobody – always have been, always will be. But, I have to admit he's made me think as well.'

Chapter 19

SHEILA MANAGED to keep up with Arty's report of his conversation with Rob even as her thoughts leapt and skittered during the usual Sunday dinner of brisket, mashed potato, carrots and tinned marrowfat peas topped off with *Bisto* gravy, followed by a slice of swiss roll and *Bird's* custard. Apparently the new vicar had been given the job of getting the parish out of the doldrums, bringing it into the different post-war world. He'd suggested Arty think about putting himself forward for the Parochial Church Council who were, according to Arty, the folk who ran the church and its business.

'Will we have to go to church? Sunday's my only day off what with washing on a Monday, then all that housework, the Co-op and, well I was lucky to get yesterday afternoon off because I had time owing.'

'Sheila, you don't have to do anything you don't want to. Never again. Rob says Lyn doesn't go regularly, only when she feels she wants to.'

'Yes, she told me, the first time me and Ellie went round.

She says she married the man not the job, but she puts in an appearance every now and again to keep people happy. She helps out with jobs, making tea, visiting people and stuff like getting them to set up the Brownies.'

'I'm going to think about it, being on the PCC, and then perhaps sit in on one or two meetings. We'll see,' said Arthur.

'I'll tell you what, Arty, it'll be one in the eye for Lady Syddall when I tell her you're on the Parochial, whatever it's called. And I'll tell you another thing, I'm going to talk to my mam again about getting an electric washing machine,' said Sheila. 'Lyn's got one and she says it's a godsend. Ha, do you get that, Arty? A god-send.'

Arthur smiled happily at his wife as he shook out the pages of his *Sunday Express*.

'Are you walking our Ellie round to the ginnel? She's safe enough walking on her own from there. I'll go upstairs and get ready.' Sheila winked. 'Ellie, go to the lavvy and get your hands and face washed, it's time for Sunday school.

∗

The catalyst of the tea at the vicarage was profound. It was a long time since Sheila had felt so good about herself. The last time had probably been the day she signed on for the Land Army. She'd accepted that her mam had the last word about her being a nurse but she had refused to accept it was the munitions factory for her war effort. She'd achieved something on her own, all those years ago. She asked herself again and again. Why had she let herself go? Why had she got herself into such a bloody mess? She reflected on her past; she'd always liked a good time but … anyway, now she was going to sort herself out good and proper.

Lyn had done it; made up her mind what she wanted to do after being told she couldn't be a doctor or nurse. She'd signed up for the Land Army as well and left home, although for her it wasn't the first time. It sounded like she'd never had a proper home where she was wanted and loved. The poor girl had been sent to boarding school when she was not much older than Ellie and Ann.

Sheila held her head high at the thought of having a friend who thought she was … well, what did Lyn think she was? Honest and straightforward. Sheila had made her decision. *From now on I'm going to be the person Lyn thinks I am. If she can refuse to go and bow to The King and get over her snobby mam thinking she's married beneath her, I can get myself sorted. First off, I'll write to Vera. She is my best friend after all and then I'll tackle Fred. Once and for all I've got to get things sorted. Then I am determined to stop pretending to Arty that I read the library books he brings. I will read for ten minutes every day.*

201 Hazel Avenue
Prestolee
Stoneclough
Nr Radcliffe
29 October 1954

Dear Vera,
I know it's been a while, but thank you for looking after me when I took bad in the furnishing and for coming to see me in hospital. I saw your mam the other day and she said Bert's put his foot down about

you coming to Stoneclough. ~~*Silly bugger*~~ *They caught
that man, his case comes up soon. My dad says he
should be flogged.*

*How are you and Christine? We are all well. Ellie
is joining the Brownies this week. I've persuaded my
mam to get a washing machine; we are keeping it at
125. Arty is getting involeved* ~~*involved*~~ *with the vicar.*

It would be lovely to see you sometime.

~~*Yours*~~

Love

Sheila

*

Sheila posted the letter on her way to work on Wednesday.
On Friday she was absorbed in unpacking a large parcel of
tea towels and sorting them into colours before arranging
them on shelves. Standing back to admire her stacked
handiwork she was startled by a poke in the back. She
turned, half, well a quarter expecting, or hoping and
dreading that it was Fred.

'Vera!'

'That made you jump. Who were you expecting? Don't
tell me…'

'No, it's not like that, not any more.'

'Sheila.' Vera shook her head. 'What am I going to do
with you?'

'What are you doing here?'

'I came because of your letter.' Vera waved across the
shop. 'Mr G, how are you?'

'I'll say it even if I shouldn't,' said Mr Gorton advancing

toward the two women, 'what with you here, disturbing my staff,' Mr Gorton gave each woman a luminescent smile, 'but you're a sight for sore eyes, Vera.' He flicked his head from side to side, looking over each of his shoulders in turn, to take a surreptitious glance down to the bottom floor of the furnishing.

'Go on, the pair of you, Sheila can have an early dinner break.'

'Thank you, Mr G,' the two women chorused.

'I'll grab my coat. Come on let's go to Togs,' said Sheila. 'I fancy an ice-cream.'

'No, let's stay here in the cafe, Bert delivers to Tognarelli's.'

'Togs! Since when?'

'Don't ask, come on let's get a cuppa and a fag.'

Settled in a corner of the Co-op cafe with a fag and an order of tea and toasted teacake the exchange of news could begin. Sheila brought Vera up to date with her convalescence after losing the baby, including her mam and Arthur's bottoming of the house. Vera knew her well so there was no need to hide her sluttish ways from the friend she'd known from when they were both in prams. The finding of the French knickers in the bottom of the wardrobe and their subsequent washing and ironing made Vera laugh out loud.

'That's done you good,' said Sheila taking a close look at Vera, 'having a bit of a laugh.'

'Yes, well,' Vera hesitated. I take it you and Fred … you know.'

'It's over, it's got to be. It should never have started again.' Sheila pressed the palms of her hands to her hot cheeks.

'Sheila?' Vera leaned back and cocked her head on one side to better scrutinise her friend. 'Are you … blushing?' Vera flapped her hands at the side of Sheila's cheeks.

'Yes, well it's me and Arty.'

'Arty?'

'Like I said, he's, well, we've… he's.' Sheila dragged in a deep breath and looked around, then bent her head toward Vera and whispered, 'you'll never believe it. It turns out he's bloody marvellous at … you know, IT.'

'What! You've been married the best part of nine years. What's been goin' on? How have you only just discovered he's good at IT?'

'We've been doing IT, obviously, but you know, a quick twiddle here, a grunt and groan and it's all over. Well,' Sheila paused and sighed, 'turns out he didn't want me to think he was depraved. That's what he said. Depraved, Vera, can you believe it?'

'So what's different?' Vera's furrowed brow and curled lip betrayed her suspicions and doubts about Sheila and Arthur's sex life. 'Never mind,' she shuddered. 'Do you think the baby might have been his?'

'I don't know. I don't want to think about it.'

'Don't get upset.' Vera pulled a hanky from her skirt pocket. 'Here, dry your eyes.'

Sheila gathered herself, and after a slurp of tea and freshly lit fags the exchange of life events continued. Bert was working every hour God sent, never at home. The business was growing, fast. He was at the bakery before Vera and Christine were up, sorting out his new offices in the afternoon and out at his new interest The Masons in the evenings.

'Does he have to walk about half undressed and do fancy handshakes?' said Sheila, her right hand grasping her left breast.

'He doesn't say much about it. Although I had a look in his little case – he doesn't have to take the stuff every time, and there was a stiff, light blue cloth, shaped a bit like a pinny and a book with funny marks in it.'

'How often… never mind.' *He's up to his old tricks.* 'It doesn't matter. Why's he still being funny about you coming down to the village?'

'He's different.' Vera gave a dismissive wave of her hand and leant her elbows on the table. 'Full of himself, bossy and,' she shrugged, 'I don't know. He's not like he used to be.'

Sheila snorted. 'He always was, full of himself I mean, even when we were at school.'

'Not like he is now. To be honest, Sheila, I'm sick and tired of being treated like a servant. He thinks he's Lord Fauntleroy and I'm his bloody housekeeper. He's forever telling me what I can and can't do. I wish we'd never moved. I was better off working here. I detest being beholden to him for every soddin' penny. I tell you, Sheila,' Vera flicked her hands, dismissing Bert and her new life, 'it's getting to the stage where I can't stand much more from that bad-tempered, foul-mouthed, miserable old bugger.'

'Vera!'

'I'm not joking, I have to mug about after him, then take our Christine to, would you believe it, elocution, ballet, and –' Vera flopped back against the chair – 'I'm fed up, that's what I am, bloody fed up. Your letter was like getting a present.'

'Come back to work. Tell him to bugger off and come back here. Mr G will see you all right.'

'I can't. It's too far and I've nobody to pick Christine up. Fred, look there's Fred.'

'Vera, me and Fred – he won't talk to me…'

'You mean since he got the manager's job?'

'No, you know, since he met Arthur, that day when he was drunk.'

Vera peered at her friend through the fog of cigarette smoke. 'I don't think it's anything to do with you and him. I suppose it could be, but then again…'

Sheila shook her head. 'What are you going on about?'

'He's courting. Didn't you know? With Betty Wilson, that little girl Marion's mam.'

Sheila felt a tide of emotion sweep through her body. Relief he was with somebody, at last. Arty would never find out. Grief it was gone now, whatever it was she had lost it, and him.

'Sheila, you look funny.' Vera stood up. 'Are you alright?'

Sheila motioned for Vera to sit down.

'I thought you'd have known; you were always as thick as thieves. My mam told me.'

'No, he's … let's just say I haven't seen him, well not to speak to and he hasn't called to see us for a while.' Sheila forced a smile. 'And now we know why. Don't we?'

'You can't kid me, Sheila, he's kept his distance because you gave him the push since you and Arthur found out how to –' Vera knitted her arms across her chest, leant forward and mouthed – 'give each other a jolly good, you know what?'

'That, but more than that. It was the baby; it was a punishment, for me not being proper with Arty and our Ellie – for losing myself.'

'Where's that hanky I gave you? Sheila, don't take on you'll look a bloody mess this afternoon. Like I've said before,' Vera nodded 'you always were an ugly crier.'

With promises to keep in touch the two women went their separate ways.

*

Sheila looked around for a job that would give her the excuse to go out into the yard. She saw the brown paper packaging from the tea towels tucked under the counter. *Right Fred, one way or another we're going to get this whole bloody mess sorted.* She scoured under the department's counters and the drawers of the sideboards and dressing tables on display. At busy times staff pushed bits of packaging and papers of one kind or another out of sight, in case management or the Chairman should happen to pass through nodding and smiling while their swirling heads took in the number of customers and staff beavering away in pursuit of the half-yearly divvy target.

She tied the detritus she'd scrounged into a bundle and shouted across the floor to the deputy manager. 'I've had a bit of a sort out; I'm taking this lot to the boiler house.'

Scuttling across the yard, she dumped her bundle and went in search of Fred. She felt slightly sick, and there was a quiet pain tapping away over her right eye. The pain became a determined thud as she made herself put one foot in front of the other on her journey to the poky room that, with Fred's promotion, had been designated as the yard office instead of the junk room. Outside the door she hesitated tempted to turn back. *I'd best knock.* She lifted her hand but before it had a chance to meet the wood the door swung open.

'Fred!' Sheila dropped her hand to her side.

'Sheila!' Fred spluttered. 'What the blazes?'

'I…I… wanted to thank you.'

He looked up and down the yard, 'Come in.' He stepped aside.

'I can't stop. Like I said, I wanted to say…you know.' She scraped under her eyes with the heel of her hands. 'I need to get back.'

'Meet me here when you finish. I'll give you a lift home.'

Sheila scurried back to the furnishing not sure if she'd done right or wrong.

*

Quarter past one, twenty to two, twenty-five past two, three o'clock, tea break, half past three. Would the afternoon never end? Sheila had never counted how many clocks were for sale in the furnishing but she was sure that one way or another they were multiplying as the minutes dragged by. They all told the same story as the hands of the clocks made their collective journey to half past five: it was a long, long afternoon. Sheila imagined her conversation with Fred. She gave a customer the wrong change, fortunately it was a regular who forgave her for being given a two-shilling piece instead of half a crown. The return of the sixpence and

Sheila's apology passed a full three minutes. She thought about writing Fred a note and pushing it under his office door. Then it was twenty-five past five, Mr G was locking the front door and it was closing time.

He was there, leaning against the car, fag in hand. The sick feeling returned. *Say what you've got to say and then go and catch the bus.* Fred shifted his glance, raised his hand and opened the passenger door. Sheila slid into the seat. *God, help me.*

'How's Elaine?'

'How's your mam?'

'You first,' said Fred, checking both ways as he pulled into Market Street.

'Your mam, how is she?'

'Fine, she asks about you and Elaine, and Arthur of course.'

'Fred, Ihavetosaysomething.' Sheila gathered her breath as words tumbled together.

'R-i-i-ight.' Fred chanced a glance at Sheila.

'Arty. Thank you for ... not saying anything. It means a lot ... to both of us ... well it would to Arty if he knew.'

'What's all this Arty business?'

'I used to call him that, at first, when you were away ... you know, in the army.' Sheila puffed out a long breath. 'And I know about you and Betty, and I'm ... well, you know, pleased.'

'I heard Vera was in earlier. Did she tell you?'

'Yes. It's not a secret, is it?'

'No, far from it.' He took his eyes off the road to glance at Sheila. 'I've asked her to marry me.'

'What?!' You hardly know her!'

Fred pulled the car into the side of the road. 'Sheila, I'm lonely. I've missed you ... but she's a good woman and the little girl likes me. It's done now and I'm sure we'll be able to make a go of it.'

'What about love? Do you love her?'

'I might ask you the same thing about Arty,' Fred said, with a sneer in his voice.

'There's no need to be like that.' Sheila made to reach for the door handle. 'I'll walk from here. I've said what I wanted to say.'

'No, Sheila, stay. Let's not leave it like this. I'll run you home.'

Sheila settled back in the passenger seat determined not to cry again. She stared out of the window lost for words.

'Sheila, can I ask you a favour? If I tell you something will you keep it to yourself?'

'Course I will, I owe it to you for what you've done for me and Arty and our Ellie.'

'You were right. Bert is Marion's dad. If I ever see that two-timing swine again, I'll knock his bloody teeth in,' Fred said, banging his hands on the steering wheel. 'You won't say anything to Arthur or Vera, will you?'

Chapter 20

A s her daddy pulled her bedroom door to Ellie turned on her side and arranged Isle of Man Teddy so that they were lying facing each other and she could stare into his eyes.

'Happily ever after,' she whispered to him. He stared back. Ellie tried to stare him out but he won. He always did. 'We's happily ever after. Ann's mummy is pretty like a fairy godmother, she can give wishes. She's made me a nice mummy. Christine is a bad little fairy. The naughty man, it's rude to say bastard, came to give Christine and me toffees and mucky my socks. Ann's mummy sent Uncle Fred back. He gave his nose a big blow after he shook Daddy's hand and Mummy cried. Why did he shake hands with Daddy? Why did my Mummy smile and cry at the same time? Mrs Taylor is an ugly sister; she puts poison in the milk. Don't drink milk at school, Isle of Man Teddy, it will make you sleep for a hundred years.' Elaine rubbed her eyes. Isle of Man Teddy was asleep, and she was still awake.

'Daddy, Mummy, can I have a drink of water?' Ellie yelled

as she sat up in bed. She didn't really want a drink but Wee Willie Winky was taking his time coming to close her eyes.

'Just a sip, little one,' her daddy said, 'or we'll be having a trip to the toilet during the night and we don't want that, do we?'

'Was Uncle Fred with our baby?'

'I don't understand, love.'

'He said he's been a bit lost. Will we find our baby now; like Marion? She was lost. Where is our baby, Daddy? Have you looked at the back of The Horseshoe?'

'Come on, love. It's time you were asleep.' Arthur patted the pillow. 'Remember what I told you about our lost baby and the seed the daddy gives to the mummy to grow the baby. Lie down and I'll stroke your hair for a minute or two until Wee Willie Winky is on his way.'

'Is we happily ever after, Daddy?'

'We are, little one, we are, and we always will be.'

*

Ellie liked reading and writing. Sums and school milk she would rather not bother with. Mrs Taylor was a witch and had poison in her pockets. The poison made the milk taste funny, except when Jack Frost was about. Country dancing and singing were nearly as good as reading and writing. Gardening was alright if the sun was shining. Ellie liked the flowers and trees but not worms and slugs. She was very interested in seeds.

Mrs Marsh had started talking to the class about Children of the World. Ellie liked seeing the little dolls dressed in fancy costumes. The dolls belonged to Stephanie;

Mrs Marsh's big girl. Stephanie was in the headmaster's class and had to call her mummy Mrs Marsh when she was at school. The girls were allowed to hold the dolls so long as their hands were clean. The boys had to keep their hands to themselves after David Turnham tried to pull the knickers off the doll from a place called France. He said he wanted to see what was underneath a girl's knickers. Mrs Marsh had a word with his mummy. At dinner break Ellie liked rounders and chasing, but not kiss chase. Rainy days were not good, sitting on prickly PE mats in the hall playing snakes and ladders and ludo was boring.

Now that she and her mammy and daddy were happily ever after Ellie was happy when it was home time. On Monday, Tuesday and Wednesday her mummy met her at the school gate. Ellie looked forward to Thursday and Friday when Grandma Crompton came to meet her. Grandad was up and about by the time they got to 125. He'd had his afternoon sleep and was ready to play. He kept Ellie up to date with the goings on of Weary Willie and Tired Tim. Sometimes he let her comb his hair and set it in grandma's curlers. Ellie and grandad sometimes made patterns with the buttons in grandma's button box. Ellie's favourite job was using the special stamp grandad had for his pile of football coupons. She stamped and grandma folded. Grandad put the coupons in an old shopping bag of grandma's and took them to his special friends.

Ellie liked the Brownies. She had been three times. The first time all the little girls had to have their mummies with them. Ann's mummy said hello to the girls and the mummies. Then another lady who said she was a Brown

Owl said what being a Brownie would be about. She was going to be like the teacher and tell everybody what to do. Ellie counted seventeen girls. Some were from Ringley School and some from Prestolee. Stephanie Marsh and another big girl from Prestolee and a big girl from Ringley were going to be something called sixers. Ellie was put in the Elf pack and Ann in Pixie. The Brown Owl lady said she had tried to mix up the girls so that friends from the same schools were not together. Some of the little girls sulked about this and one cried. Ellie and Ann shrugged their shoulders at each other. Ann's mummy had already told them that they would not be together all the time. The Brown Owl told the mummies that they should only buy the uniform if the little girls still wanted to be a Brownie when they had been three times.

Ann looked good in her uniform. It hadn't been turned up like Ellie's. Ellie wished she didn't have a turned-up uniform. Hers was lumpy round the bottom. She remembered that her mummy had told Aunty Vera she was 'bloody useless with her hands.' The new mummy was the same as the old mummy at sewing things. Ellie liked the necktie but the brown beret was itchy. Best of all she went to bed late on Brownie nights, but she didn't get a story.

∗

Arthur shook his head, startled as the familiar music signalled the end of *The Archers*. He'd missed the episode, his thoughts tossed and tangled. He'd made his decision and would stick to it. He wasn't a coward. He could face what lay ahead. After all, it was only a meeting of the

Parochial Church Council. What is there to be afraid of? he asked himself. Rob had taken him through the minutes of previous meetings. It seemed pretty ordinary stuff; repairs to the church windows, concert parties, loaning equipment out, church flowers and setting up the Brownies. Come on, man, it's a parish church in a village in industrial Lancashire. It's hardly on a par with the cessation of the British occupation of the Suez Canal or the state visit of Haile Selassie. He told himself it would be good to see Rob being the vicar. Even though he has that quiet arrogance, that attitude that he has a right to belong, the same as Pammy that came from being part of the Bolton School crowd, there was also something humble and selfless about him. Perhaps it's because of his dad being a bookie, albeit it a legal one. Or perhaps it's his war service 'behind enemy lines'. Or perhaps it's because of his quiet faith that endures despite … well, despite everything that had happened because of the war.

*

Geoff Taylor who lived back-to-back and whose parents had the house next door to Arthur and Sheila was a good neighbour. He worked at the factory with Arthur and he and his wife were regulars at Holy Trinity. Geoff's wife Joan was on the PCC. Over the back fence Geoff encouraged Joan to let Arthur in on the inner sanctum goings on.

Joan reported that the vicar was considered to have a common touch and be interested in the history and times of the three villages. He was keen to stick to the low church ways not like that new vicar at Ringley who had folk bobbing up and down till they were dizzy and swinging the nonsense and to top it all wanted his congregation to call him Father.

The vicar's wife Jocelyn was considered to be a different kettle of fish from her husband. A bit too much on the posh side for most people's liking and she talked nineteen to the dozen. As far as anybody could make out, she wasn't a regular at any particular service and when she was, she couldn't keep her kiddies under control. The two boys were a handful who could do with their bums smacking or locking in the coal hole for half an hour or so.

Joan paused before leaning forward over the fence. She hesitated. 'There's them, and let me tell you, Arthur, I'm not one of them, as is not so sure about,' she glanced around and, satisfied that the whole of Prestolee was not hanging on her every word, continued, 'as wonder why you,' she nodded vigorously, 'you know, want to join ... become one of us, you know?'

'Joan, that's not what I meant when I asked you to have a word with Arthur.'

'No, it's a fair question.' Arthur winked at Geoff. 'And one I've asked myself.'

Joan crossed her arms. Geoff stroked his chin. They waited on Arthur's response. 'Rob ... I mean the vicar suggested it. His wife ... well, she's got friendly with Sheila.'

'I'd heard that.' Joan sucked her lips.

'She's a smashing woman by the way, Joan. I'd say she natters on to cover her nervousness.'

'You were sayin' about wanting to join us on The Council.'

'Well, I feel I want to give something back, to do

something worthwhile, for' his voice dropped, 'for coming home, when so many didn't.'

'That's good enough for me,' said Geoff with a nod. 'Well lass, are you satisfied now?'

'Yes, but what about God and all that?' said Joan.

'What's that got to do with anything? It's about the church standing for something good and folk having summat to look up to,' said Geoff. 'Come on, you've had your answer, let's get back in t'house and get that kettle on.'

*

Lyn answered Arthur's knock on the front door of the vicarage.

'I'm not early, am I?'

'No. Relax, Arty. Mrs Taylor is here, she was asking if you'd arrived and the verger is with Rob in his study. Give me your overcoat and go on through.' Lyn turned in answer to the bang of the front door knocker.

Arthur pushed open the door and blinked as he adjusted his eyes to the gloom. The light cast by the shaded bulb suspended over the dining table gave off so little light it was hardly worth bothering about. A standard lamp by the fireplace and a table lamp in the window bay provided dim pools of isolated light. Arthur sniffed; he smelt damp and something vaguely rotten.

'Like as not there's summat dead under these floorboards,' Joan said. 'Come on over here, you'll catch your death if you sit with your back to that draughty window.' Arthur pulled out the chair next to Joan.

'The secret is to get here early so's you don't sit in a

draught and don't sit with your back to the fire. That way you neither freeze to death nor get burned at the stake,' said Joan. 'The sooner they've finished repairing the Sunday school roof the sooner we'll be able to see each other across the table at meetings.'

Arthur had no sooner settled himself than the places at the table were filled. He counted nine people, four men and five women, then Rob and himself.

'Good evening, shall we bow our heads,' said Rob.

'Lord, in the name of your son, our Lord Jesus Christ, we ask you to bless our meeting. Guide our thoughts and help us to make considered decisions about the issues before us. Help us to welcome our friend Arthur as he seeks to find his place in our parish.'

'Amen,' chorused the members of the Holy Trinity Parochial Church Council.

Over the next few weeks Arthur attended the half past nine Holy Communion and the six o'clock evensong on alternate weeks. He settled on evensong as his preferred service. The flow of the music, the words and the absolution soothed him and gave him time for quiet reflection. He began to look forward to the service and was hesitant to agree with Ellie that she was a big girl and would sit still if she and Ann could attend the service with him. Attend they did and sat quietly; Ellie watched her daddy join in the responses and bow his head in prayer. She noticed his face; it was soft and gentle like when he stroked her hair when they were waiting for Wee Willie Winky. Ellie followed Ann's gaze to see what she was looking at. She was watching her daddy as he said the prayers.

Chapter 21

THE WEEKS slipped by as the vibrant leaves of early autumn gave way to the misery of the grey days and damp of November. Ellie took home a letter from school saying that she had been chosen to be the Archangel Gabriel in the infants' nativity. Ann was to be Mary.

Mr Gorton and Sheila continued with their Wednesday afternoon cookery lessons. Sheila and Arthur's cleaning schedule was more or less established, with gusto on Arthur's part and a more devil-may-care attitude on Sheila's. She couldn't see the point of shifting everything off the sideboard every week – a quick dust around the doilies every now and again disturbed the dust enough for her liking.

Vera managed to get to the Co-op once every few weeks and have her dinner with Sheila.

Fred, with encouragement from Arthur, brought Betty and Marion to the Working Men's for an hour after tea on Saturday. The welcome from Sheila's mam and dad encouraged the fledgling family to make the visit a regular part of their weekend. Sheila gasped when, in a pause to consider the layout of the snooker balls, she overheard Fred asked Arthur to be his best man.

'You're alright with that … Arthur being Fred's best man? It was my idea. What with you and Fred being close since you were young,' Betty said, 'only you seem a bit taken aback.'

'No, I'm fine, course I am.' Sheila took a deep breath to steady her heart that was beating against her ribs with the force of an enthusiastic child pelting a football against a wall. 'It's just I hadn't realised the wedding would be so soon.'

'We thought we'd go for New Year's Eve. What do you think?'

'… it's up to you. Where will it be?'

'Fred wants it to be at Holy Trinity. He's always gone there, well, he did as a lad … course you'd know that.' Betty took a slurp of her port and lemon. She paused, the glass in mid-air on its journey back to the table, as she gave a soft burp. 'He's told me about you and him.'

Bloody hell. Sheila spluttered and reached for her glass. It was empty.

'Yes, you know. How you're like a sister to him.' She held up her glass to Fred. 'Can we have another one, love?' Betty meemawed.

Hell's bells. Brother and sister? I think there's a word for that sort of thing.

'Yes, well, since we were kids … you know.'

'Sheila?' Betty inched herself towards Sheila on the banquette and lowered her voice. 'I know he's told you about our Marion. I were vexed at first, but then I realised, if you're family to him and Arthur's his best mate… Well, my best friend Hilda knows, so I've seen sense about him telling you.'

'Bert? Believe me I know. Vera…' Sheila shook her head.

'Vera! You've not said owt to Vera, have you? She seems a good sort. I wouldn't want her bothered.'

'No, I promised Fred and I keep my promises, well I try to. Betty, you do know that Bert's a two-timing bugger? Always has been and always will be. I warned Vera years ago, before they were married, but she thinks the sun shines out of his backside. Although, having said that, she's beginning to change her tune.'

Arthur and Fred finished their game, replaced the cues in the frame and joined the two women at the table.

'Where are the girls?' Arthur looked at his watch. 'It's time we were thinking about making a move.'

'Talking to my mam behind the bar, supposedly helping stack beer bottles.'

'I saw you two having a chinwag. Betty's told you then?'

'About us being like brother and sister?' Sheila raised her eyebrows.

'Yes. No, the wedding.' Fred twitched his nose. 'Arthur being best man?'

Sheila forced a smile.

Fred wiped his forehead with his hanky and encouraged Betty to talk about the wedding arrangements. They'd been to see the vicar, who Betty said was 'the salt of the earth.' She'd felt obliged to tell him that Marion was born – she dropped her voice and whispered out of the side of her mouth 'on the wrong side of the blanket'. The wedding would be in the afternoon of New Year's Eve. The ceremony would be at three with a tea at Fred's mam's after the church service.

'Are you going to live with Fred's mam?' asked Sheila.

'No, we'll start off at Betty's and then,' Fred shrugged, 'we'll see. What do you think, Sheila, about Arthur being best man?' Fred's voice held a note of pleading.

'If it's alright with everybody else,' Sheila took a deep breath, her heart bouncing, and forced herself to look at Fred, 'it's alright with me. Why wouldn't it be?' *Dear God, Fred, what do you want me to say?*

'Sheila, I meant to say, you won't mind if,' Betty hung her head as a red flush seeped upwards from her bosom to her face, 'I don't know how to put it.' She paused, unsure of herself. '...Vera doesn't come. If she comes, it'll look bad if we don't invite that two-faced bugger and I can't trust myself to be near him,' she said as Fred held up his clenched fists.

'That's not what I'm trying to say.' Betty sliced the air in front of her with her hands. 'Sheila, I feel obliged to ask Hilda to stand for me. She's stuck by me, and at my age, and with having had a child before I were wed, well... I don't think it's right to have a fancy do with bridesmaids, otherwise I'd have asked you.' Betty hung her head to hide her tears. One hand clutched her chest while the other covered her mouth and nose. 'I could do with a word, in private,' she mumbled between her fingers.

'Arty, why don't you get us another round?' Sheila gave a shooing motion with her hand, while flicking her head towards Betty. 'Fred'll carry the drinks. Won't you, Fred?'

'Is summat up, love?' Fred looked from Betty to Sheila.

'No, we're just nipping to the Ladies,' Sheila lowered her voice, 'for a quiet word.' She cast her eyes around the room to check for eavesdroppers. Sheila ushered Betty into the Ladies. Inside the cubbyhole of a room Sheila motioned for Betty to take the hard-backed chair facing a rickety card table whose green baize was scarred with bald patches. Sheila gave the closed lavatory cubicle door a push. The two women were on their own. Edging herself into the small space behind the chair Sheila contemplated Betty through the mottled mirror balanced precariously at an angle between the table and the wall.

'Betty, love, don't get yourself in a state about me not being a bridesmaid. I'd only look like mutton dressed as lamb in a long frock. To say nothing of it being freezing in that church.'

Betty's reflection gave Sheila a weak smile. 'You really are a tonic, Sheila. You and Arthur and your Ellie.'

'Tonic?'

'I know you must think Fred's settled beneath himself,' Betty scratched at a piece of loose baize, 'taking me and Marion on.'

'Beneath himself? How?'

'It's good of you and Arthur to act as though I'm one of you ... that I fit in. Let's face it; we're the talk of the three villages since our Marion was taken.'

'Betty, love, it's a nine days' wonder. People were worried about Marion. Look how many turned out to search for her, and then my mam had that collection for her when she was in hospital.'

'Wherever I go there's bother. I'd just got myself settled when our Marion got taken. One minute she was playing on the front while I pegged washing out, and the next minute she was gone. They blame me, I know they do. Unmarried mother, disowned by her mam and dad.'

'Who are "they"?'

'People. Watching and listening, nosing into other folk's business.' She pushed her hands through her hair. 'My last landlady asked to see my marriage lines. When I told her they'd been lost she told me I could get lost and chucked me out. That's why I went to him, Bert, as a last resort. Then I prove everybody right, that I'm not fit to be a mother, letting my kiddie run wild.'

'That's rubbish, you're a good mother. And anyway, what about our Ellie and Christine? They were out on the street on their own.'

'You and Vera are married women, and your girls had more sense because they've been brought up right, with a mam and a dad. I hardly dare let her out of my sight, even at night. It's a godsend being here like this with you and Arthur and your mam and dad.'

Sheila considered Betty's tirade. 'At night?'

'She sleeps with me.'

'What about after the wedding?'

'Perhaps she could have a little bed in with us?'

The door opened to admit two women.

As the four women danced around each other to swap places Betty whispered to Sheila, 'Will you look after Marion for me, on the wedding day? That's what I wanted to talk to you about.'

Sheila pulled Betty to one side once they were out of the Ladies. 'I thought she was ... not hurt?'

'He didn't touch her,' Betty gestured toward her crotch, 'you know, down there. But she won't talk about it. She clams up if I mention it; screws her eyes tight shut and puts her hands over her ears. She rocks back and forward, back and forward. It's enough to break your heart.'

'Poor little bugger,' said Sheila glancing over to the bar where Ellie and Marion were talking to her mam. Betty followed Sheila's gaze.

'I've had her to Dr Kelly. He says to leave it alone, she'll sort herself out in time.'

'I'm sure she will. But for now we'd best get them home to bed. And Betty, Marion needs to have her own room.' Sheila hesitated then whispered, 'Have you ever been to bed, a proper bed, with a man?'

'No. He used to take me for walks and then we'd ... you know.'

'I'd try and coax her into her own room, if I were you.'

Betty looked bemused, then gasped as understanding dawned. 'I see what you mean, but I wouldn't want the light on, doing it's bad enough without seeing what's going on.'

'Believe me it would be best if she had her own room.' *I'd best have a word with Fred.*

The wedding arrangements sorted the two families went their separate ways. Sheila and Arthur linked arms, each caught up in their own thoughts, as they made their way home.

'Is everything alright? You're quiet,' said Arthur.

'Just thinking about Betty and little Marion. Fred'll be good for them. He'll help them to be a family, like us.' *I want us all to be happy, to be able to put everything behind us.* 'And, Arty, I think with being best man you'd best look for a new suit; we can afford it, the divvy pays up before Christmas,' Sheila said as Arthur put the key in the front door. 'I'll wear that new frock and get my mam to ask my aunty if I can borrow her fur coat and hat. Ellie can wear her Christmas box, a new frock and coat from my mam and dad.'

*

Ellie had never been to a wedding. She had heard about them in happily ever after stories. Each time she saw Uncle Fred and Aunty Betty she tried to imagine them dressed up like the pictures in her storybook. Her mummy had told her Aunty Betty would be wearing a costume not a white dress like the one mummy had worn when she married daddy.

In Ellie's storybook Cinderella looked beautiful in the dress that the fairy godmother had given her instead of her rags. The gold dress with its long train and puffed sleeves and the lace collar with the matching gold slippers made Ellie sigh. The prince looked handsome in his darker gold, nearly brown suit. The baggy pants were tucked into boots that reached up to the prince's knee. Best of all was his big hat with the swirling feathers. Ellie had never seen Uncle Fred wear a hat. Uncle Fred and Aunty Betty would look really nice in their costumes.

The wedding and the nativity as well as Brownies and

visits to the vicarage, Weary Willie and Tired Tim and the promise of Father Christmas meant life for Ellie was very busy. Isle of Man Teddy was given a quick kiss each night and then left to his own devices. Ellie liked Mrs Marsh again, she hadn't said rude things about the children, and she had told Ellie that she would be a really clever girl if she would slow down and take more care with her work. Mrs Taylor had stopped poisoning the milk and calling people snots. Ellie was happy.

*

'Amen,' the pupils of Prestolee Primary School responded as the headmaster closed his big prayer book at the end of assembly.

'Leave your chairs where they are and sit down again,' he said in his do as you're told voice. Chairs shuffled and little voices rose at the unexpected turn of events. The headmaster clapped his hands. 'We have a visitor in school today. A nurse has come from the clinic to see how clean you all are.' Ellie watched him raise his bushy eyebrows, smile and shake his head at Mrs Pugh sitting at the piano. Ellie understood it was something to do with ragged children. She felt squirmy. She glanced at Ann who raised her eyebrows and shrugged her shoulders at Ellie.

'You will go to your classes, carry on with your lessons and when it is the turn of your class your teacher will lead you to the sick room. You will be quiet and do as you are told at all times. Do I make myself clear? Good,' he said without waiting for a reply. 'We will start with my class. Stephanie Marsh, lead on.'

Ellie was tracing a picture of a castle when she heard a sharp rap on the classroom door.

'She's ready for you now, Mrs Marsh,' said Mrs Taylor from the doorway.

The class marched through the hall and up the stairs that led to the dining room, sick room and the caretaker's cubbyhole. The smell of polish, disinfectant and cooking tickled Ellie's nose. The girls at the front of the line whispered. The boys at the back pushed and shoved each other and fell about laughing as one of them let out a noisy, stinky trump. Mrs Marsh shifted her position to the back of the queue giving David Turnham a clip round the earhole as she walked past him.

'What's your name, deary?' said the nurse as she reached forward to pull Ellie toward her lap. 'Turn around for me, and bend your head.'

'Ellie Brooks.'

Ellie felt the nurse lift the hair at the back of her neck. Then she fiddled in the hair behind Ellie's ears. She then turned Ellie around and asked her to spread her hands out like stars.

'No scary bees, in pet I go, some eggs but no rice,' Ellie heard the nurse say to the other lady who was writing in a book.

The headmaster's letter to the parents of his pupils was the talk of village shops, post office, chemist, pubs and Working Men's. It occupied the bus queue and the canteens of the mills. Every child in the school had nits. Many had lice. In certain families scabies and impetigo were rife. Involuntary scratching was the shared action of the village. The chemist had a mad rush on nit combs and *Derbac* soap. Over the remainder of the week, boys attended school with shaved heads and girls with shorn hair. The most unfortunate had chilly heads and bodies daubed purple, their bodies a canvas for gentian violet.

Sheila and Lyn teamed up in an effort to rid their children of infestation and to prepare for the nativity. Sheila offered to nit comb and wash the children's hair with the foul-smelling soap. After she'd dragged the fine-tooth comb through each child's damp hair, she finished off the nits she'd farmed once and for all by squashing them between her thumbnails.

The Brooks family and the vicarage family were in the elite position of hosting nits only. It was reputed that Stephanie Marsh had nits, lice and what looked like scabies. Sheila and Lyn shook their heads in sympathy at the school gates and chortled to each other over their scones and tea about the comeuppance of ruffian teachers. In exchange for rendering her children nit free, Lyn offered to make Ellie's Archangel Gabriel costume. Three nights after the initial set to with the nit comb and soap Sheila called in at the vicarage on her way home from work to check her handiwork.

The boys were clear. Ann was not, although Sheila declared that the nits looked as though they were probably dead.

'Can't you dislodge them, Sheila? Mummy's visiting next week,.' Lyn said.

'I'm frightened of hurting her when I drag the nit comb through the length of her hair.'

'I don't mind, Ellie's mummy, really I don't,' said Ann.

'Keep still, love, while I have another go. Lyn, hold her head.' Sheila looked around the bathroom. 'What are you looking for?' Lyn had her head in the large cupboard over the sink, pushing jars and bottles to one side.

'Scissors. Cut it off, Sheila. You said you trim Ellie's hair.' Lyn thrust the scissors at Sheila. 'Go on and slice it off. Oh God, I can't bear to watch.'

'Only now and again, she mostly goes to the barber with Arty, and look, there's none in further down where her plait would be.'

'You don't understand, Sheila. It's Mummy, she'll create a hell of a fuss. She'll insist the children go away to school. Please, I couldn't bear it. She's a thousand times bigger snob than Mrs Marsh. She hates Rob being in places like Salfor...'

'Like here, like Prestolee you mean?'

Lyn hung her head. 'Yes,' she whispered. 'She's dreadful. I sometimes think I hate her.'

'Righto, we'd best get on with it. Give 'em to me, the scissors,' Sheila said holding out her hand.

'Mummy, don't cry. I want to have short hair so that I can stay here at school with Ellie.' Ann nodded to Sheila as she straightened her shoulders. 'I'm ready, Ellie's mummy.'

*

The washing machine had been drained and pushed back into its place in the kitchen. The clothes airer above the fire in the front room and the maiden positioned in front of the fire were draped with damp clothes. Socks, knickers and underpants were stretched out in the hearth. The air in

125 was steamy and damp. Sweat glistened on the foreheads of mother and daughter who faced each other across the dining table that filled the middle of the front room. A solid brown teapot, cups, milk jug and sugar bowl held centre stage. Each woman drew heavily on their cigarette.

'Thank God that's over for another week. I'm well and truly jiggered,' said Sheila.

'I never thought you'd hear me say it, but thank God for that washing machine,' said Mrs Crompton.

'So I can, sometimes, get things right?'

'Sheila? You're not frettin' again,' Mrs C peered at her daughter over the top of her misted up glasses, 'are you? Me and your dad were worried sick...'

'No. I'm fine … honest I am.' Sheila picked a speck of tobacco off her tongue and paused.

'Mam? I never want to be like that again, like I was before… you know … the baby and all that.'

'What's brought all this on again?'

'I've been thinking about one thing and another. Lyn, she's frightened of her mam … Mummy she calls her. I think our Ellie… She didn't like me much before.'

'What's done is done and you've come to your senses. Fred getting himself sorted with that Betty's been a godsend, if you ask me.'

Sheila's hand shook as she lowered her cup back to the table. 'What are you saying, Mam?' Her voice quivered. Sweat slithered down her back. *Bloody hell how did she know? She can't have known.*

Mrs Crompton took her time wiping her glasses on the bottom of her apron. The air hung heavy in the cluttered room. 'Fred's sniffed around you since you were no more than kiddies.' Mrs Crompton reinstated the glasses on her nose and fastened her eyes on her daughter. 'I always thought that tale about being pals, working a bit of overtime together were a bit far-fetched.' She shook her head and took a deep breath. 'If you ask me summat were going on between you before that to do with the baby.' She shrugged her shoulders, raised her eyebrows, dipped her chin and looked Sheila in the eye.

Sheila hung her head, she breathed deeply. She opened her mouth to speak but her mother continued, in a softer voice, almost as though she were speaking to herself.

'Perhaps it's best left, there's no good will come of opening up old wounds. You've come to your senses, and like I've said before, me and your dad, over the years, have come to like Arthur. Fred's sorted, that's good.' Mrs Crompton nodded as if confirming her own thoughts. She contemplated Sheila across the table. 'Now look at you, friends with toffs. I'll say this for you, Sheila, you keep me and your dad on our toes.' She gave a rueful smile.

'Mam?'

'Leave it, love. There's nobody as goes through life without regrets. If they say they do, they're bloody liars.'

Sheila felt her breathing settle. She gulped the last mouthful of tea. It was cold. 'Mam, do you have regrets?'

Mrs Crompton took a shuddering breath. 'I shouldn't have stood in your way with the nursing. I realised that when you signed up for the Land Army.' Her eyes closed for a second, she looked somewhere over Sheila's shoulder then shook her head. 'Never mind, tell me about Lyn and her mam.'

Sheila recounted the tale of the big game hunt at the vicarage including Lyn's fear that her 'mummy' had the power to stick her nose in and send Ann and the boys away to school. She shared her realisation that Lyn had been embarrassed when she'd confessed that her snotty mother thought that Rob's last parish in Salford and the likes of Prestolee weren't good enough for Lyn and her children.

'Perhaps her mam doesn't know any better. She's 'appen never met ordinary working folk before, and if them teachers and Irene Taylor think they're better than the rest of us they want their heads seeing to, stuck-up buggers.'

'...and Bert, look how he's turned out. Going all hoity-toity with the Masons, Vera's had to have an evening dress made,' said Sheila.

'...and Arthur wants to better himself,' said Mrs Crompton warming to the subject of social mobility. 'He's got in with that Holy Trinity crowd, going to church and all that. Perhaps there's summat else going on with Lyn and her mam?'

Sheila hesitated. 'It's about not being the right sort of daughter, not doing what they want her to do and letting her mam and dad down. She did the same as me, signed up for the Land Army and now she's living with ruffians, lousy ruffians at that, and she's married a bookie's son.'

'Like I said, Sheila, her mam's probably only ever known her own kind. Tell Lyn to fetch her round here for a cup of tea. I'll get my best tea service out, that one I won playing dominoes.'

'Mam, while we're at it.' *Keep your trap shut, Sheila.* 'Me and Fred, it's…'

'Sheila, leave it, love. It'll do no good. Don't upset yourself, again. Tell me what they're doing about their wedding.'

Chapter 22

ELLIE LOOKED forward to practising for the nativity play. Ann's mummy had made an old white sheet into a long frock with wide sleeves that reached to the floor for Ellie's Archangel Gabriel costume. Even when she stood with her arms outstretched the pointy bit at the end of the sleeves touched the floor. It was hard work for Ellie to stand for a long time with her arms out, so Mrs Pugh said she could cross her hands over her chest some of the time. The Archangel's costume had a gold-coloured belt that had once been the fancy trim from round the top of some dusty old curtains from the vicarage. Ann's mummy washed the trim in *Lux* before she made the belt. Ann looked lovely in her blue dress; it was one that her mummy had finished with. Ellie's mummy said Ann's mummy was 'bloody marvellous' being able to make costumes out of old stuff. The boys in the nativity wore dressing gowns and tea towels on their heads. Ellie was glad she wasn't a boy. Ellie thought a lot about the words that she and Ann had to say when the Archangel told Mary about baby Jesus.

Archangel Gabriel: You are truly blessed. The Lord is with you.

Mary: How can this happen? I am not married.

Archangel Gabriel: The Holy Spirit will come to you.

Mary: Let it happen as you have said.

Was The Holy Spirit a seed? If it was, why didn't the Archangel Gabriel say 'the seed will come to you'?

Ellie had asked Father Christmas at the Co-op for a sewing machine, a Famous Five book and a weaving set. She knew it was a man dressed up pretending to be Father Christmas. The real one was too busy in Fairyland getting everything ready for Christmas Eve. He was so busy that he had to send for Weary Willie and Tired Tim to help with packing his sleigh. Grandad said it was the only time of year the little buggers lift a finger to earn a crust.

Ann's brothers had been very naughty – they told Ann and Ellie there was no such person as Father Christmas. Ann and Ellie had asked their mummies if it were true. Ann's mummy told them that if they believed that a fat man with a long white beard dressed in a red suit and matching hat was real, then he was real for the time being. Then she said that the boys weren't naughty and they would still get presents. Ellie and Ann's voices spiralled into a surprised united, 'W-h-y?'

Ellie's mummy said, 'Because a Y is not a Z.'

Ellie was very puzzled. What did 'for the time being' mean? Everybody knew a Y wasn't a Z. Perhaps Father Christmas had to have his desk next to the teacher's desk when he was a little boy if he didn't know the difference between a Y and a Z. Best of all Grandma Crompton,

Grandma Brooks, and Ellie's mummy and daddy were coming to see her be the Archangel Gabriel in the nativity. Uncle Fred, Aunty Betty and Mrs Baker, Uncle Fred's mam, were coming as well. Marion was only a sheep. Ann's mummy and daddy would be there. Her daddy would be wearing his vicar's costume and saying a few words. Ann's granny and tickly grandad had vowed never to set foot in Prestolee again. Vowed must be a naughty word Ellie decided. Ann's mummy had cried and said a lot of other bad words when she told Ellie's mummy about vowed.

*

In the run up to Christmas Sheila was dashed off her feet in the furnishing. It seemed as though every house in and around Farnworth had decided to have a new three-piece suite. She liked being busy, talking to customers and making suggestions. Sheila was pleased when people commented on the way cushions and antimacassar sets had been displayed on the suites. It had been Sheila's idea to combine the soft furnishings with the suites. Mr G hadn't been keen on relieving the antimacassars of their shrouds of cellophane but he'd changed his mind when he saw that soft furnishing sales had gone up. When she suggested they set up the space in front of the big window as a sitting room with a suite, a sideboard decorated with ornaments and Christmas cards, a rug and most daring of all a Christmas tree in the corner, as well as a couple of pillowcases masquerading as Father Christmas's sacks with boxes wrapped in Christmas paper inside, with a teddy and perhaps a train set sticking out, Mr G had hesitated a minute and then agreed. The window display was the talk of the Co-op. Passers-by stopped and pointed, some came in and were tempted to buy.

Sheila would have liked a fireplace with a carrot for Rudolph and a bottle of *Guinness* for Father Christmas but Mr G thought having alcohol on the premises was 'a step too far.' When the Chairman paused on one of his 'meet the troops' missions he asked to speak to Sheila. She was flabbergasted. He congratulated her and although Sheila felt creepy when he eyed her up and down, she managed to nod and smile. She could have kicked herself when the odd haitch crept into her replies to his questions. The upshot was that in the New Year she was to spend half a day a week working with Miss Syddall and the manager of the men's tailoring department to help them improve their 'boring' window displays.

It was reported that Miss Syddall had to be helped to the staff room when the Chairman called in at the drapery to pass on his brilliant idea.

*

Arthur paced up and down, a box of *Black Magic* in his hand. He couldn't decide whether to leave them on the sideboard or hide them under a cushion or let Sheila sit down and then slip them onto her knee. He was fizzing with excitement. He glanced at the clock; it was ten to six. He craned his neck and peered over the television to get a better view out of the window. He realised he'd made a mistake in not drawing the curtains together. Sheila would wonder why they were open. He was reaching up to pull

the curtains when he saw Sheila sashaying along. He waved
and moved toward the front door.

Sheila quickened her pace so that she was nearly running.
'What's up?' Sheila fumbled with the latch on the gate. 'Is
something wrong?'

'No, love. Come here.' Arthur opened his arms as the
gate thudded shut.

'Daddy's bought you a box of chocolates,' Ellie announced,
peeping out from behind her father.

Arthur laughed as he ruffled his daughter's hair.

'Chocolates!'

'For your good news yesterday, the window job, a-n-d
my good news today and life and happiness.'

'When can we open the chocolates?' said Ellie, stroking
the black box sitting on the arm of the settee. She looked
up to see her mummy and daddy kissing each other. They
were always doing it, snuggling up to each other and sort of
pecking at each other's lips. She watched, fascinated. 'Does
it taste nice doing that sucky, chewy thing with your lips?'

'Let's open the chocolates while you tell us your news,'
said Sheila tearing back the cellophane wrapper. 'Only one
before bedtime, Ellie.'

Arthur had been promoted to charge hand. He had
written to management to raise his concerns about the
processes used in the production of batteries. He was
concerned about the way that sulphuric acid and lead were
handled in the different workshops. The men sometimes
had orange wee, and the visiting doctors found lead in
their blood when they took routine blood tests. Arthur
had noticed how often the conversation in the canteen was

about men who had recently retired dying before they had managed to see a full, sowing, growing and harvesting year on their allotment or having the chance to see out a crown green bowling season.

From the brief notes he'd made over a couple of years, he was sure there was a connection between the extraction of harmful acid and lead resulting in early deaths and other conditions affecting the men. Management had taken his letter and his notes seriously once they realised that he wanted to improve the men's working conditions and not disturb the generally good working relationship between the workers and the managers. He had taken pains to stress that the men knew about his concerns and respected their bosses' reputation as good employers.

The upshot was Arthur was going to spend part of his working week with one of the scientists to look at how working conditions might be improved. The men in his workshop had clapped and cheered when he told them. He was happy that his work had been acknowledged by his bosses and accepted by his workmates. It meant he was doing something, giving something back. The perpetual drag of the guilt he felt at surviving the war, against all odds, would perhaps now be eased and his conscience salved. The bonus of a rise in his wage packet was unexpected but welcome. He had made up his mind: Sheila and Ellie deserved the best, they were going to move to buy their own house. Arthur had thought long and hard about it; they would stay in the village. But he would be a homeowner; a man of substance. He was sure Sheila, the different Sheila, would go along with his plans.

'Who would have thought it, Arty, both of us getting a pat on the back in the same week? It's bloody marvellous.'

'Happilyeverafter,' Ellie mumbled around the caramel sticking to her teeth and the chocolate seeping out of the corners of her mouth.

'Wipe your face,' Sheila pointed to the kitchen, 'and you can have another toffee, and then it's up the wooden hill for you, Miss Ellie. Me and your daddy have a bit of celebrating to do.' Sheila put her arms around Arthur's waist and squeezed him as she wiggled her chest against his back. 'Don't we, Daddy?'

*

Propped against their pillows and satiated by their lovemaking, Arthur and Sheila shared a cigarette, passing it backward and forward.

'Sheila,' Arthur inhaled deeply, 'I've been thinking about us moving, but staying here in the village.' He turned to stroke his wife's cheek. 'What do you think?' He held his breath.

Sheila gave a slight nod. 'Yes, let's do it.' A ghost of a smile played across her face. 'Dock that cig,' she said as she hoisted herself on top of Arthur.

.

Chapter 23

THE SCHOOL nativity had one or two minor events that lifted it out of the ordinary. The vicar's mother arrived in full evening dress and fur stole. She bore more than a passing resemblance to the Queen Mother, nodding and smiling with quiet grace as she looked around for a seat. It was later discovered that she and her husband were going to a posh 'do' at the Albert Hall in Bolton. The vicar's father, splendiferous in full evening dress, followed his wife down the narrow aisle nodding and calling out 'how do' and 'season's greetings' to the rest of the assembled audience perched on gym benches and midget chairs. The stately lady regally accepted the full-size chair at the end of a row. She was delighted to chat to the headteacher from the newfangled and revolutionary George Tomlinson Secondary Modern School, whose ideas on education corresponded with her son's. The lovely man was so solicitous of her comfort, helping her with her stole and offering her his programme that she missed the performance of her husband.

To steady himself in the acrobatics of lowering himself into the curl required to facilitate his rounded backside meeting the narrow, low, wooden gym bench, he was forced to support himself by grabbing hold of Grandma Brooks' shoulder.

'Thank you, love,' he said reinforcing his gratitude with a pat on Grandma Brooks' knee, 'How the bloody hell, whoops, sorry, language,' he murmured casting his eyes to his wife. 'How come she managed to get a proper chair? Honestly, love.' He patted Grandma Brooks' knee again. 'If she fell off the Co-op she'd fall on the divvy,' he said, attempting to ease two fingers between his neck and his shirt.

'I wanted 'em to go to Bolton School, our Ann and them lads. I were happy to pay. But our Robert said "no, Dad, they'll go to the local school". He's one of them socialists, believes everybody deserves a chance in life. Well we gave him the best, the very best, let me tell you. I expected him to be summat proper.' He shook his head, drew breath and gave a deep sigh. 'But he's a good lad and that lass—' he nodded and attempted to wave to Lyn but found his arms were held rigid, sandwiched as he was, between Grandma Brooks and another proud grandparent. At the sound of his reverberant voice his daughter-in-law had turned around in her seat, and despite the warning finger on her lips had a twinkle in her eyes for her sociable father-in-law.

'Hello love,' he called to Lyn.

Lyn shook her head and turned her attention back to the stage, her shoulders shaking.

'She might be posh, upper crust and that, but we think

the world of her, we do that, me and the missus.'

'Very nice, I'm sure,' mumbled Grandma Brooks, overcome by the biographical details of the vicar's family, the knee patting and the indirect attention of the proud parents and grandparents of the village who had forgotten their cramped discomfort as the pantomime of the vicar's father unfolded before their eyes.

The main performance of the evening commenced by the school hall being plunged into darkness a second or so before Mrs Pugh gathered herself to plonk out the opening bars of *O Come All Ye Faithful* and a procession of children shuffled down the aisle to climb up the steps toward the makeshift stage. The actors jostled into position muttering and murmuring.

Proud guests stretched their backs and craned their necks nodding and pointing as their child found their allocated spot and peered out into the darkened hall, seeking the reassuring faces of their guests. A fleeting silence was broken when a sheep in the flock with Marion attempted to give a surreptitious, forbidden wave and was given a sharp kick by a shepherd and told 'you'll cop it after'.

The vicar rose from his front row seat and, facing the audience, lifted his hands to invite silence. The vicar was robbed of his introduction by a desperate cry.

'I'm goin' to be sick,' a shepherd predicted before projectile vomiting all over the manger and the baby Jesus doll. Without further ado Mrs Marsh swooped onto the stage made up of tables whose legs were bound together with string. The stage wobbled, swayed, and wobbled again. The audience gasped. One or two attempted to stand but were jammed rigid by the close confines of their neighbours and were temporarily paralysed by having their knees folded under their chins. Mrs Marsh scooped up the shepherd with one arm and the manger with the other and whisked them from view. Ann and Ellie in their roles of Mary and the Archangel Gabriel were rooted in their set positions wide-eyed, while Joseph shouted for his mam and wet himself. Two shepherds clung to each other, whimpering. The waving lamb took the opportunity to pick at a scab on her hand. The cows were about to start a fight while the wise men fell about laughing from their position of comparative safety, sitting on the steps waiting for their grand entrance.

To distract from the chaos Mrs Pugh took it upon herself to pound out *There'll Always Be an England*. Disaster averted, and with the audience and actors feeling better from the rousing singsong, the nativity continued to a successful conclusion, despite the lingering smell of vomit and urine and the absence of the Christ child and his manger.

*

Christmas with the Brooks was different in 1954. Arthur and Ellie went to the early morning service at Holy Trinity while Sheila tidied away the wrapping paper from the presents. For the first time for a long time she and Arthur had gone to the trouble of giving each other proper presents, not just shaving cream and a box of chocolates. Sheila bought Arthur a pen and pencil set as well as the usual shaving stuff. Arthur had visited the Co-op chemist in secret and asked the assistant about the boxes of Max Factor make up. Sheila was thrilled to bits and itching to have a go with the powder and lipstick. It had given her an idea; the notion of being dolled up for Christmas and then the wedding. She'd decided to get her hair cut and permed between Christmas and New Year. It would be a surprise for Arthur and Fred. *Let it go, Sheila. Let him go. It's done. This time next week he'll be a married man. You don't deserve happiness you trollop, you good-for-nothing, selfish woman.*

The rat-a-tat of the front door knocker and Ellie's piping voice supplemented by Arthur's baritone singing *Away in a Manger* roused Sheila. She gathered herself and plastered a smile on her face and opened the door. Ellie bounced into the front room wriggling out of her new best coat.

'Mummy, we're going to have a new house. Tell her Daddy, tell her.'

'I thought you'd gone to church.'

'We did.'

'… and the man…'

'Ellie, love, calm down. Pick your coat up and let's all sit on the settee.'

Sheila's dark mood evaporated as Arthur told the astounding story of how the local builder had wished him Happy Christmas and asked if he could have a word. Sheila had known the builder all her life, he and his men put bets on with her dad and she'd gone to school with his lad. He and his wife had a daughter who'd come as a bit of a surprise, and was a good ten years younger than her brother and, if village gossip were to be believed, was a bit of a one. She'd always been full of herself, good at art, dressed in odd clothes, talked posh and carried big folders about with her. Sheila realised she hadn't seen her for a year or two.

The builder had asked Arthur if it was true that he was interested in buying a house in one of the villages. He'd been doing a job in the vicarage and during a tea break had told Rob that he had a house for sale. He'd been doing it up for when his girl came back from Art College in London. She was supposed to be getting married to a lad from Kearsley who was training to be an accountant. Turns out she'd eloped with a sculptor with long hair and a beard, and would be living in London supposedly earning a living from painting.

'He and his wife are devastated. He wanted to walk her down the aisle at Holy Trinity. She told her mam and dad she cares for them but despises their narrow-minded lives. It's been a real kick in the teeth.'

'So, the house?' Sheila was trying to make the pieces fit.

'He says he wants rid of it, but…'

'What's up with it?'

'… it needs a bob or two spending on it to get it reet,' said Ellie, glancing from one parent to the other.

Sheila and Arthur smiled at each other over Ellie's head.

'W-e-ll, that's as maybe, little one. The upshot is he's said we can look at it on Monday. Now come on, we'd best get a move on, or your mam and dad will wonder where we've got to.'

*

One feature of Christmas stayed the same: the Christmas

dinner. Sheila had offered to cook but was relieved when her mam and Arthur insisted that they kept the tradition of eating at 125. They used the excuse of the size of the dining table, but Sheila sensed conspiracy.

'It would have been nice to see the Queen on yon television of yours, but never mind, she'll sound just as nice on the wireless,' Mrs Crompton said, taking a dripping dinner plate from the draining board. 'Here, Sheila, there's still gravy on this,' she said, dropping the plate into the sink full of hot suds.

Sheila bit back a retort and carried out an exaggerated inspection of the next plate. The kitchen straight, postprandial snoozes over and the Queen loyally listened to, Christmas afternoon crept on with the opening of Ellie's compendium of games.

'Before we start a game, your dad has something to tell you,' Mrs C said with a warning look at her husband.

'I've given in, been beaten down.' He smiled at his wife. 'Taking bets.'

'Tell them the full story. It was that or the Working Men's.'

'Committee didn't like it, the rozzers calling round. So that's it, the committee and your mam have got to me. She never wanted me to do it in the first place, so she's gone and done it; made an honest man of me at last.'

'He liked the danger, the threat of being caught…You did–' Mrs C held up a finger in warning– 'don't argue.'

'What about your friends, Grandad? Will you never see them again? Christine was my friend and I don't see her any more.'

'I'll still do the coupons – they're legal. You'll still need to help me and your grandma with the stamping and folding.'

'Even if we move?' said Ellie.

'Move?' Grandma and Grandad said in unison.

The story of the potential move was told.

'Yes, well it goes to show it's what I've allus said. Education is wasted on lasses. He's wasted all his hard-earned cash sending her to them colleges and before you know it, she'll have a kiddie and it'll be goodbye to all her fancy ideas. Complete bloody waste.'

'Please can we play snakes and ladders now, p-l-ea-se?' said Ellie.

The board was set up and counters arranged. Ellie anticipated the first throw of the dice when the grown-ups started talking again.

'How much is he asking for it?' Grandad said.

'Can I open my selection box?' said Ellie.

'£650. Yes, but only one or two pieces of chocolate,' said Arthur.

*

As Sheila, Arthur and Ellie turned into Church Road on Monday morning, a red van pulled up outside the middle of the terraced houses facing Holy Trinity. The driver touched his cap to the family walking toward him.

'Hello, Merry Christmas. It is still Christmas, isn't it?' Arthur said.

Aw, poor Arty, he's as worked up as me. Sheila nodded and smiled.

'Can I play with Ann after we've moved?' Ellie said, giving the vicarage a wistful glance.

'We're not moving today, love. Just looking at the house.'

'Come on in and see what you think.' The builder put the key in the lock, and with one foot on the doorstep paused and turned to face the family hovering behind him. 'Missus says as I aft t' warn you before you step inside, our lass has funny ideas, summat to do with all that schoolin'. She's bin in London too long the missus says.'

For God's sake let us in. For one thing, we'll freeze to death if we stand on this path much longer and besides that Arty's that pale he looks as though he's going to faint.

'…It's all to do with that there Festival of Britain, her queer ideas. Come on,' he turned the key, 'step right in.'

Sheila gasped. The inside of the house was nothing like she expected from the few times she'd been in one or other of the houses on the street as a girl, playing with school friends or running errands for her mam. It was like nothing Sheila had ever seen.

'It's a right eyesore. In't it?' said the builder. 'What wi' all them walls knocked down so's you can see reet through t'kitchen. Didn't I say it were queer?' The builder gave Arthur a plaintive look. 'Missus says I've to let it go for £625, that is if you're interested in taking it on because sure as hell is hell, summat like this'll never catch on round here.'

'Is it alright,' Arthur waved his hands toward the staircase, 'if we wander round?'

'Course it is. Take your time. I'll wait in't van.'

'Well, what do you think?' Arthur whispered as the front door snapped shut.

'Where are the walls?' said Ellie from halfway up the stairs.

'I think it's bloody wonderful,' said Sheila wandering around the open space, her arms spread wide and her head swivelling from side to side. 'Fancy me … well, I never thought I'd feel like this about a house. Ellie, love, watch yourself on them stairs. Who'd have thought of taking the wall off the side of the stairs and knocking everything into one big room?'

'I've read about the new designs, about The Festival of Britain, but never thought…'

'There's a lavvy and a bath in the same room. Come and see,' Ellie shouted from upstairs.

'It'll need hardly any cleaning with it being one big room,' Sheila spread her arms wide again and turned full circle, 'and what about all the bookshelves, Arty? You can have your own library.'

'It reminds me of the airmen's huts at Snaith.'

'Snails?' said Elaine jumping off the bottom stair.

'No, love. Snaith – where I had to live during the war. Spartan but somehow homely.'

To the amazement of the builder his white elephant of a house was sold if Arthur could secure a mortgage. Overcome with the enormity of their decision Arthur relaxed his family rule that it was bad manners to call on others without invitation and agreed to visit the vicarage. Caught up in the excitement Lyn couldn't wait to see inside the house so with no further ado the two families trooped across the road to peer in the front window.

'Our furniture'll look out of place against all that plain white,' said Sheila.

'Not if you paint it white,' said Lyn.

'The sideboard and the table and chairs?' Sheila was dumbfounded at Lyn's incredible suggestion.

'Yes, I've seen photographs from the Festival. That's a great idea,' said Arthur.

'Are you getting the new designs in at work, Sheila?' Rob said.

'In Farnworth?!' Sheila said, shaking her head.

Chapter 24

EXCITEMENT ABOUT the house was put to one side as the New Year's Eve wedding approached. Arthur collected his new suit from the men's tailoring at the Co-op. Sheila took a small suitcase to her aunty's house and returned with the prized fur coat and hat. Ellie's new tartan wool dress was sponged down and the Brooks family were all set for Fred and Betty's wedding.

The church was freezing cold. The penny number of invited wedding guests were joined by members of the parish who had come to watch the wedding. Marion's abduction and escape earlier in the year had marked her out as a child of special interest, and Fred's dad's family were a branch of one of the older village families. The undertone of whispered voices was augmented by the more or less melodic playing of the assistant organist who was new to the village and had still to get to know the vagaries of her instrument.

Rob, Fred and Arthur appeared out of the vestry. The groom and best man took their seats in the right-hand front pew while Rob, smiling and nodding to his flock, began to make his way up the aisle toward the front door to greet the bride. On the way, he stopped to have a word with Sheila, Ellie and Marion and Lyn, Ann and the boys, who were sitting in adjacent pews. Sheila caught the whiff of whisky on Rob's breath. *Lucky buggers, is it any wonder they all look rosy-cheeked. The rest of us are frozen through.*

The organ was silent while the organist adjusted her sheets of music. There was an expectant silence broken by a cough. Rob strode back down the aisle and bowed to the altar cross. Turning to face the congregation he signalled for Fred and Arthur to stand. With the groom and best man in position, Rob turned his attention to the bride and her escort waiting by the font at the top of the long aisle.

Sheila caught her breath as she watched Fred's face soften when he turned and saw Betty. *I thought he would only ever look at me like that.*

'Mummy, why are you crying?'

'Shush, love.'

Music reverberated around the church. The winter sun sparkled through the jewel colours of the stained-glass windows to cast shimmering patterns on the cream walls as Betty and Hilda's husband walked to meet Fred, Rob and Arthur. *God bless you, Fred, for your cockeyed love. God bless you forever. I wonder if they've done it yet? Sheila, you're in church!*

'Dearly beloved, we are gathered here in the sight of God, and in the face of this congregation to join together this man and this woman in holy matrimony…'

I'll never forget you, Fred, my first love… What would

have happened if you'd written during the war? What would have happened if Arty had not been friendly with what's his name? Giles, that's it. Too late now. It's time to look forward, Sheila. The past is the past. You need to begin to forget.

'...let him now speak or forever hold his peace.'

*

Checking the post became an obsession for the Brooks family. Ellie wasn't sure what her mummy and daddy were waiting for the postman to bring. She understood it was something to do with moving to the house across the road from the church and the visit they'd made to Bolton to see the fat, bald man who looked at them over the top of his glasses. She'd like to go and see him again. He'd given her a cough toffee even though she didn't have a cough.

She'd sat very still for a very long time listening to the man talk to her mummy and daddy. They did sums and talked about something that would happen in 30 years. Her daddy looked poorly and his hand was shaking when the man gave him pieces of paper to write his name on. Now they were waiting for the postman to bring something and then Ann's mummy and her mummy were going to paint the sideboard white 'when, and if, we get IT'.

*

Sheila toyed with the idea of calling to see Vera's mam. *What will I say? How's your Vera, and Christine? What would her mam say other than that they're alright? Did her mam know that Bert had banned them from coming into the village unless he was with them? Did her mam think it was odd that Vera, Christine and Bert weren't invited to the wedding?* It was too risky. Vera's mam was nobody's fool, she'd soon start asking her own questions and Sheila didn't want to betray Betty's confidence about who Marion's dad was. She owed Fred and she kept her promises.

Sheila decided to give it until after the weekend. Then if Vera hadn't called in the furnishing she'd write, even though Vera had said that Bert had a cob on if he thought she'd been in touch with Sheila. She'd use the excuse of the house and then if Bert opened the letter he would see there was nothing about him or Vera and Christine.

Sheila's life was full and happy. Her only concerns were worrying about getting the mortgage and mithering herself about Vera. She was fascinated by the books that Arthur had borrowed from the library about the Festival of Britain. The bright colours of the posters and paintings drew her in. She studied them again and again until she could see them with her eyes closed. Rothko, Kandinsky and Matisse were magic names. *That builder's daughter knew a thing or two.* Sheila was desperate to move, to get into that house with its open space and white light. *Who would have thought it?* Sheila asked herself time and time again. *Me, Sheila Brooks, interested in something like this? I bloody love it.* She gave up trying to get interested in novels. Big colourful books with pictures of furniture in strange shapes and bright colours were better than stories. *Please give us a mortgage, please,* she begged the god of all things financial.

*

Sheila, Mr Gorton and his deputy manager were behind the

counter on the ground floor of the furnishing department, contemplating a pile of trade catalogues.

'Go on then. We'll get one three-piece with spindly legs and one of the funny shaped chairs. Although who in Farnworth and Kearsley will go for a black, basket weave chair with red legs Sheila, I do not know,' Mr Gorton said.

'We need to put a time limit on the sale,' said the deputy manager, turning up his nose, 'then we'll see who's right and who's wrong.'

Awkward bugger.

'Vera?!' The glass in the front door of the showroom rattled as the door slammed shut.

'Vera, what on earth have you done to your face?' Mr Gorton rounded the counter, 'Sheila, look at Vera's face.'

'Another drama for Mr Gorton and his girls. I thought it was too good to last,' said the deputy manager with a snarl.

'Bugger off,' said Sheila pushing him aside, 'Vera, dear God…'

'I've left him. Why didn't you tell me?' Vera's unswollen eye turned to Sheila. 'I wondered why we weren't invited to the wedding.'

'Sheila, take Vera into the back. Customers, the Chairman… you never know who's about.'

The job of clearing a space to sit down in the back shop gave Sheila a minute or two to think. *Vera's found out about Marion and faced Bert. She's finally told him she's had enough. Fred's been round to face him and Vera's ended up in the middle of it. Or…*

'Vera, what the hell happened?'

'You'll never believe it, Sheila. He's…' Vera touched her

swollen eye and winced. 'He's told a young girl, she can't be above twenty … well, he's asked her to marry him, she's having his baby.'

'Bloody hell. Start at the beginning.' Sheila hitched herself onto the wooden draining board that faced the door. 'I can see what's going on from here and see if anybody's coming. Go on.'

Vera had been in Christine's bedroom listening to her read when there was a pounding on the front door. She wasn't expecting company, so she had a quick look through the curtains and there she was, a youngish girl standing on the doorstep with a suitcase.

'Well I thought she'd come to the wrong house. I went down and opened the door and asked if she was lost. She said, "no this is the address they gave me at the bakery".'

Sheila nodded encouragement for Vera to continue.

'Bakery? says I, all innocent like, and she says "yes, Bert's bakery. He's my fiancé".'

'Bloody hellfire,' mumbled Sheila.

'Turns out she's expecting. Her mam and dad found out and chucked her out.'

'But what happened? How come you ended up looking like this?' Sheila pointed at Vera's face.

'I couldn't speak at first I was that flabbergasted, then our Christine arrives downstairs in her pyjamas and, well, you know what she's like, she says to Irene, that's her name, Irene, "Hello, what's in that case? Can I open it?" The girl… Irene, says, "I don't understand" and she looks from me to Christine like she can't make sense of anything, "where's Bert?" Our Christine told her he was at work and that he'd missed her bedtime – again.

"'Daddy?" The girl looks as though she going to faint, she's speechless. Well so was I to tell the truth. "Daddy?" she says again looking round gormless, like. "Daddy?".

'Yes, love,' says I, 'and I'm his soddin' wife.'

Vera told the rest of the tale to a shocked Sheila. He'd told Irene a pack of lies. He was separated from his wife, waiting for a divorce. They'd never got on, it was all a mistake. She didn't understand his needs as a man. Bert and Irene had been at it in his car. He'd given her a little diamond chip, she was wearing the thing, it looked like it came from Woolies. Once they were engaged he'd coaxed her to have his wicked way with her. She was five months gone. Her mam had done what Sheila had done and noticed that the *Dr. White's* weren't going down. The mam had packed a suitcase and told Irene to bugger off before her dad got home from work. Irene phoned the bakery and got Bert's address. He'd told her some cock and bull story about living with an aunty who didn't like him having lady visitors.

'Go on, what happened next?' said Sheila.

'I made us a cup of tea, with a slug of whisky. I needed time to think, and believe it or not I felt sorry for the kid.'

'How could you?'

'It's hardly her fault, she's only young. Then I bundled Christine back upstairs. I didn't know it then, but she sat at the top of the stairs and well, she heard and saw it all. I was coming downstairs when I heard his key in the lock.'

Sheila's hand flew to her mouth; her breathing was shallow. 'Is that when he…' she waved her hand in the direction of Vera's face.

'Honestly, Sheila, I don't know where I got the strength from. I say to him, calm and reasonable, "we've got a visitor". He looks surprised. We don't get company turning up, not since we moved. "Your fiancée." Well, you should have seen his face. He barged into the lounge. She's sitting there in the corner of the settee, shaking. He turns round to me. I remember I had my arms folded across my chest. I say, "Apparently, we're separated because I don't satisfy your manly needs. Every night, and back and front on a Sunday aren't enough then?" Then he hit me, again and again.'

Back and front on a Sunday?!

'I remember Christine sobbing. I think I was sick, I must have been because Christine had it all over her pyjamas, that and blood from my face. Next thing I remember he's dragging her, Irene I mean, out the door, but before he goes, he shouts, so the whole street can hear, "You stupid bitch she's not the first, ask Betty Wilson, and if I have my way…" I slammed the door after him.'

'What happened next?'

'I rang next door to my mam and dad and asked if they'd get my dad to ring me back. Him and my mam came straight away. They stayed all night. This morning my dad got that builder you're buying that house from, he told me it's a right mess by the way, to come and change the locks. My dad's gone, all guns blazing, to the bakery. My mam's got our Christine and well, I needed to get away from my mam, so I told her I had to come and see you before all the village finds out and well, I want you to take a message to Betty for me.'

*

Sheila returned to the shop floor when Vera made her way to
the pharmacy to be given the once-over by the pharmacist.
Aware of the lurking presence of the deputy manager Sheila
forced herself to quieten thoughts of Vera and focus on the
job in hand. She was in quiet contemplation of the space in
the window, mentally making plans of how best to show off
the revolutionary – for Farnworth – three-piece suite and
single chair, when her concentration was disturbed.

'Is it okay if I have a word with Sheila?'

'Arthur?' Sheila spun round to see Arthur talking to the
deputy manager, while Ellie was trying out a rocking chair.

'Be my guest,' he said with a dismissive wave of his hand.
'It's like a three-ring circus in here.'

Miserable bugger.

'Can we tell her now?' Ellie's energetic leap from the chair
left it see-sawing and creaking.

'My God.' Sheila skirted round the obstacle course of
furniture to throw herself at Arthur. 'We have, haven't we?'

'I couldn't wait.' Arthur glanced over his shoulder at the
deputy manager who was glowering at them. 'Have I got
you into trouble?'

'He's full of himself, take no notice.'

'Mummy we're moving, we'll be near Ann. We're moving.'
Ellie pushed herself between her parents.

'I know, love, I can't believe it, but Arthur I'll have to go.'
Sheila sensed danger when she saw the deputy manager
gesticulating to Mr Gorton. 'Vera's in the pharmacy. She's
in a right mess. Go and see her, she'll tell you what's been

happening. Mr G doesn't mind about you coming in but I can't say the same for misery guts.'

'Arthur, Ellie.' Mr G made his way to them all of a dither. He held out his hand to Arthur and patted Ellie's head. 'Sheila, he's threatening to go to the top floor…'

'I'm sorry, Mr G,' Sheila pecked at Arthur's cheek. 'With one thing and another, I'm dizzy. Arty, go and see Vera, she's in a bad way. She'll be glad of your company on the bus back to Stoneclough.'

*

Ellie thought a lot about the words she heard grown-ups use. She tried to find meanings from the way grown-ups said the words; she looked at their faces to see if they were smiling or sad or cross. She noticed that their voices went up and down. When their voice went up at the end of what they were saying it meant they wanted an answer even when they hadn't asked a question. She understood the word disappointed. Mrs Marsh was always saying it.

'Children, I am disappointed,' shake of the head, 'that I could not leave the classroom without you making a noise.' Or, 'David Turnham, I am disappointed.' Hand on hips, screwed up lips and popping out eyes. 'Don't tell me you have come to school without a handkerchief ag-a-in?' Or, 'It is very…' glance out of the window and choking sound, 'disappointing that it is raining today.'

Disappointed meant sad or fed up. Ellie was fed up with the mortgage, moving, Aunty Vera and the moon and stars. The moon and stars had disappeared. Ellie liked to have her curtains open when she went to bed so that she could see the stars, and the moon as it changed shape each night. Waxing and waning, her daddy said it was called. She liked to see the stars twinkling and think about children in other countries looking up at them at the very same time that she was looking at the dark sky. Her daddy said the moon and stars were hidden by the clouds tonight. Everything felt hidden and out of Ellie's reach. The mortgage had come. The postman had delivered a letter. Ellie had expected the mortgage to come in a giant parcel tied up with lots of string and daubs of red sealing wax. Her daddy had twirled her round and shouted out 'we've got it, we've got it'. Where was 'it'?

Then instead of making the beds, emptying the ashtray, washing the pots, taking out the ashes and banking up the fire, her daddy shoved their library books in a bag and set off for the bus. Ellie didn't tell her daddy she hadn't cleaned her teeth and that he'd forgotten to tie a ribbon in her hair. At the library they left the books from last week at the desk and went without choosing any more books or talking to the library lady. Ellie felt in need of Pippi Longstocking's special powers.

Usually after the library on a Saturday Ellie and her daddy walked home and called in at Simmonds' and then had pilchards on toast for their dinner. Today they walked to Farnworth. Ellie got a stitch in her side because her daddy took long giant strides. Perhaps they'd have an ice cream in *Togs*. Ellie liked the ice-cream parlour with its big windows and the big bright pictures of funny shaped boats painted on the walls. The ice cream came in little glass vases with wafers sticking out and a long spoon to eat with. When they were passing *Togs* she pulled on her daddy's hand and dawdled. He shook his head and said, 'Hurry up, we need to tell Mummy the good news.'

Mrs Marsh would have been disappointed in the goings-on in the furnishing. The little man who looked like the bad man from the war, the one who stuck his hand up a lot, was very cross. He was shouting down the telephone and giving mummy dirty looks. Ellie didn't like dirty looks. Mummy was glad about the mortgage but sent them to see Aunty Vera in the farm a sea. The man in the white coat waved to Ellie and gave her a barley sugar stick. He was dabbing at a lady's face – the lady was Aunty Vera. She'd tripped up and fallen and landed on her nose and eye. Christine was at her grandma's, but she wouldn't be able to play because she was 'out of harm's way'.

Ellie pressed the wobbly bit of her little girl nose against the hard, woolly strands of Isle of Man Teddy's nose. She would never be disappointed with him, he was always where she expected him to be and he never said anything that made her feel mixed up. He was a good teddy.

*

Arthur contemplated his wife. He saw a woman who was happy, relaxed and glowing with fulfilment. It was a look he'd seen often in the last few weeks. Fair enough she'd been upset about the mess with Vera and Bert. He had hoped the look of ease and contentment came from her expecting again, but it wasn't to be. The contrition and guilt he felt when he thought of the way he'd dismissed her theory about Bert being Marion's long-lost father had taught him that she was a woman to be listened to. He thought long and hard about those days when Sheila was in hospital and delirious. She'd wanted to tell him something else but he couldn't catch the memory when he played the hospital scenes in his head. Should he ask her? He toyed with the idea and had opened his mouth more than once but stopped himself. He didn't really know what he wanted to ask and was it wise to revisit bad memories?

She had a talent, Mr Gorton confirmed it. She might not be much good as a cook and her cleaning was, at best, rudimentary, but Sheila had an eye for design. Window dressing and the introduction of modern furniture to the Co-op were marvellous innovations according to the top brass at Farnworth and Kearsley Co-operative Society. They wanted Sheila to go on a course in Manchester. Who'd have thought it, Sheila wanting to go to college? Arthur berated himself. He was doing it again; doubting Sheila. She had ambition, she'd wanted to go to the grammar school and had had her heart set on nursing, but they'd been denied her. Well she wouldn't be denied this time.

How things worked together to influence each other fascinated Arthur. He liked to make notes of how events connected and interweaved, at home and at work. If Rob and Lyn hadn't moved into the village and Sheila and Lyn hadn't taken up with each other and the two girls had disliked each other, where would they – he, Sheila and Ellie – be today? How different would their lives have been? Did God work in mysterious ways his wonders to perform? If Rob hadn't introduced him to the builder they wouldn't be here in this house with Sheila happy and interested in modern furniture, colourful paintings and books on design.

Yes, life was grand. The one thing he vaguely missed was his well-cooked tea on a Wednesday. Mr Gorton still visited but instead of setting to in the kitchen he and Sheila went to the vicarage to paint furniture. Rob complained that if he or the children stood still for more than a few seconds Lyn eyed them up with a pot of white paint and a paintbrush.

'It's cathartic for her; sanding down her mother's furniture and painting it white. She's blanking the old bag out of our lives,' Rob told Arthur.

Chapter 25

THE CLUMPS of snowdrops in the wooded area at the edge of the river made Sheila smile. *It'll soon be spring. I'd best be thinking about window displays – yellow and white. The daffs won't be long now. We could have vases of fresh flowers on the sideboards, and piles of yellow and white towels in the drapery. Yes, and yellow cushions on the suites. Dear God, Sheila, listen to you.* She looked around. She was tempted to run or skip. *What a pity I've dropped our Ellie at school. She loves having a bit of fun skipping and imagining things, making up stories and having a bit of a laugh together.*

Sheila was brought down to earth when she pushed open the back door of the furnishing. The deputy manager tightened his already immaculately knotted tie before brushing past Sheila with such vehemence that she overbalanced and caught her arm against the doorknob.

'What the bloody hell do you think you're doing?'

'Don't you be using foul language with me, Mrs Brooks, or the chairman will be hearing you have a dirty mouth.'

'Hang on a minute. What's with the Mrs Brooks, and the pushing and shoving?' *As if I didn't know.*

'Don't play innocent with me. I'm not,' he put one hand on a hip and made a limp wrist with his other arm, 'Mr "isn't our Sheila a clever girl" Gorton, who you can play for a fool … you stuck up bitch.'

'Watch who you're calling a bitch.'

'… and like I was saying, you,' he all but spat at Sheila, 'are the same rank as me so don't you forget it.'

Rank! I ask you, what's all that about?

'Watch yourself, mate,' said Fred, stepping back to avoid the deputy manager as he barrelled out of the door.

'Have you been rattling his cage again?'

'Me? Would I do something like that? Our Ellie thinks he looks like Hitler.' Sheila pressed her lips together, patted her hair and smiled into Fred's eyes. 'Are you passing through?'

'Yes. No. I wanted a word, on our own.'

Not again? Surely, he can't want to start up again?

'Don't look so worried, there's nothing up. It's just, well I wanted you to be the first to know. Betty's expecting. She can't stop eating Pontefract cakes.'

'Fred–' Sheila threw her arms around him– 'that's good, better than good, bloody marvellous in fact.'

'You're alright about it?'

'Fred, I'll have to go.' Sheila grimaced and nodded over his shoulder. 'He's got it in for me … Adolf. Tell Betty I'll see her tonight at Brownies.'

*

Sheila dispatched Ellie and Ann to the charge of Brown

Owl. She looked around but there was no sign of Marion. *Funny how do you do. It's not like Betty to be late.* Sheila lingered on the steps of the Sunday school and watched Betty roll herself out of the front seat so that Marion could scramble out of the back of the car. *How far gone is she? She's like the side of a bus already.*

'I'll take her in.' Betty straightened Marion's brown woolly hat. 'Why don't you sit in the car with Fred? I won't be a tick. He said you were coming round for a cuppa after the girls were dropped off.'

*

Sheila took the opportunity to have a good look round Fred and Betty's front room. *You could eat your dinner off that lino.* Sheila scrutinised the skirting boards. *I'm getting more like my mam every day. Clean it might be, but stylish it isn't. A tin of white paint would go a long way in here.*

'Thanks for coming round. I can see you sizing things up, you'll have us moving the furniture round ... Betty won't be a minute, she's upstairs. Something to do with her,' Fred rubbed his hands over his belly, 'corsets.'

Having settled the two women with a cup of tea Fred excused himself to take a load of firewood to his mother's house before he picked Marion and Ellie up from Brownies.

'I, well me and Arthur are pleased about you expecting.' Sheila nodded toward Betty's abdomen.

Betty reported on her visit to Dr Kelly. Her speech was hesitant, and her hands shook so that tea slopped into her saucer.

'Is something up?' Sheila said as she leant forward to take

Betty's cup and saucer.

It turned out that Betty was overcome with Fred's kindness and care. Her pregnancy with Marion had been fraught with worry. She'd hidden it for as long as she could from the warden at the NAAFI hostel and then she'd come home with a cheap ring and a tale for her mam and dad about a dead soldier.

'Then there's all that mess with Vera and Bert, the good-for-nothing that he is,' Betty said.

'Was he rough, nasty with you, with his fists and that?'

'No. Well, not really violent, a bit of pushing and shoving. Is she going to report him?'

'Report him? Who to? The police won't do anything and anyway he's in with that Masonic crowd, same as half the police. And let's face it, they're known for looking after each other, that's why half of them join.'

'Don't get me wrong, I'm not sorry it's out in the open about me and him. It doesn't take away that dirty feeling, but at least I've got a ring on my finger.'

'You're not still blaming yourself about Marion, are you?'

'Who else is to blame? I hope I can be a better mother this time round.'

'Tell me who says you are a bad mother and I'll soon sort 'em out.'

'You and Arthur are the best, the very best. Fred looks up to him like a brother.'

Shine on, what next?

'You don't think badly of me, do you, Sheila?'

'Why would I do that?'

'Going with Bert and not being wed. You and Arthur, I

bet you didn't.' She shook her head and touched her lips. 'Sorry, I shouldn't ask.'

'To tell you the truth, Betty, we hardly knew each other before we were married. We wrote to each other and saw each other a few times when we got leave together and then before you could say boo to a goose it was wreath and veil and six bridesmaids, and we were living at 125 with my mam and dad.'

'You were lucky.'

'Well, you could say that, I suppose. What about you? Did you meet Bert when you came down here before the war? Did you know him from then?'

'No, it was during the war when I came to the youth club. You're all a year or two older than me. I recognised you from when you were home on leave. You got me up dancing once, made me join in. Fred says him, Bert and Vera, must have been away doing their bit and all that, and besides that I didn't realise he lived down here in the village. He told me he lived…'

'…with an aunty who didn't like him having lady visitors. There's still one thing I don't understand. What made you move down here from Little Lever?'

'Like I said before, I was desperate after that miserable cow of a landlady had given me notice. I saw his name on one of his vans and thought, what have I got to lose? I'd never asked him for a penny. I needed to look after Marion, to keep a roof over her head and food in her belly. I never wanted to upset Vera. When I met her at the May walks, I could see she'd no idea about anything.'

'Well, she had and she hadn't. Me and Fred tried to warn

her often enough. He was always on the lookout for a touch up at the back of the lavvies, but she wouldn't have it, she was besotted with him. Are you alright, you and Vera?'

'More or less. We'll never be the best of friends.' Betty shrugged. 'Not like you and her … she thinks I should go after him for money, but Fred won't have it.'

'Has he never,' Sheila inclined her head, pursed her lips and rolled her right hand forward in small circles, 'given you anything?'

'He found me a job and had a word with somebody on the council about a house. Oh, and pushed some money in my hand at the May walks, and he was very good, he helped,' Betty fanned her hands in front of her face, 'when' she dropped her voice, 'our Marion was taken.'

'Betty! He's a two-timing bugger! Don't start making excuses for him.'

'He's Marion's dad, and I loved him.'

'You've got Fred now, and the baby coming.'

'Yes, like I said. I've a lot to thank you for, encouraging Fred to ask me out.'

Well that's one way of putting it.

'I never thought I'd have this, a husband to look after me, to make me feel clean, not shoddy. Now I'm like you and Marion is like your Ellie, and it's Vera and Christine who have nobody.'

All because that two-timing, jumped-up bugger can't keep his thing in his pants and his fists by his side. Dear God, Sheila, hark at you. You are a two-faced trollop with a very short memory.

Chapter 26

ELLIE WORRIED about what was right and what was wrong. Most of the time she understood what led to being told she was a good girl, or that a job was 'well done', but sometimes grown-ups said and did things that made her feel muddled up. She worked hard to say please and thank you and mind her manners. She noticed that grown-ups smiled and said nice things when children were well behaved. Her mummy and daddy were pleased when she did jobs like putting the cornflakes and bottle of milk out on the kitchen table in a morning. Once or twice she slopped the milk and poured out too many cornflakes but her daddy said it didn't matter. He said that it was more important that she was trying to help.

Brownies and school were very good, especially when she was with Ann. Being with Ann made Ellie feel shiny and clean, like having a bath and her hair washed on a Friday night. One of the things that muddled her up was how grown-ups treated Marion. Her mummy and daddy said she had to be kind to Marion and look after her at school and at Brownies. Ellie sometimes turned away and tried to pretend Marion wasn't near her in the school playground or waiting in the milk queue or sitting round the toadstool. It was wrong to turn away and when she did Ellie felt the way she did when she had to do a number two at school and the lavatory paper had run out. She tried not to do number twos at school, she hung on until she got home or to Grandma's. Ellie didn't like the hanging on feeling.

Marion smiled at Ellie when Ellie was kind to her. Ellie smiled back and sang the words of her Sixsong in her head. 'This is what we do as Elves, think of others not ourselves.' Ellie did not want to be a bad Elf. But why did grown-ups smile at Marion as though she was something special, like that might break, like the tea set Grandma had won at dominoes? Ellie wasn't allowed to touch the cups, saucers, tiny plates and the big bread plate. The muddle was to do with the bastard man in the shiny black car. Grown-ups said Marion was a brave little girl and 'she'd not come to any harm in the long run'. Why was Marion good when she and Christine had been in bother with PC Plod and they hadn't even got in the shiny black car? How far was a long run?

*

Sheila was concerned about Mr Gorton. His mother was in hospital. She'd tripped and fallen downstairs while he was at work and had ended up lying in the hall, behind the front door, for most of the day. She had a broken hip, pneumonia and a bad bang on her head. Mr Gorton was exhausted from visiting her in hospital every visiting time; Monday,

Tuesday, Thursday and Friday evenings and Wednesday, Saturday and Sunday afternoons.

Sheila offered to visit on Wednesday or Sunday afternoon to give him a bit of a rest. He refused the substitution but asked Sheila if she would visit with him. As Sheila and Mr Gorton sat side by side in quiet contemplation at the bedside, Sheila had to steel herself to glance at the elderly lady who bore little resemblance to the quiet, gentle soul who used to visit the shop to see her son and have a chat with her and Vera. Sheila thought of the Turkish Delight and Aeros that Mrs Gorton had brought in for Ellie and Christine before the move. Sheila had never had the heart to tell Mrs Gorton that neither girl liked the vaguely scented tasting Turkish Delight. A subtle change in Mrs Gorton's breathing made Sheila shift her attention from her thoughts to the old lady in the bed. Her pale skin had taken on a waxy sheen and she seemed to have diminished, shrunk in on herself. *She's near the end, poor Mr G. He'll be lost without her.*

When the Sister paused at the end of the bed to say that they could stay on after visiting ended, he didn't seem to understand why.

'You can stay with your dad and your grandmother, until the...' the Sister mouthed the word 'end,' as she nodded toward Mr Gorton, 'if you think it would help him.'

'Thanks, but he's my boss ... and my friend, not a relation.'

'Do you think he is aware?' the Sister whispered.

Sheila shook her head. 'No, I don't think so. He thinks she's going to get better. Is it alright if I stay with him for a bit? Then I'll have to go, my husband'll wonder where I am.'

'Of course, I'll get one of the nurses to make you a cup of tea. Mr Gorton, would you like a… Mr Gorton?'

'Why is she breathing like that?' Mr Gorton turned to the Sister as his mother took a last shuddering breath.

∗

Arthur glanced at the clock. Quarter past six, visiting was three to four. Say it took ten minutes to leave the hospital and get to the bus stop, then ten minutes into Bolton, if they caught a bus straight away. Then ten minutes to walk to the Farnworth bus stop and wait for the next bus, twenty minutes to Farnworth and then ten minutes down to the village. Sheila was late; something must have happened. She'd be upset for Mr Gorton, if and when his mother died. Perhaps she'd seen him home? Arthur pondered his options.

'Ellie, leave your book and get your hat and coat. Let's go and see if your mummy is on the next bus.'

'Where is she?' Ellie scrabbled off the settee and glanced at the window. 'It's gone dark.'

'Probably on the next bus. If she doesn't arrive, we'll go to the telephone box and ring the hospital to ask about Mrs Gorton.'

Hand in hand Arthur and Ellie hurried through the heavy air of the dreary March night. The River Irwell tumbled and twirled in dark eddies under the bridge separating the island of Prestolee from the thoroughfare of Stoneclough.

'Slow down, Daddy, my side has got a stitch.'

'Sorry, love.' Arthur slowed his pace. 'I forget that you have to hobble along on little legs, but look there's the bus coming round by The Hare and Hounds. Can you manage a quick run?'

Huffing and puffing and focused on the oncoming bus, father and daughter didn't notice a group of boys in a side street tormenting a mangy-looking dog with a ball. The ball bounced high and hard and then bounced again onto the main road. The dog leapt after the ball.

*

Sheila watched as the Sister leaned forward in her chair and dipped her head to try and engage Mr Gorton's attention, but he failed to respond to her offer of eye contact. He sat in the chair adjacent to her desk, his right elbow lodged on the corner, his head down and shoulders slumped. *Poor bugger, he doesn't know what's hit him.*

'Will you be able to get him home?' The Sister glanced down at the watch dangling from the bib of her starched white apron. Sheila registered the smell of cooked food: boiled cabbage and some sort of stewed meat. She forced a smile.

'We'd best be on our way, and let you get on with things.'

'If you're sure you can manage.' The Sister rose from her desk, ready to usher Sheila and Mr Gorton to the world beyond the ward. 'It's just that we're short of staff this evening.'

'Don't worry. I'll take him home with me.' Sheila glanced at the telephone. *Perhaps I could ask to ring the Working Men's. Best not, she's busy.* 'We'll be on our way then.'

'Come on, Mr G,' Sheila held out her arm, 'let's get you home.'

'Home?' He looked around, bewildered.

'Yes, I'm taking you home with me.' *Arty'll wonder where the hell I am.*

'What about my mam?'

'Don't worry, we'll get you to our house and then Arty'll know what to do next.'

Sheila linked Mr Gorton to pull him along beside her. After an initial stumble or two he managed to settle to a lurching gait that saw the couple onto the corridor and toward the revolving door at the hospital exit. *Bugger! How the hell do I manage this?*

'In you go, Mr G,' Sheila shoved him into a segment of the door. 'Face the front,' she mee-mawed through the glass partition before sliding into the next portion and pushing the door forward. The revolving door spewed them into the dark evening air. A sharp breeze swirling round the solid Edwardian building rocked Sheila's body and slapped her face. The cold jolt startled and refreshed her.

'It's not far to the bus stop. We'll soon be home.' She took a deep breath in and let it out in a reverberating phew. *Come on, Sheila, you know you can do this. Put one foot in front of the other and keep on walking. Dear God, if you're there, please help me. I want to be at home with Arty and our Ellie.* 'Come on, Mr G, let's keep moving.'

Once in the town centre, Sheila tugged Mr G forward as they crossed Bradshawgate and trudged into Mawdsley Street.

'Come on, there's a bus in. We'll soon have you warm and cosy.'

'Where are we going? I have to see to my mam. Has she

really gone, Sheila?'

'Keep moving, Mr G. Come on.' Sheila waved to the bus driver who was making ready to drive away. 'Hurry up. He's seen us.'

'All aboard.' The conductor helped Sheila haul Mr G onto the platform of the bus as the vehicle lurched away from the pavement. 'You've got your hands full there, love.'

'You're telling me,' Sheila said as she folded herself into the seat next to Mr G. 'His mam's just died and he's taking it badly. He's not himself.'

Once in Farnworth and queueing for the number 25 bus to Stoneclough, Sheila felt her shoulders relax at the thought that the journey would soon be over. When she saw the bus heave into sight and pull into the bus stop she felt like crying with relief. *Home at last; warm and safe. I'm going to leave everything to Arty once we get home. I could murder a cup of tea and a ciggie.*

'Come on, nearly there, Mr G, we're passing The Hare and Hounds.' Sheila nudged his elbow; he'd nodded off. Sheila shuffled along the bus onto the platform. Mr G bumbled along behind her. The cold air felt good. She breathed deeply; the familiar tang of the river tickled her nose. *Home at last. What the…*

*

Ellie heard boys shouting and laughing and a dog yapping and barking. One of the voices sounded like David Turnham. Ellie secretly liked David even though he was naughty, smelled a bit and lived in a prefab. He winked at her when no one was looking and sometimes gave her two straws for her milk. She let go of her daddy's hand so that she could look around and see where he was.

'Daddy, come and see.' All of a sudden there was a flash of movement and Ellie saw a ball flying high in the sky and the blurry shape of a dog darted past. The dog barked with excitement as it chased the bouncing ball into the road. After a teeny, tiny speck of silence there was a loud crash, a bang and another loud crash. Ellie saw big shapes smash together. She shook her head and closed her eyes. There were screams, frightening screams, and shouting, lots of shouting and the smell of something that hurt her nose. Grown-ups ran toward the noise. Ellie stumbled as a man brushed against her.

'Daddy? Daddy, where are you?' Ellie peered into the darkness. She was frightened, lost and alone. 'Daddy?' she screamed. She was shaking. 'Daddy?'

'Come over here, love. Let's get you out of the way.' A lady put her arm round Ellie's shoulder and ushered her into a garden. 'What's your name?' The lady bent down and looked at Ellie's face. 'Are you Sheila's little girl?'

'Yes... My daddy, where's my daddy? I want my daddy.'

The lady put her arm around Ellie and guided her into a house. Ellie blinked as she stepped into the bright light of the front room. She looked around the crowded space. It was like Grandma's with all the furniture squashed up together. She was frightened to be in a strange house. Where was her daddy? What was all the noise? Voices shouting, people running, and bells ringing, lots of clanging bells. Car lights flashed as they whizzed past the window, lots of lights.

'Come on, let's take your coat off and get you nice and warm. You're cold from all that wandering around outside. Come and sit close to the fire. Will you be alright on your own while I go and see…?' Ellie and the lady turned toward the vestibule as the front door clattered open.

'George, what's happening? How bad is it?'

'Carnage, bloody carnage … bodies … we need towels, blankets … who's this?'

'Sheila Crompton's, as was, kiddie, she got separated from her dad.'

The man staggered to one side and waved his hands about. He shook his head.

'Keep her here, for God's sake, keep her here. She can't see, mustn't see…'

'Why … what…?'

'Sheila… and some lads and…' He shook his head. 'I'll get word to Maisie or Billy that the littl'un's here.'

Ellie turned her head to look from the lady to the man trying to understand what they were saying. Why were they talking about her mummy when she had lost her daddy?

'Don't worry, I'll keep her here. You stay with her a minute while I find you some towels and blankets.'

The man pulled a funny face at Ellie – perhaps he was trying to smile. He bounced from foot to foot and rubbed his hands together. He pulled another funny face and looked toward the window. 'Hurry up, love,' he shouted.

'Have you seen my daddy?' Ellie swallowed hard. She didn't want to cry. Her tummy rumbled. More blue lights flashed past the window. 'I let go of his hand…'

'Your dad's with your mam, love.' He shook his head as

he turned away to look out of the window again. 'She was on the bus.'

'But why…' Ellie took a deep breath when she heard the lady clomping down the stairs. The man was mixed up. The lady was kind.

'Here.' The lady appeared with a pile of blankets and towels. 'Best not say anything else to her–' Ellie saw the look that grown-ups give to each other when they want to keep secrets from children– 'until we know what's what.'

'Come on, love, away from all these…' She waved her hand toward the window. '…goings-on. How about a nice piece of cake and some Ovaltine?' She held out her hand.

Ellie looked toward the door. 'Why is my daddy with my mummy on the bus?' She watched the lady knit her arms across each other and rub her elbows. She looked frightened, like it was her turn to recite the four times table.

'She … I think she might be … well, your daddy will be with her wherever she is.' The lady moved toward Ellie.

'Is my mummy dead?' Ellie sagged back into the chair and stared into the fire. 'I don't really want a wicked witch to come for her. Not now.' Hot tears spilled down her cheeks as she gasped for breath. The lady shuffled herself onto the armchair and hauled Ellie onto her knee.

'Cry it out, love. Cry it out,' she said as she stroked Ellie's head. Her pinny smelled of baking and cigarette smoke like Grandma's did. Ellie closed her eyes.

'Can I go to my Grandma's?' she muttered against the comfort of the lady's chest.

'Soon, love.' She eased Ellie off her knee and shuffled up out of the chair. 'Let's give your face a wash and find you summat to eat.' She wiped her eyes under her glasses with the corner of her pinny.

A rat-a-tat-tat on the front door halted their progress into the kitchen.

'Mummy, Daddy.' Ellie darted toward the door. It was Ann's mummy. Ellie fell into the outstretched arms of the familiar figure and sobbed.

'Thank you for being so very kind and looking after her,' Ellie heard. 'It doesn't look good...'

Ellie was aware of being folded into her coat and of Ann's mummy holding her hand as they went out into the cold, dark night with big shapes and blue lights down the road near the bus stop. Then she was cuddled tight in the back of Ann's car and being told to close her eyes and not to look. And then she was in the vicarage in Ann's big cosy bed with her asleep beside her. Ann's daddy said a prayer to ask the doctors and nurses to make her mummy and other friends, especially the children, better and to send her daddy home to Ellie. He said, 'Suffer the little children to come unto me.' Her mind flitted to David. She hoped he wasn't wandering about on his own in the cold and dark. Then Ann's mummy was sitting on the bed, stroking Ellie's hair, humming *Silent Night*. Ellie closed her eyes.

Chapter 27

ARTHUR WAS relieved to be sitting by Sheila's bedside in the eerily quiet ward. With the dimming of the lights the overwhelming turbulence – the noise, the acrid smell of burning rubber, the sight of bodies, torn and mangled and Sheila, lying spread-eagled, yards from the bus, like a puppet without its strings – felt like a distant mirage that was hovering out of reach.

'Touch and go,' that's what they told him she was, 'touch and go.' She had a badly broken leg. Her head was heavily bandaged. She might have brain damage and there was concern about internal bleeding. Arthur's eyes were fixed on Sheila's chest. He watched, anxious and alert, for each slight rise and fall of breath. Her face under the oxygen mask was waxy and ashen like the faces of the bodies he'd seen on the streets in Poland.

She lay very still. Arthur held her hand as he asked the God he had begun to trust questions. He prayed and bargained and pleaded and offered his life instead of Sheila's. If he'd died, on one of the times he was shot down, she might have married a farmer in Cornwall and been safe, away from him and... A nurse appeared at the bedside to check Sheila's blood pressure. She pumped up the black cuff wrapped around Sheila's upper arm and watched the monitor in the long wooden box, then she repeated the procedure. She felt Sheila's pulse and watched her chest rise and fall before recording her findings on the chart at the bottom of the bed. She disappeared without a word or explanation. A doctor arrived.

Arthur stood up and moved to the bottom of the bed while the doctor felt Sheila's pulse. Then he put his stethoscope to her chest, shone a torch in her eyes and then nodded to the nurse facing him across the bed, who turned back the covers. The doctor moved his hands over Sheila's body, pressing and tapping. He straightened up and nodded again to the nurse, who rearranged the covers. Arthur felt sick with fear and anticipation.

The doctor cleared his throat. 'Your wife is bleeding internally and requires urgent abdominal surgery. We have no option but to operate.' He paused. 'We will do our best, but you must prepare yourself for the worst. We do not hold out much hope.'

Arthur clutched the bottom of the bed and fumbled for his handkerchief.

'We need to get Mrs Brooks ready for theatre. You'd best get home and get some rest,' said the nurse.

*

The last bus from Bolton to Farnworth was long gone. Head down, Arthur slogged the six miles home on foot. In a distant nightmare, he'd dragged his body along like this in another world, another lifetime. *I want to die,* he thought. *This time I want to die. If Sheila dies, I want to die.* Snot and tears mingled on his face and he scrubbed them on his mac sleeve. *Dear God, where's Ellie?* He had a vague recollection of a woman, Lyn perhaps, telling him Ellie was safe. *I'll live. Sheila will live. We've got to, for Ellie's sake. She's invincible is Sheila. Together we're strong. Let me wake up from this god-awful nightmare, from this world of nightmares.*

He stood gazing up at the house in Hazel Avenue. *What was he doing in Hazel Avenue?* He looked around the keyhole at the dark houses, the windows curtained against the black night and his despair. *I'm out of my mind,* he told himself as he turned to drag his weary body through the ginnel toward home.

*

The darkest black shifted. Shades of grey bubbled and fizzed far away. A great weight dragged her down. Faraway shouts and curses, bad words, rude words. Light grey, soft voices, then shouting, loud, aggressive shouting. Sheila listened, the coarse, grating voice stopped. *Thank God.* Prods, pokes, pestering. Voices, wheedling voices. Wet skin, turning, rolling, pushing, pulling, cold, damp. *Shove it away. Can't move. Leave me alone. Bugger off, let me go back. I'm going back. Sinking back down. What's that? Gerroff.*

'She's bitten me.'

Tired, bone weary, fizzing again. Shouts. Touching. Cold. Sharp scratch. Black. Light grey, like a dirty lace curtain, patterns, shapes. What's it called? Face. A face! Faces. Mouths moving. Waitresses? Waitresses with sharp scratches and wet clothes, smearing. Ugh, cold water. Prodding and poking – stop it. Mumbling voices, talking.

'Mrs Brooks? Sheila? Can you hear me?'

Sheila tried to nod. Her head ached. *Where's that mucky curtain gone? Back, get back, behind the lace.* Bustle and noise. She chanced opening one eye. *Bugger, that hurts.* She screwed her eyes tight shut against the too bright light. Risking the light and the pain Sheila lifted her eyelids a smidgen. *Bars? A gate? Locked in? Prison? Where the hell is this? What am I doing in prison?* Through the bars, bodies in blurry mauve check and another body in navy blue and white and then legs of grey covered in white were on the other side of the prison bars.

'S'leavemealone,' Sheila heard a voice that felt as though it rumbled from deep within her, 'go away.'

The prison bars fell away, and a flowery cloth appeared behind the waitresses and the grey legs of the men.

'Mrs Brooks, do you know where you are?' the old waitress said.

'Flowerth.' Sheila gazed at the curtains surrounding her bed. 'S'not prison then?'

'No, my dear. You are in hospital.'

'Hospital! Swhatfor?' Sheila smacked her lips together. 'Steeth, wherethmiteeth?'

*

Ellie stood on tiptoe to look at the photograph of her mummy and daddy on grandma's sideboard. It was a wedding photograph. Her mummy looked pretty dressed in her white dress and carrying a big bunch of branches and flowers. Her daddy was smart in his uniform. They were linking arms with each other and smiling. Ellie reached to pull the photograph to the edge of the sideboard so that she could see her mummy's face. She had to try hard to remember her real mummy. Sometimes when she tried very hard a picture of the bad mummy from a long time ago came into her head. Ellie felt tingly and shaky and a bit sick when that picture flitted and dithered in her head. She remembered wishing a wicked witch would take the bad mummy away and boil her in a cauldron. She chanced a glance at her daddy in the photograph. He would be very cross if he knew that Ellie had been a very bad girl and asked for her mummy to be boiled in a cauldron. The wicked witch had waited too long to grant Ellie her wish. The witch had got mixed up and taken the wrong mummy. Ellie wanted her good mummy to come back. She was a bad girl. A very bad girl. She had killed her mummy.

'Elaine, love, come on.' Grandma came through from the kitchen, gave the photograph a quick wipe with the edge of her pinny and pushed it back into place. 'Dry your eyes. Your mam's going to get better ... we think.'

In the long time that her mummy had been away Ellie had settled into living at 125. Her daddy slept at the new house and called for his tea at Grandma's. After the crash, he had been very sad and quiet. His eyes never crinkled and he looked sleepy. He sat Ellie on his knee and read her stories plodding through one word after another without letting his voice change for the different people in the stories. Grandma was always busy; baking, cleaning and washing and ironing. She used bad words when she clanged and banged the pots in the kitchen sink.

When she had a minute or two, Grandma took Ellie onto her knee and held her close to tell her tales of her mummy when she was a little girl. Sometimes Ellie and Grandma used the same piece of rag to wipe away their tears and blow their noses. Grandma told people, 'Our Billy's torn to shreds.' Grandad had given up his job at the Working Men's. He cried a lot. Kind meant caring and looking after and helping. Ann's mummy and daddy were kind. Ann's daddy took it in turns with Uncle Fred to drive Daddy and Grandma and Grandad to the hospital. Uncle Fred and Aunty Betty and Aunty Vera and Ann's mummy were kind. They all looked after Ellie because she couldn't go to the hospital; she wasn't twelve yet. Ann and Marion were kind. Ann played quietly with Ellie and let her have the top, crusty half of the scones and the chewy end pieces of malt loaf.

Marion was the other big reason Ellie knew she had done something very wrong. People in the Co-op, the paper shop and post office looked at Ellie in the sad way they had, once upon a time, looked at Marion. Ellie squeezed her shoulders upwards and ducked her head ready for heavy-handed pats on the head and benedictions of 'God bless her'. She accepted strokes on her cheek and the whispered chant of 'poor little bugger'. Ellie's mummy was in the hospital cauldron and it was Ellie's fault for being wicked and not loving the old mummy. Marion had only taken some toffees from the bastard man and she had to sleep behind The Horseshoe like Hansel and Gretel, but without the leaves to cover her up and keep her warm. Marion had been a very brave girl, everybody said so. And now David Turnham had a leg missing. Had he been punished for being a naughty boy, for pulling faces and giving cheek to the teachers?

Ellie trembled when she thought about how bad she had been, making naughty wishes. She was waiting for her punishment. She'd tried curling up on the back doorstep of 125. It had been hard and cold. When would it happen? Would it be the bogeyman that came for her and left her somewhere on her own in the dark? Ellie wanted to ask Marion something but she couldn't quite catch the words to make the question.

*

Slowly at first Sheila made progress from being in bed all day to sitting out of bed for increasing lengths of time. She sipped drinks through a straw and was fed mashed up food. With the help of a physiotherapist she learned to use her arms and legs. Then she began to feed herself and walk to the lavatory. Day by day she developed her physical strength. Her head presented her with different pictures. Sometimes she understood her predicament; she had been in a bad accident, she was in hospital, she was getting better.

On good days she was glad to be visited by the thin man and the older couple who the nurse said were her husband and mother and father. They seemed nice. At first, no matter how many times the doctors and nurses asked her, she couldn't remember how she came to be in hospital. Then a pattern developed when the nurses were making her bed, they asked her the same questions. Her name, how old she was, her address, her husband's name, her daughter's name and how she came to be in hospital. When she hesitated, they told her the answers. The first day she remembered her name was Sheila the little student nurse cried. The day she remembered Arthur's name the nurses hugged her and each time they went by her bed they asked her his name. One visiting time, her favourite student nurse hovered a distance from the bed to hear Sheila say 'hello, Arthur'. It was a tearful few minutes. Sheila was judged to be making progress when she turned the tables on the nurses and asked them their names, ages, addresses and what they had been doing before they came on duty.

She developed confidence in her legs; they took her to places away from the boredom of her bedside. Heartened by the congratulations of the nurses when she made it to the toilets and back on her own, Sheila wanted to impress them even more, so went to explore further, but then sometimes lost confidence on her return journey to her bedside. She tried out different beds, sampled fruit bowls on the different lockers, had a sit down in the Sister's office and rearranged the fridge in the kitchen in an attempt to understand her place in the strange world of beds and bustle and routines. Her sense of adventure led her to wander to the big doors in halfway down the ward. She poked her head into the bright entrance hall where there was no one about. The warmth of the sunlight through the windows drew Sheila on. She stepped out of the ward. It was good to have a proper leg stretch. She nodded and smiled to the people she met on her long walk up one corridor and down the next.

When she arrived at a big revolving door she felt suddenly tired and sad and lost. The nice man behind the counter sorted her out by using the telephone on his desk. Sheila was surprised he knew her name. He told her she was a regular visitor.

Slowly she came to understand that she was Sheila Brooks, married to Arthur and mother of Ellie. The little plump old lady was her mam and the tall man with the grey hair and sad blue eyes, who cried a lot, was her dad. When she got used to them, other people came to visit. Fred, she remembered Fred. He'd been her boyfriend a long time ago. Lyn, her posh friend, married to Rob the vicar and Vera, lovely familiar Vera, who Sheila was staggered to hear was separated from Bert. Then she was told that Mr Gorton didn't visit because he was dead, killed in the same crash as the one that had landed her in hospital. Poor Mr Gorton, her lovely boss and friend. She was sad and cried at the thought of his mangled body. The nurses told her it was a good sign that she was upset and felt sad. Then on a special day the nurses helped Sheila do her straggly hair because Ellie was coming to visit.

She wasn't allowed on the ward, but the ward Sister gave Sheila special permission to sit on the benches outside the ward.

'Mummy, Mummy.' The little girl ran down the corridor toward Sheila then, suddenly shy, she skidded to a halt. 'Mummy, is that ... you?'

Sheila held out her arms, Ellie hesitated and then skidded onto the wooden bench and slid into her mother's embrace. Arthur knelt in front of his wife and daughter. The tableau bent their heads together so that the confluence of their tears spilled over each other's cheeks.

Chapter 28

NINETEEN WEEKS and three days after the accident, Sheila was due to be discharged from hospital. She could walk with a slight limp and manage to see to what was needed in the lavatory and bathroom. She used a small, shiny red notebook that had the times tables and other useful information in tiny writing on the back to keep list and prompts. Sheila had carefully recorded the names of Lyn and Rob's boys, the dates of family birthdays as well as a list of the routines of home – Wednesday Brownies; Saturday Arty and Ellie go to the library; Sunday Arty goes to church, sometimes with Ellie.

Sheila was sad when she thought about the gap on Wednesday afternoon that held a reminder of Mr G's visits to cook and paint furniture. Thinking about him prompted thoughts about the life she remembered. The house with the big white room that she loved with a quiet passion. Arty, she shivered with pleasure at the thought of lying in his arms, in their bed, with the streetlights shining through the gap in the curtains.

Ellie, little Ellie, the way she tilted her head when she was puzzled, her endless questions, her laughter and warm little body. Her mam – always on the go, always wanting things to be sorted and to have everything neat and tidy. Sheila paused in her meanderings about her mam.

Why does she never stop? I've never thought about it before. Why does she never have a proper natter? I know loads about my dad; what he thinks about things, like voting Labour, what women should and shouldn't do. What he thinks about hanging and who needs to be strung up. Who should win the Cup Final and the best way to keep a bowling green in tip-top condition. What do I know about my mam? She went to America for two years in a huff to see my Aunty Flo because my dad wanted to wait to get married. When he begged her not to go and asked her to marry him she still went, stayed two years and then came home and married him. She had a bother having me and was damaged down below. When I think about her going to America, it was my dad that told me the tale. She's never told me anything about herself. She works hard, likes baking. Loves our Ellie and likes Arty… What does she think about me? Let's think. She thinks I'm useless at housework. Well face it, Sheila, she's not wrong there. She knew there was summat up with me and Arty. She worries about me; that's why she stopped me from going nursing because of the things I'd see and have to do. What sort of daughter doesn't know her own mam?

'Sheila? Are you alright?'

Sheila opened her eyes and leant forward in her chair. The young staff nurse stood behind the medicine trolley at the bottom of Sheila's bed.

'Fine thanks, staff. Just thinking.'

'Do you need any pain relief?'

'No thanks. I've not had a headache for days now. Staff?' Sheila hesitated. 'Do you mind if I ask you something?'

'Ask what you like, Sheila.'

'Do you get on with your mam?'

'Yes, mostly.' The young woman twisted her mouth and looked thoughtful. 'She goes on about things; me not having a steady boyfriend, no sign of grandchildren, that sort of thing. Truth be told, she'd like me married with a houseful of kids and,' she shook her head, 'it's not going to happen, well not for a while anyway. I'm off to do my midder in Glasgow, and let me tell you, Sheila, she won't like that one bit. To be honest, I keep putting off telling her.'

'Does she try and tell you what to do all the time?'

'She tries.' The staff nurse glanced down at the watch holding up one corner of her apron bib. 'What's brought this on? You're not worried about anything, are you?'

'No, like I said, just thinking.' Sheila stroked her chin. 'What about your dad?'

'He's a different kettle of fish. He likes the same things as me, reading and, would you believe it, cricket? He keeps score for our village team; he took me with him from being a child. Sheila, pleasant as this is, it isn't getting the medicines done.' The Staff Nurse looked closely at Sheila. 'Are you sure you're not worried about anything?'

'No, honestly, thanks for talking to me. Will you still be on duty when it's time for me to go?'

'I wouldn't miss seeing you off, Sheila. It's not often we see a patient as badly injured as you were recover the way you have.' She shuffled her papers and pushed the trolley on to the next patient.

Sheila turned her attention to the times table at the back of her notebook.

1 x 7 = 7

2 x 7 = 14 ... I can remember, I can and will bloody well remember – everything.

3 x 7 = 21

*

Arty relented, against his better judgement, and told Ellie she could go with him and Rob to collect Sheila and bring her home from hospital. After the visit to see Sheila, the little girl had been upset and disturbed for days. Somehow, she had got it into her head that the accident had been her fault.

She woke screaming, distraught by her nightmares, something about witches and cauldrons, blue lights and the bogeyman. Tired and washed out himself from worry about Sheila, as well as trying to keep going at work, and keep up the punishing schedule of hospital visits and making time to be with Ellie at some part of every day, meant he was at breaking point.

Ellie's nightmares frightened his overwrought in-laws, so he'd taken his little girl to sleep at home. Her night-time torment and distress took him back to the black days of his own night terrors. As she screamed and thrashed he had an insight into the pressure, exhaustion and worry he'd caused Sheila as he relived his time as a rear gunner shot down over Poland and then Yugoslavia. He was perplexed about the agitation his innocent child felt. He interrogated himself with questions. *How could she be in such a state? What had she seen the night of the crash?*

'I can't understand it. What can I do to help her?' He appealed to Rob and Lyn as he tried not to collapse into the evening meal they were sharing with him.

'Let her come and stay with us for a few nights,' said Rob, putting down his cutlery and turning to Arthur.

'It's too much to ask yet...' *I'm buggered.*

'Go and fetch her things, and take advantage of it being a no visiting evening and go to bed early. Please, Arthur,' Rob's voice was sharp and insistent, 'for your own and Ellie's sake, let us help.'

Dear God, I'm lost, so lost.

'Excuse me...' Arthur stumbled from the kitchen table and into the hall to sit on the bottom stair and, as despair and hopelessness devoured him, he let the tension and pressure have their vengeance. He was aware of Rob squeezing next to him on the stairs and pulling him into his arms.

'Come on, Arthur, the girls are upstairs.' Rob squirmed to reach into his pocket. 'Don't let Ellie see you like this.'

Arthur sat up, took the proffered handkerchief, wiped his face and breathed deeply.

'Get a breath of air while you go for her things and then come and say goodnight.'

Arthur stood, closed his eyes, nodded to his friend and reached for his coat slung over the newel post.

A few nights became a week. Arthur didn't know what they did or how they did it, but when Ellie moved back home she was calm and, cuddled up to Isle of Man Teddy, she slept through the night.

∗

Ellie snuggled back into the corner of Ann's daddy's car. They were going to bring her mummy home from the hospital. Ellie felt sorry for her daddy. She knew he was tired. If he sat down for a minute or two he dozed off. She was going to help her daddy look after her mummy. Ann's daddy had helped Ellie say prayers when she stayed at Ann's house. There were no witches, or wicked fairies or bogeymen. Jesus knew what was good and what was bad. Ellie liked Jesus; he was kind and could forgive bad things.

∗

One of the first things Sheila intended doing when she was settled at home was to go to the hairdressers. Her hair was lank and lifeless. She chanced a glance in the bathroom mirror. *I look like a bloody witch.* She was desperate to go home, but at the same time scared.

How'll I cope with everything? I'm worn to a frazzle when I've spent half a day in occupational therapy. What if Arty's gone off me while I've been in here? What if our Ellie's gone back to thinking I'm a useless mam? She did think that, I know she did, before I lost the baby. Get a hold of yourself, Sheila, you've come this far, you can bloody well get yourself sorted and back to normal. Whatever normal is...

'There you are. Come on, your husband's here,' said the Staff Nurse poking her head round the bathroom door. 'Come on, let's get you dressed and on your way.' She held out her arm to offer Sheila support.

'Thanks Staff, but I have to learn to manage on my own now.'

'You're a fighter, Sheila, a real fighter.' The Staff Nurse said as she handed Sheila a battered suitcase. 'I'm going to miss you.'

With the curtains drawn around her bed Sheila contemplated the clothes Arty had brought. They looked odd; clothes from another life, a suspender belt and stockings, a bra, her best skirt and blouse and a cardigan. She pulled the knickers on under her nightie. *Bugger, the elastic's gone.* She dragged her nightie up and wriggled into the bra. *What the blazes?* Sheila looked down at her body. *I'm like a bag of bones.*

'How are you getting on?' said the Staff Nurse as she appeared from behind the bed curtains. Sheila stepped away from the bed so that the Staff Nurse could see her body. 'Don't look so glum. A roll of bandage and some safety pins'll hold your clothes up.'

'I look a right mess.'

'You'll soon put weight on, once you're home with your family and you've got some good home cooking inside you.'

Chapter 29

SHEILA STROKED the back of Ellie's hand. She was overwhelmed when the little girl slid into the back seat of the car and snuggled in beside her. They felt for each other's hand and having found each other sat, hands clasped, throughout the journey. The conversation between Arty and Rob drifted around Sheila as she drank in the familiar sights of Farnworth and then Stoneclough Brow, the station steps and the terraced houses.

'Good God! Oops, sorry Rob. What's happened to the corner of The Grapes?'

'It's good to have you back, Sheila,' Rob said with a smile.

Arthur shuffled round to look at Sheila in the back seat. 'It was the accident, love,' Arthur said. 'You're not going to get upset, are you?'

'No, no I'm alright. Is that where it happened?' Sheila twisted her head to peer backwards at the damaged pub covered in a skeleton of scaffolding.

'Let's concentrate on getting you home, eh?' said Arthur.

'Can I show Mummy what we've got? Can I?'

'Ellie, I thought we agreed,' Arthur lowered his voice in a mock whisper, 'it's a surprise.'

Ellie's hand flew to cover her mouth, her eyes wide.

Sheila hesitated in the middle of the front path. She lifted her face to the summer sun and closed her eyes.

'Mummy, come on.' Ellie stood in the doorway hopping from one foot to the other. 'We've got something to show you.' She held out her hand. 'Close your eyes.'

Sheila was guided into the big room.

'You can open your eyes now.'

Sheila took in the room she loved; the white walls, the colourful pictures, the bookshelves, the painted sideboard and –

'The three-piece from the furnishing. Arty, how? When? Why?'

'Mr Gorton's money'll pay.'

'Ell-ie.' Arthur put his hands on his hips and gave his daughter a mock scowl. 'Remember what I said.'

'Yes, I'm sorry, Daddy.' Ellie paused. 'But when are you going to tell Mummy that Mr Gorton left her all his money?'

Arthur laughed. Sheila, flummoxed, dropped down onto the new settee. Arthur settled next to her and took her hand. Ellie squirmed against the other side of her mother.

'It's true, love, he thought the world of you.'

'Why me? I don't understand.' Sheila stretched her arm around Ellie and pulled her close.

'He left a note for you. We've read it,' Ellie said bending forward. 'Haven't we, Daddy?'

'It was an open letter. He'd left with his solicitor, with the will. Would you like to read it, love?' said Arthur.

> *46 Harper Green Place*
> *Farnworth*
> *6 January 1955*

Dear Sheila,

With the start of the New Year I am carrying out a resolution I determined on some time ago.

I have talked it over with Mother and she is in full agreement with my decision. For many years there has only been the two of us. Father was killed in a pit accident. We have been happy with our quiet lives. I had my work at the Co-op and Mother has the Church. We have few visitors and keep ourselves to ourselves. Our only relative is a second cousin of Mother's, who lives in Morecambe.

What I want to say, Sheila, is I can never thank you enough for being the light of my life, more so this last few months. The day you walked into the furnishing when you were a girl of fourteen you made me see the world from a different point of view. You make me smile with your comments about how the Co-op is run; the divvy and the Chairman and lots of other things. Then when you invited me into your home to spend time teaching you to cook, well let's just say it was very special to me. More importantly, you let me get to know Arthur and Ellie as well as introducing me to Lyn and Rob. Who would have thought painting furniture white would be so much fun? You, Arthur and Ellie have been a tonic to me.

My greatest wish is that our friendship continues for many years and that I am in my dotage when you get this letter from my solicitor.

To thank you for everything you've done for me and with Mother's agreement I am leaving you the residue of my estate other than Mother's jewellery – there's not much, but she wants it to go to her cousin. It may be that the cousin will go first – who knows. I have left £60 to Lyn and £25 to Vera.

Sheila, all I ask is that when the time comes for you to inherit, that you use the money to fulfil your life. Follow a dream, for me.

Yours sincerely,

Alphonso Gorton

✳

'Alphonso?' said Sheila, looking up from the letter. 'I knew he was called Alf, but Alphonso? She flopped back wafting herself with the letter. 'What does it mean, Arty? I don't understand.'

'He was a lovely noble man, who kept himself shut away for a reason,' Arthur said, relieving Sheila of her fan. 'We need to keep this safe.'

'What reason?' said Ellie, reaching for the letter.

'He … he thought it was for the best, that's all,' said Arthur. 'Now why don't we go and get Mummy a cup of tea and one of those scones you and Ann made? Are you alright, love?'

Sheila nodded. 'Will you take me to his grave, Arty?' She reached up her sleeve for her hanky. 'I still can't believe he's gone. That I'll never see him again.'

✳

Arthur, flat on his back, stared at the twinkle of light from the streetlamp. Sheila's head rested on his shoulder with one of her legs hooked across his body. He breathed deeply. Sheila was at home, more or less safe and sound. He reassured himself that life would, at last, settle down and get back to normal.

'Arty? Why is our Elaine called Ellie these days?'

'Do you not remember–'Arty stopped himself to rephrase his reply. The consultant had advised him not to keep asking if Sheila remembered incidents and events. 'It was after you lost the baby, you wanted to shorten her name. It caused a hell of a fuss at school.'

'Yes, yes, I can remember.' Sheila rolled onto her back. 'Gladys Taylor and snots.' She turned to snuggled back into her position at Arthur's side. 'It will all come back, Arty. I am determined.'

Arthur heard Sheila's breathing change; she was fast asleep. He focused on the light shining between the curtains and turned his thoughts to the being that had sustained him through the long weeks of trial and tribulation. Thank you, he whispered, for listening to my prayers, and keeping my family whole. Give me strength for whatever lies ahead. As the soft shadows of sleep crept over him, Arthur rehearsed The Lord's Prayer.

Chapter 30

ARTHUR HAD arranged to take two weeks' holiday to coincide with Sheila's discharge from hospital. He wanted to be with his family and catch up on jobs around the house. The patch of front garden was a tangle of cramped rose bushes covered in greenfly interspersed with weeds. The back yard would benefit from a whitewash and the moss between the flags would soon join up to form a bowling green. Their first summer in the new house would soon be gone. Arthur sighed when he thought of his thwarted plans to grow tomatoes against a startlingly white wall. Still, there would be other summers. It had been March one minute and now it was August; days, weeks and months had been and gone in the whirl of worry, work and hospital visiting and now here they were, his girls safe under one roof.

'Arty, me and Ellie are going to go for a walk,' said Sheila, making her way downstairs. 'Don't look so worried, we'll be alright. Won't we, love?' Sheila looked behind her.

'I'll look after Mummy,' Ellie announced, jumping down

the bottom two stairs.

'Where are you going?

'The hairdressers – I look like a bloody witch what with my clothes hanging off me and my hair all limp and straggly,' Sheila pulled at her hair loosening a hair grip. 'Ach. I can't stand it.'

Arthur made to get up from his chair.

'Stay where you are, you're worn to a frazzle. I'll be alright with our Ellie with me. Read. Have a cup of tea. Let's hope she can fit me in now. Don't worry. We'll be home as soon as we've got me sorted.' Sheila held out her hand. 'Come on, my little nurse.'

Arthur waved from the window as his wife and daughter set out on their journey. He stood sentry until long after they had moved out of sight.

*

Ellie slipped her hand into her mummy's hand. Jesus wanted her to be a big girl and show she loved her mummy and daddy. Ann's daddy had explained bad, scary feelings couldn't be taken away by wishing for wicked witches, bad fairies and cauldrons. Ellie understood from her talks and prayers with Ann's daddy that there were wicked people in the world, but no such things as witches or fairies or bogeymen. Ellie spent a lot of time thinking about Weary Willie and Tired Tim. She was beginning to think there might be 'little buggers' in the world, just as there were wicked people, but no such things as little elves that lived in Grandad's weedy garden and under the stalls on Farnworth market.

'Mummy.' Ellie slowed her walking pace and squinted up at Sheila. 'Is there such a person as Father Christmas?'

Sheila pulled up short in the middle of the bridge linking Prestolee to Stoneclough. 'It's the middle of August, love. What's brought this on?'

'Witches and fairies and Weary Willie and Tired Tim and Bogeymen.'

'I don't understand,' said Sheila, shading her eyes against the glare of the sun to contemplate her daughter.

'They are imagined, imaginary. That's what Ann's daddy said.'

'That's true,' said Sheila. 'Look at the suds, the gypsies have been busy today.'

Ellie nodded. She gasped, perhaps her mummy didn't know about imagined people doing imaginary jobs. She'd pray to Jesus to ask his help in telling her mummy the truth.

*

Sheila felt better with her hair shorn off and an appointment made for a perm. While Ellie examined the penny tray in Simmonds', Sheila was the centre of attention. The shopkeeper, the centre of the village gossip network, insisted on bringing a stool around the counter for Sheila. By the time Ellie had made her choice of a sugar mouse, changed her mind to a sherbet dip and then plumped for a sugar mouse again, Sheila had a banging headache and felt exhausted from the barrage of questions. The shop was stifling, even with the door open. Sheila felt sweat run down her back. She scrubbed at her forehead with a moist hand.

'Ellie, we need to...' Sheila staggered toward the door. 'Run and fetch your daddy, I don't feel right.'

'Here, you've not paid for that sugar mouse,' said the shopkeeper to Sheila who was leaning against the doorframe.

'I think I can run to a penny,' said Gladys Taylor, licking her fingers before delving into the biscuit tin to choose half a pound of loose biscuits. She blew into the paper bag she was holding. 'Add it to my bill. That kiddie is a lovely child. I've been keeping my eye on her, making sure she's alright,' Gladys said in an exaggerated whisper. 'They are somebody, you know; friends with the vicar.'

Snots and in with the vicar. I wonder what you'd say if you knew about Mr G's money, Gladys? Sheila pushed herself away from the doorframe to focus all her attention on crossing the road. She felt sick and woozy. *I'm going to black out.* Gasping for breath, she staggered toward a garden wall. *Thank God.* She took deep breaths and gave a weak wave to Arthur and Ellie scurrying round the corner. Arthur sprinted toward her leaving Ellie trotting behind. Step by slow step, with Sheila leaning on Arthur and holding Ellie's hand, the family shuffled home.

'I think I might have overreached myself,' said Sheila as she sank down onto the settee. At home with her feet up, a cup of tea in her hand and a piece of her mam's fruit loaf balanced on her knee, Sheila felt wobbly but protected and loved. 'I want to get back to normal, Arty. It's time we stopped relying on other folk, kind as they are.'

'It's going to take time, for all of us.'

Sheila and Arthur, with helpful interjections from Ellie,

came to the conclusion that they all had to start out on the road to Sheila's recovery together.

'I'm going to help Mummy. I can cook and clean and go shopping.' Ellie's serious face and vigorous nodding made her parents smile. 'I am. I really am. Ann's daddy said I should show Mummy how much I love her by doing jobs and things. Don't cry, Mummy.'

'Come here,' Sheila put down her cup and held out her arm, 'and give your old witch of a mam a cuddle, love.'

Ellie froze.

'What's the matter, precious girl?' said Arthur. 'You look as though you've seen a ghost.'

'Mummy,' Ellie threw herself against Sheila, 'you are a … lovely princess not a wicked witch. I, I…'

'Come on, love, we're all overwrought,' said Arthur stroking Ellie's hair. 'We're hot in this boiling weather, tired and frazzled.'

'Ellie, I want to do something special with you,' Sheila whispered against her daughter's sweaty forehead. 'Like when you go to the library with Daddy, I thought we might do something, just me and you.'

Ellie lifted her head to peer at Sheila. 'What sort of things?'

'We could … draw … and paint pictures.' *Where the hell did that come from?* 'The lady in occupational therapy said I was good at drawing. I was bloody useless at basket weaving, that's for sure.'

'I like drawing.' Ellie shuffled off the settee. 'Should I get my paints out now?'

'I think Mammy needs to rest.'

'I do, Arty, but there's something been festering in me. Something I need to do. I want to be a real person to our Ellie, not a mam who she doesn't really know.'

'I'll go and get my paints,' Ellie made for the stairs, smiling.

'Sheila...'

'Arty, it'll be fine. I'll be fine. Fetch us some newspaper to cover the table and find us an old jam jar for water. Me and our Ellie are going to knock up a, what's his name? Rothko. That's it, see I can remember. We'll show the Festival of Britain and that builder's daughter a thing or two.'

Over the following two or three days the Brooks family settled into a holiday routine. Sheila had breakfast in bed; tea and toast made by Ellie, under the close supervision of Arthur. The tea on toast was served on a biscuit tin lid. The family promised themselves a tray, out of their inheritance. With the fine weather continuing and the household jobs done and dusted, Sheila, Arthur and Ellie set out to visit their friends who were at home during the day; Lyn and Rob, and Betty and Marion.

Sheila's mam had made herself responsible for providing a hot midday meal at 125. In the early afternoon, Sheila rested on the bed, Arthur read for an hour and Ellie played with Ann at the vicarage. Life began to settle down as the routines of hospital slipped away, and Sheila became more accustomed to life at home. At the end of the first week Sheila felt and looked a hundred times better; her hair was permed, Lyn had taken in two dresses and a skirt and Sheila's skin had lost the sallow washed out look of a long-term hospital patient. Arthur was pleased with his steady progress on the front garden; he'd cut back the tangle of weeds choking the roses. The roses had been sprayed with a solution recommended by the librarian and the drooping blooms had been deadheaded.

Ellie grew in confidence when she was with her mummy. She chattered away about her life at the vicarage with Ann. She was determined to be helpful so that Jesus would be proud of her. She informed Sheila that she was going to be a vicar's wife, or a nurse or a painter when she grew up. On the Monday of the second week of Arty's holiday, a letter arrived from his mother inviting the family to Singleton for a day or two before Arthur's return to work. Sheila, pleased to be at home and safe with Arty and Ellie, hesitated to accept her mother-in-law's invitation. She was reluctant to pack up and leave the home she loved so much, but then it dawned on her that not only did Arty's mam want to do her bit, but also that if they went to Singleton her mam and dad, Lyn and Rob and Fred and Betty could relax, free from the commitment of supporting herself, Arty and Ellie. *They all deserve a bloody medal for what they've done for me, Arty and our Ellie.*

'Let's go, a bit of country air'll do us all good, but can we leave it till Wednesday. We've got Vera and Christine calling tomorrow afternoon, and I'd like to see Vera and catch up.'

Chapter 31

ONCE HE'D seen Sheila and Vera settled with a cup of tea and a piece of cake, Arthur excused himself to tackle the back yard. Ellie and Christine had disappeared to call for Ann and play hopscotch on the front.

'Well you look a damn sight better than when I saw you at the hospital,' said Vera, not bothering to disguise her interest in the open plan room. 'I don't know as I like this idea of knocking down walls and having them strange looking pictures.'

'I love it. Who'd have thought I'd get taken in by something like this?'

'When I think about it, you always were one for doing something a bit different.' Vera paused to cock her head on one side. With a dramatic flourish she raised her right arm and swung it metronome style while she listed: 'Signing up for the Land Army, going to Cornwall, marrying Arty,' she halted her swinging arm, 'a toff from out of the village. These pictures—'

'He isn't a toff. Anyway,' Sheila paused, crossed her arms

and dipped her head and, looking sideways at Vera, she smiled, 'let's have it then, what's that totally unreliable, cocksure, lying toad of a village lad been up to?'

'I deserved that. I bloody hate him for what he's done to me and Christine.' Vera paused for a breath and a slurp of tea. 'How's Betty, by the way?'

'Like the side of a bus, but say what you like about her, her heart's in the right place.'

'She seems nice enough, I've met her a couple of times in Togs. She won't go after him for money; she says Fred doesn't want anything to do with him.'

'Which when you look at it, and I'll give it to you, he is a bugger, he's lost a lot; all his friends, respect of folk in the villages…'

'For God's sake, Sheila, you surely don't feel sorry for him?'

'No.' Sheila shook her head. *I've been bloody lucky. It could have been me, disgraced, outcast, living over the brush.*

'Sheila, what's up? You haven't half gone a funny colour.'

'I'm fine,' Sheila shook her hand as Vera made to move toward her, 'so much has happened … to us all.'

The two women rehearsed the events of the previous year and a half, ending with the death of Mr Gorton, his mother and their inheritance.

'So, have you found out how much you'll get?' Vera said.

'No, it's "in the hands of the solicitor", Arty says. He's had to leave a lot of the sorting out to them.'

'The funeral was really sad; two coffins and no relatives. It was a damn good job there was a good turn out from the Co-op.'

'Arty's going to take me to their grave when we get back from his mam's.'

'Your friend Rob and Mrs Gorton's vicar gave them a good send off, but to die like that on the same day, and nobody to mourn you. It was terrible.'

'Do people know about the money at the Co-op and in the villages?'

'As far as I know it's common knowledge. Why?'

'My mam and dad know, and Fred and Betty. I didn't want people to think me and Arty had, would … get above ourselves.' *Gladys Taylor did know, the creep.*

'It's nothing to do with anybody else. You were good to him, in all sorts of ways, without knowing about his will. That's what matters. And he always thought the sun shone out of your backside.' Vera cocked her head to one side. 'Will you go back?'

'I don't know, I'm not ready to think about it yet,' Sheila shrugged her shoulders. 'I don't think I can face Lady Syddall and, according to Fred, little Hitler's the manager now.'

'Here, Sheila I've been meaning to ask. Has your Elaine, sorry, your Ellie, been having elocution lessons? She doesn't half talk proper these days, and she's different somehow – more grown-up, less of a soft kid.'

'She's spent a lot of time at the vicarage,' said Sheila. *Soft kid, huh? At least she's not a know-it-all little madam.* 'Do you want another cuppa?'

Despite Vera's protests that he wasn't worth wasting their breath on, Sheila pursued the hot topic of Bert. Her morbid interest in his affairs was like picking at a scab on a bruised and battered knee; she couldn't resist measuring what she had, despite the accident, with what might have been if she'd run off with Fred. Vera gave a scant report that he was as cocksure of himself as he'd always been. The poor kid, who turned out to be eighteen, had given birth to a boy the previous week. The new family were living in a terraced house next door to the bakery.

'Our Christine'll have more brothers and sisters than she has fingers to count 'em on if he carries on putting himself about. It makes my blood boil just thinking about him.' Sheila could see the evidence of the blood boiling. Vera's face and neck were red, and her hands shook as she lifted her cup. 'What do you want to keep harping on about him for?'

'We all grew up together and we were once his friends.'

'You take the biscuit, you really do, Sheila. After what he's done, beating me up in front of our Christine. How can you feel sorry for him? That bang on the head has something to answer for.'

'I'm sorry.'

'Forget it, and him. I'm trying to. My dad had a word with the local bobby. He said nothing would come of making a fuss. "It was only a domestic." Like I said, it takes the biscuit. It really does.' Vera paused and blinked as though surprised to find herself sitting next to Sheila. 'Let's talk about something else and sod that bugger. I wish I'd never clapped eyes on him. You and Fred must have known what he was like when we were kids. Why didn't you say anything?'

Sheila shook her head. For once in her life she was

speechless.

*

Ellie sat on the pavement with her back to the cool of the shaded garden wall. She'd been winning and then chanced a skimming shot. Her stone had skittered out of her target of the 8 square giving her time to watch, listen and contemplate. There was something different, funny, wrong and strange. Ellie liked to think about words and their different meanings. She listened to Christine giving instructions to Ann. It reminded Ellie of reading out loud at school. Mrs Marsh told children off for saying bath and master and made them say barth and marster and cuck instead of cook. She often linked her telling off with the words heathen, common and northern. Ann talked nicely. Ellie copied the way Ann said words. When she and Ann talked it sounded nice. When Christine talked it sounded funny. Even though Marion talked common, Ellie liked her. She had been kind when her mummy was in hospital. It was good that Christine lived in betterclassofplace with her mummy.

Chapter 32

ARTHUR TOOK a tentative step onto the brown sludge of the riverbank. He had promised himself he was going to cross the river. Somewhere at the back of his mind was the promise of a view of the Lake District and the peaks of Beacon Fell. Yet it was staying upright, controlling his body as the brown sludge pulled at his feet and offered to drag him down that was the real challenge.

He intended to swim once he got into the deeper water in the middle of the river coursing at its benign low tide. His right foot sank an inch or two into the mud. Arthur relished the cool rush of water and gunk between his toes. Tentatively he placed his left foot forward; he balanced his body and repeated right foot, left foot until he reached the edge of the river's main flow. He stepped in. Yes! He plunged into the deeper water and swam. It was glorious. The slight pull of the current threatened him. He stretched his arms into a confident crawl, his legs kicked, he was in control, moving forward, he was winning … shallow water, he had arrived on the other side. Time to rest and contemplate the view.

'Daddy, daddy.' Ellie waved from the safety of the grassy bank. 'We're looking for crab apples.'

Arthur waved back at Ellie and watched her skip after his mother and Sheila as they set off along the opposite bank. He braced himself for the frisson of current and cool water. He was refreshed and energised; ready to return to life on the safe side of the river.

*

Happy days of doing nothing much but enjoying each other's company and helping with odd jobs around the site came and went. For the first time since leaving hospital Sheila slept beyond five-thirty, the routine start of the hospital day. Snuggled in the enveloping nest of the feather bed with its profound memories of the glorious intimacy that had been the epiphany of their marriage and life together, Sheila and Arthur rekindled their passion for each other. Relaxed in each other's arms, the penultimate day of their holiday in front of them, Sheila sighed.

'What are we going to do? What am I going to do, Arty?' Sheila said, shifting herself to sit up with her back against her pillows. 'I'm happy,' she smiled down at her husband, 'but floating, lost.'

'Let's enjoy today and think about the future once we're at home,' said Arthur.

They heard a shuffle, whispers and a giggle, a knock on the door and a pause.

'Are you decent?' 'I've made your breakfast.' Arthur's

mother and Ellie said in tandem. Sheila slid down the bed and fished under the covers, 'just a tick,' and then dragged her nightie over her head, 'come in.'

As she turned to leave the room her hand on the door handle, Arty's mother turned to face the family on the bed. She paused.

'I've been thinking. I don't want to interfere, or anything...'

What's coming now? Sheila glanced at Arty who was giving his mother a wry look.

'That usually means you've made your mind up to something,' Arty said. 'Come on, out with it.'

'Well what if ... Sheila, love, why don't you and Ellie stay on with me and dad? I could do with some more advice about setting up the shop in the shed. Only if you feel up to it.'

'Yes, I'll stay.' Ellie scrambled from between her parents and threw herself at her grandma, her arms clasped tight around her waist. 'I can sell things.'

Sheila gulped and swallowed. *What do I do now?* 'Thanks, Grandma Brooks, we'd like that.' *Bloody hell where did that come from?* Sheila sat open-mouthed, amazed at the independent articulation of her mouth.

*

Sheila adjusted to the idea of staying in Singleton without Arty. She reasoned that she could make herself useful to her in-laws by helping set up the shop in the shed. The campsite was three miles or so away from the local village post office and general store. While a nearby farm supplied eggs and milk, the odd tin of peas, packet of cream crackers, bottle of salad cream or bar of soap and roll of toilet paper were hard to come by at short notice.

Grandma Brooks had arranged with the village store to share the profits to the mutual benefit of herself, her chalet owners and the store. Grandad had negotiated a lean-to extension of their chalet with the man who he'd contracted to erect new chalets on the camp. Arthur, with instruction from Sheila, had painted the inside of the shop. Now Arty had gone home to go back to work and Sheila and Ellie were stranded in Singleton. *There's nothing for it, I'll show everybody I can be a good wife and mother and daughter-in-law for that matter. I can set up a little shop in a shed, after all look what I managed at the Co-op with my displays. Get your finger out, Sheila, and show 'em what you're made of.*

Sheila contemplated the pile of wooden crates; she scrutinised the space on the shelves and the floor. She adjusted the position of the sturdy old kitchen table that had metamorphosed into a shop counter. Shifting the tins, bottles and packets around on the shelves to display them to best advantage, Sheila realised she was enjoying herself creating a shop from an empty, limited space and filling it with the everyday necessities that fuelled people's lives. She stood back and admired her work. She now knew what she wanted to do with Mr Gorton's money, if Arty agreed.

*

Ellie, fed up of watching her mummy pile tins of pears and peaches up, then stand back and look at them and then start all over again, wandered outside. She meandered to the chicken coop. Grandma had bought some chickens and was hoping to get eggs to sell in the shop. Grandad didn't like the chickens. He was going to 'wring their bloody necks and stuff 'em in a pot,' if the cockerel kept waking him up early. Ellie risked poking her finger through the wire in the chicken shed. Grandad was right; they were horrible creatures who nipped fingers. The one with the wobbliest neck reminded her of Mrs Pugh whose class she would be in when she went back to school. Perhaps all creatures with wobbly necks were bad-tempered with children. Ellie became absorbed in thoughts of scary Mrs Pugh who made you stand on your chair if you coughed or scratched your nose or forgot your hanky. The list of do's and don'ts was endless. Ellie shivered. If he didn't watch himself, David Turnham would go dizzy from being so high up all the time. Then she remembered his lost leg. Poor David... Ellie, deep in thoughts of school, jumped as she emerged from the shadows of the outbuildings and a passing car peeped.

Judith and her mummy. She waved back and then was suddenly shy. She straightened her back and prepared herself to remember the lessons she learned from watching and listening to life at the vicarage.

*

Sheila took the proffered cup of tea from her mother-in-law. The two women stood in the doorway of the shop admiring Sheila's handiwork.

'It's a real credit to you, love. I'd never have thought of using old cups and saucers with the packets of tea. Or the cake stand amongst the packets of biscuits, or a scrubbing brush with the soap.'

'Had you thought of selling some of your baking; tarts and pies, and biscuits? I think homemade biscuits would go down a treat.'

'Sheila, you're a godsend. Are you sure you need to go home?'

'No, she needs to come and keep me company,' said a voice from behind them.

'Pamela!'

'Hello, Mrs Brooks.'

Sheila watched the elegant women bend to give Arty's mother a peck on the cheek. *I feel a real frump against her. She looks like something out of Women's Own. What's with the kissing business?*

'How are you, Sheila? I was so very sorry to hear about your accident and the death of your friend.'

'Fine ... getting better, back to normal. How harr, *bloody hell,* you?' Sheila seethed at herself, at the unnecessary aitch, as a surge of heat suffused her chest and began its intrepid journey to her cheeks.

'Ellie tells me Arthur is at home and you and she are helping Mrs B.' She leant between the two women to poke her head into the shop. 'Wow, this looks terrific, you've got an eye for detail. I admire your ... talent. That's the word – talent.'

Sheila wafted her hand in front of her face. *I bet she never sweats and turns beetroot red and puts aitches where there aren't any – never.*

'Come on, let's sit down. I made some lemon tea earlier,' Arty's mother said, leading the women into the kitchen.

'How long are you here for, Pamela?'

'Until next Sunday. I've come to get some peace and quiet; I've an editorial deadline to meet and dad's patients keep coming to the door at all times of the day and night.'

'He's a good doctor; he was always kind to us.'

'Patients first, family second has always been his motto. Sorry, Mrs B, but … well here I am out of the way.'

'Well at least Judith will have Ellie to keep her company, while you get on with your … whatever it is you do.'

That's telling her, Grandma B. She's not that fond of her. I wonder why?

*

Sheila was relaxed, happy and a touch nonplussed that she was enjoying her stay with her in-laws. She had made herself useful setting up the shop and each day she asked 'is there anything I can do?' while simultaneously dreading the answer. Mrs B was a quick, efficient, whirling dervish of a housewife. Ellie rescued her mummy from washing up and the potential embarrassment of her slapdash technique; it wasn't unusual for food to still be clinging to plates, knives and forks, pie dishes and cake tins when they landed on the draining board with Sheila's dip, dunk and drain method. Ellie, kneeling on a chair, washed up according to the teaching of Brown Owl who was preparing selected Brownies for a badge. Relegated to drying up, Sheila felt safe and secure that she could complete the task without showing herself up.

'I see Pamela's arrived,' Grandad Brooks said from behind his newspaper.

'This morning,' Grandma Brooks said as she eased the table leg back into position and folded down the extended leaf of the table. 'She's an ungrateful girl at times, not like you, Sheila, always willing and helpful.'

Sheila gulped, amazed at the unexpected compliment. 'Why?'

'My lads came home; she doesn't understand how her father must feel.'

'Her brother was killed, and her mother, well... who knows?' said Grandad.

'...and her dad, he was always a good doctor before, but now, well she can't see he works every hour God sends so he doesn't have to think, to remember. And that tale about Judith appearing from nowhere. Well, I ask you, does she think we were all born yesterday?'

'Mother,' said Grandad, lowering his paper and nodding toward Ellie.

'She's invited me round for an hour tonight, when I've got Ellie in bed.'

'You go, love, but watch yourself, there's something about her I've never trusted.' Grandma Brooks flicked a look in Ellie's direction, 'Well, least said...'

*

Sheila contemplated the few clothes drooping from the hangers in the wardrobe. It came down to one of the two skirts that Lyn had taken in and a blouse that was new before the accident but that now fitted where it touched. She'd have to make do. Perhaps she'd have some clothes once Mr G's money came through. The image of the elegant woman she was destined to spend the next couple of hours with swam before her.

I could say I've got a headache, that I'm tired. Bloody hell, Sheila, it's a cup of tea not a bloody audience with the Queen. Watch your aitches, or better still, keep your trap shut. She's always got plenty to say for herself. Think of what Arty, Fred and all the other lads went through in The War; shift your backside. A shop, of my own, and a few new clothes, and whatever Arty wants, books, and money on one side for Ellie's schooling. That's what I'm going to do with the money.

*

Sheila returned the wave from Pamela who was standing at the open window looking out onto the quadrangle of chalets.

'Come in, come in.'

Conscious of her cobbled together clothes Sheila eyed the blue and white polka dot circle skirt and white, sleeveless cotton blouse. She took in the matching blue pumps. As an avid reader of *Woman's Own* before her accident, and with little to do in hospital but leaf through magazines, Sheila was well versed in the latest trends in ladies' fashions. *I feel like a bloody tramp. It's a good job I made an effort.* 'You look … lovely,' Sheila was aware of the stretched, strained cheeks of her forced smile, 'smashing.'

'Mrs Critchley, she's my dressmaker,' Pamela patted down the full skirt. 'She's tremendous. I'll give you her address if you like.'

Sheila felt the heat of the red flush starting in response to the perceived criticism.

'I'm sorry, Sheila. That was clumsy of me.'

'It doesn't matter… I know I look a sorry sight.' Sheila flicked away the threat of hot tears with the tips of her fingers. *Bloody hell. Where's my hanky?*

'Look, let's start again.' Pamela crossed her hands over her heart. 'I do so want to get to know you.' She turned to indicate a low table with a jug of brown liquid with what looked like fruit salad floating in it. 'I've made us a jug of *Pimm's.*'

'*Pimm's?*' Sheila coughed to cover the squeak in her voice. '*Pimm's*, that's … nice.'

'You'll love it. We used to have it at garden parties at university.'

Put up and shut up. Sheila chanced a surreptitious glance at the clock on the mantle. *Half an hour and then I'll go.* She perched herself on the end of a chair to watch the complicated process of decanting the brown drink and the fruit into the two waiting glasses. *Wait till I tell Vera and Lyn. Pimm's! With cucumber and mint, as well as a load of fruit!*

The stilted conversation meandered over the weather, the life and times of Ellie and Judith and their return to school after the long summer holiday, then the setting up of the shop in the shed. Sheila watched the fingers of the clock drag themselves onward. Pamela excused herself to check on Judith.

'Sheila,' Pamela said as she settled on the edge of her chair and repeated the performance of pouring the *Pimm's* into the half empty glasses, 'may I ask you a personal question?'

'Y-e-s.' *Bloody hell what now?*

'No, it's intrusive of me,' she settled back into her chair and sipped at her drink. 'I'm a nosy cow.'

'I can always tell you to bugger off,' Sheila mumbled into her drink.

'I knew you were my type; calling a spade a bloody shovel.'

'What?!'

'Straightforward I mean, no frills or… See I've done it again, embarrassed you.'

Sheila took a good swig of her drink and leaned forward to settle her glass on the table.

'I'd best be off, thanks for the drink.' She eased herself up from her chair.

Pamela waved to Sheila to sit down. 'I'm so used to my own company. Please, I haven't had a decent adult conversation in I don't know how long. Please stay.'

'Why?' Sheila paused. 'I thought you worked – went out to work I mean.'

Pamela settled back cradling her drink. She described in a few short sentences her life as an editor for a London-based publishing house, working mostly from the home she shared with her father and Judith.

'I love the work; it's absorbing and when I go to London I meet interesting people, but … well, I'm marooned in a sterile house with ghosts and misery.'

'But your dad? Arty's mam said he was always busy.'

Pamela described her life at home with her self-absorbed family doctor father. They shared the same address but lived separate lives. He only showed signs of life when he responded to his patients' ever-present calls at the front door and increasingly on the telephone.

'But why do you stay with him, if it's so bad?'

'Judith, school and family. My aunty and uncle live nearby and, if the truth were told, they provide the family life she needs.'

'I don't understand.' Sheila slurped her drink. *This is bloody good.*

'My older brother, Tim, was killed early in the war. Then a few years later I came back from a stint of driving ambulances in Leeds with a baby and a,' she paused, 'a missing husband.'

'Missing?' *Arty said there was something up.* 'Dead? Killed?'

Pamela eyed Sheila over the top of her glass. 'Non-existent. Come on, into the kitchenette, we need another jug of this.'

Sheila was staggered by Pamela's story. She liked men; different men. She'd been with … too many to count. She'd ended up pregnant, bought a wedding ring and invented a whirlwind courtship and a sudden death in action.

'That's why Mrs B can be a bit stiff with me. This is better,' Pamela licked her lips, 'more *Pimm's,* less lemonade.'

'Stiff?'

'She thinks I think that Arthur wasn't, isn't I mean, good enough for me.'

'Wasn't, isn't?'

'When in fact he is, was, too good for me. He's far better off with a straightforward girl like you.'

Sheila plucked at a cotton thread in the seam of her skirt. She paused. 'Were you and Arty … courting?'

'No, not really, he was too kind, too gentle. I'm selfish.

There's something wrong with me. I don't want all that, what my parents had…they shut us, well me out.'

'You?'

Back in the front room Pamela contemplated the picture over Sheila's shoulder. 'Tim was the golden boy, older than me. I was a mistake, a surprise, an afterthought.' She moved her eyes from the picture to look directly at Sheila and shrugged. 'My mother…well, life wasn't worth living without him.'

'What!' Sheila sat forward. 'Arty's mam said she had an accident.'

'Oh yes, everybody believes the tale, the lie that she fell downstairs, but then again we don't usually mention the gin.'

Arty's dad doesn't believe it. Gin! Did she say gin?

'Everyday lies, Sheila. The lies we tell to protect ourselves. The lies that trip us up and tell us who we really are.' Pamela covered her mouth with her free hand and raised her eyebrows. 'Forgive me, I'm being maudlin and obtuse,' she muttered through her fingers. She shook her head.

'Everybody does it. Tells lies I mean,' Sheila said, in part to console Pamela and in part to challenge herself. 'Don't they?'

'As far as I'm concerned most of life is a lie; a construction we deceive ourselves about,' Pamela shrugged. 'I'm a miserable cow. Ignore me and tell me about you. Cheer me up with your life story.'

'There's nothing to tell. I'm ordinary; from a village in a valley, with mills and a mucky river. What's interesting about that?'

'Sheila, I would like it if you would be my friend. Please,' she muttered.

It's the drink talking. Sheila nodded. 'I'd best be going.'

'Stay a while longer.' Pamela hefted herself out of the low settee. 'I'll make a pot of coffee.'

Sheila felt a nip in the air as she staggered, ever so slightly, back to her in-law's chalet. *I'll never sleep thinking about this lot. Oops watch out, you clumsy bugger.*

'Sorry,' she mumbled as she fell onto the large square boulder that served as a doorstep to her in-law's chalet. *Lavvy, best go.*

*

Two more days and Arthur would be back in Singleton for the weekend. He was relaxed; the tot of whisky with Rob after the PCC meeting had rounded off the evening. The nomination and seconding of him as secretary to the PCC had been a pleasant surprise. He had initially hesitated, not sure if he was ready to take on the job what with Sheila's convalescence and one thing and another. Then he understood; it was his chance to repay Rob and Lyn's friendship and kindness as well as the thoughts and prayers of the Holy Trinity congregation. He belonged; he was part of something in the village now as well as at work. His promotion to charge hand had passed almost unnoticed with everybody's attention being focused on the accident and Sheila. *With Ellie back at school and Sheila well and truly on the mend we can get back to normal. The post, I've not opened the post.*

In his dash to get to the house after work, have a

quick swill and get across to the vicarage in time for his tea he'd dropped the two envelopes on the sideboard. A handwritten envelope was addressed to Sheila. An official typewritten envelope was addressed to Mr and Mrs Brooks. Arthur slid his thumb under the flap and eased open the envelope. It was from the solicitor. *Bloody hell. How much?*

*

Sheila closed her eyes, not because she was tired but more to stop the picture of a bird on the wall facing the bed from lurching into flight. With her eyes closed she felt as though she were on a crazy fairground ride. *How can pop and a bit of fruit salad do this? She's a one; everyday lies. Well she's had a go at telling a few. Fellas, how many is hordes? Not Arty though, he isn't one of her hordes. Do men grow up knowing about – how's your father? He's never been with anybody else. Has he? When? No, not Arty. He could give lessons.*

Sheila belched. *That's better. Lemonade always makes me windy. Everyday lies, I've told a few; Fred, the baby, although it could have been Arty's. That's a lie. It was Fred's. Pretending to dust. I'll start shifting the doilies. What else, who else? My dad, dodging the police with his bets…and his stories. Weary Willie and Tired Tim…gypsies' washing. Are they fairy tales or lies or fibs? My mam, she covered up for my dad, when the police came knocking. Lyn and God? Betty, Bert, Fred, all everyday liars. Bogeymen? Father Christmas? Everyday lies, she has a point. Does anybody tell the truth? Mr G! God help me! He had to pretend; to lie all his life. He couldn't help the way he was. Poor man, poor, poor man.*

Sheila rolled onto her side and sniffed. She fell asleep

with her wet cheeks soaking the pillow.

*

Ellie was at the sink when Sheila appeared in the kitchen. She'd abandoned her wobbly chair and kneeling for the stability of standing on wooden crates from the shop.

'Look, Mummy, I can wash up better stood up. Can't I, Grandma?'

'Dad says she fed you that *Pimm's* stuff last night,' Grandma Brooks said, taking a sudsy plate from Ellie.

Sheila nodded.

'She might be Miss Clever Clogs, but she lacks for common sense. I ask you?'

'I thought it was pop.'

'Fancy ways…'

'What's fancy waves? Is the tide in?' said Ellie looking at each grown-up in turn.

'In or out, watch yourself with her. I don't trust her any further than I can throw her. There's tea in the pot, love, and a hunk of bread on the table and some best butter.'

Sheila settled herself at the table and sawed at the bread.

'What was she on about? She's a jumped-up madam, you know. Her mother, God bless her, and her father, salt of the earth, and her brother – Tim. Lovely lad. But her,' Grandma Brooks paused, turned and looked surprised for a second or two. 'Now what was I saying?'

'Pamela,' Sheila chewed the chunk of bread and swallowed, 'you were talking about Pamela.'

'She's bigger than you, Grandma,' said Ellie.

'Who is, love?' said Grandma.

'Judith's mummy. How will you pick her up?'

'Grandma meant… Never mind. Are you going to help me in the shop today?'

'I'd rather play out with Judith.'

'The child's turned out well. Course that's down to her aunty and uncle.'

Sheila drank down the last of her stewed tea and piled her breakfast pots together. 'I'm off to get ready for the opening of the shop.' She slid the pots into the washing up bowl. 'We should have something, a ribbon or a cord, across the door for the first customer to cut.'

'Arthur's far better off with you, a sensible girl as is not afraid of a bit of work.' With a humph that shook her body, Grandma dried her hands. 'I've an old pyjama cord rolled up in a drawer.'

'Mummy, why is Grandma cross?' Ellie jumped down from the crate. 'And why does she want to throw Judith's mummy into the river?'

'Grown-ups don't always mean what they say.'

'Is that telling lies?'

Everyday lies or fibs or fairy tales. 'Not really, it's a way of exaggerating, of making a point. Now, play nicely with Judith or the bogeyman will…' *Fibs, lies and fairy tales, Sheila.* 'Ellie, you do know that the bogeyman isn't real, don't you?'

Ellie shook her head and smiled at her mammy.

'That's an old-fashioned look. Ellie Brooks, come and give your old mam a cuddle before you disappear for the day.'

The balmy late summer day passed quickly for Sheila

and Ellie. The pyjama cord was untied by a young primary school teacher who was using her parent's chalet for the weekend before she faced the prospect of the new school year. She made a little speech, in the manner of a lady mayoress, thanking Mrs Brooks for her sound business sense in opening the shop and saving the time of herself and other visitors, who relied on a bike or their legs to reach the post office. She was effusive in her praise of the homemade scones and malt loaf for sale. Pamela, Ellie, Judith and a second customer clapped and cheered. Flush with the success and fun of the cord untying, Sheila urged Mrs Brooks to leave her to manage the shop while she took her time and walked round the site to spread the word that the shop was open for business. Pamela stayed on 'to keep Sheila company,' while the two girls disappeared to practise for the concert they intended to perform the following day.

*

Ellie and Judith decided on a two-handed play, with songs, in which one of them was stuck in the mud on the riverbank and was rescued by the other. Sloppy daw-daw, made by saturating rock-solid soil at the edge of the garden with buckets of water lugged, slopping and spilling from the standpipe, took the place of mud from the riverbank. The dangers of the riverbank without the presence of a grown-up, had been impressed on both girls. Slow progress in converting the edge of the garden into a treacherous trap for an unsuspecting child to drown in drained the enthusiasm of the thespians. A simple song and dance routine was the final concert of choice for the sodden, slutch-covered girls.

'Sheila, listen,' said Pamela from her seat in the sun on the doorstep boulder, 'they're singing.'

'...*blackbird has spoken like the first bird*...'

Sheila stuck her head out of the shed. 'I hope nobody's trying to have an afternoon nap.'

'I'll go and see what they're up to,' Pamela said, stretching out her arms. 'Thank you, Sheila, you are an inspiration. I'll give them a drink and a biscuit and then perhaps we can take them for a walk when Mrs B's back to take over the shop.'

Chapter 33

SHEILA PAUSED at the end of the short garden path. They were home. It seemed ages since she'd been discharged from hospital. Yet it was only two weeks and a few days since she'd returned home to stand on the same spot to contemplate the front of this house that felt like a haven, a special place. A place that had made her realise so much about herself and what she wanted to be, what she wanted to do with her life – with or without Mr G's money.

She turned to take in the view; the church across the road, the vicarage, the trees showing the first signs of autumn. *At long last; home and back to normal. What the hell is normal?* Sheila turned to join her husband and daughter in the house to face their future.

'Once we've got ourselves sorted and you've had a rest, we need to think about going to see your mam and dad to tell them about your money,' Arthur said, rolling his shoulders. 'What's in these bags?'

'Enough food to feed an army, Ellie's birthday presents

from your mam and dad, Pamela and Judith and Ellie's books and her stone collection.'

'Stone collection. It's no wonder my back aches.'

'They're magic,' Ellie said, kneeling on the floor to rootle through a duffel bag, 'and precious.'

'It's OUR money,' Sheila said, reaching to straighten a brightly coloured picture over the fireplace. 'It's for all of us. That's what he would have wanted.'

*

Sheila relished the feeling of bliss. The pleasant warmth of the bed cocooned her awakening from the depths of a deep, calm sleep. She kept her eyes closed and, conscious of the rise and fall of her chest, she slipped into a state of tranquillity. She floated, serene and content, only being roused as the edge of the bed shifted.

'I thought you might like a cuppa,' said Arthur as he drew back the bedroom curtains, 'then we'd better get ourselves off to 125.'

'I've been thinking,' Sheila hitched herself to a sitting position, 'let's say we're not sure about what we're doing with the money. That we haven't had time to think about it.'

'That's more or less true. Isn't it, love?'

'W-e-ll we are sure about saving for our Ellie's schooling and, well, I don't want to say that outright – not to my dad. I don't want him thinking I'm having a go at him because of the grammar school business with me.'

'Let's say we're opening a savings account for her, for when she's older,' said Arthur.

'Good idea.' Sheila swung her legs out of bed. 'And the

shop, they'll worry themselves daft and, like Pamela said, I need to think about it, do some research before I, we, commit ourselves to anything.'

'Sheila.' Arthur perched on the side of the bed. 'I don't say it often enough, but I love you.' He stroked her face. 'We've been to hell and back over the last eighteen months, but we've come through it – together. That's all that matters.' They leant towards each other. Their lips met.

'Mummy, Daddy. Where are you?' Feet pounded up the stairs. 'Is it time to go to Grandma and Grandad's? Ugh! You've been kissing – again?'

Ellie

Wants the school holidays to last forever. She wants both her mummy and daddy to be at home when she gets in from playing or school. She doesn't want to think about school and Mrs Pugh and standing on chairs and David not being there. Her best friends are Ann and Judith. Christine is going on a boat to a place called Canada. Marion's mummy is having twins.

Arthur

Wants a quiet, peaceful life with Sheila and Ellie. He wants take time to think about what has happened to them and why it happened. He thinks God and the Church might provide answers, but he still has doubts and questions. He knows that Sheila had deep feelings for Fred at one time or another. Her disorientation and ramblings in the hospital helped him put two and two together. Whatever those feelings were, they were in the past and the future was theirs. His and Sheila's and Ellie's.

'Forgiveness is the fragrance that the violet sheds on the heel that has crushed it.' Arthur quotes one of his favourite authors, Mark Twain, to himself on a regular basis. Would Sheila forgive him if she knew about his time with Yvette in the mountains of Yugoslavia?

Sheila

Wants to get on with her life. To be the best wife and mam – mummy she can be. She wants to be the person that the people she's come to like, nay love, think she is – her in-laws, Lyn and Rob. Pam she's not sure about. She's sad that Vera is upping sticks and moving with Christine to live in Canada. She needs to check that Fred and Marion will be alright while Betty sits out the rest of her time in hospital. Sheila wants her mam and dad to be proud of her. She wants a shop of her own. A shop that sells lovely things for the house; pictures, cushions, ornaments and ashtrays.

Acknowledgements

Thank you to my caring and supportive family and friends for your encouragement.

Friends, including the wonderful Kearsley Girls, particularly Judith Thorpe who knows the manuscript nearly as well as I do. Judith Seddon for getting in touch and remembering our times together in the 'three villages.' Carol Fenlon, Rhona Whiteford, Jackie Farrell, Elizabeth Gates and Dennis Conlon – fellow writers and the best ever critique group.

UK Book Publishing for their help and professionalism.

My sisters: Lynne Powell, Claire Turnham and Helen Turnham for permission to use family images for the cover.

James, Heather, Olivia, Charlie and Lillie Cole: for the joy you bring to our family. Special thanks are owed to Charlie for his inspired cover suggestions.

And thank you, Ron Cole, for everything.

Printed in Great Britain
by Amazon